THE WRESTLER OF PHILIPPI

A TALE OF THE EARLY CHRISTIANS

BY
Fannie E. Newberry

Fredonia Books
Amsterdam, The Netherlands

The Wrestler of Philippi:
A Tale of the Early Christians

by
Fannie E. Newberry

ISBN: 1-4101-0172-X

Copyright © 2003 by Fredonia Books

Reprinted from the 1896 edition

Fredonia Books
Amsterdam, The Netherlands
http://www.fredoniabooks.com

In order to make original editions of historical works
available to scholars at an economical price, this
facsimile of the original edition of 1896 is
reproduced from the best available copy and has
been digitally enhanced to improve legibility, but the
text remains unaltered to retain historical
authenticity.

The Wrestler of Philippi.

A TALE OF THE EARLY CHRISTIANS.

By Fannie E. Newberry.

CHAPTER I.

THE LOST AMULET.

"WHY, what is this?"

The speaker dropped the heavy door-curtain he had just drawn aside, and strode rapidly across the stone floor to a figure at the further end—a girlish figure resting on a divan, and doubled up with weeping.

She did not answer instantly, and the young man stood beside her looking down with a helpless patience for a moment, as if uncertain what to do or say. Presently he spoke again:

"Has anything happened, Salome?"

"Happened? How can you ask?" the other managed to sob out in a voice of almost petulant reproach.

"I mean anything new," he hastened to explain with an air of meekness. "Of course—"

"Of course you cannot or will not understand, Hector. You never do. Is a grief the less keen because it grows older daily? Can I ever get used to this?"

"We do get used to things," he returned slowly, gazing down at her from his superior height, as a good-natured but lumbering camel might gaze upon a fawn. "We have to control our grief or it would kill us, you see. Come, try and stop, can you not? It is time for the evening meal, and I am hungry."

"Hungry! Men are always thinking of their comforts. Have you not one thought for our poor lost Herklas, wandering no one knows how, or whither?"

The man's face twitched with some internal emotion, but, absorbed in her own luxurious sorrow, Salome did not see it. After a moment he said gently:

"But is there anything new, dear? I left you quite bright, this morning. What have you heard?"

"Nothing. But I know now all is over. Herklas will never return." Then rising and facing him, with her dark eyes awed to steadiness, she whispered solemnly, "Hector, I have lost my amulet! The gods have given me over to the fates, and sorrow is to be my portion."

"Bah!" cried the brother, throwing back his broad shoulders and letting out a merry laugh from his splendid chest. "Is that all? I was sure you had news that Herklas was in prison at least, if not sent to the galleys—or even dead by torture." He shuddered a little. "And it is only your amulet?"

"Only!" Her red lips curled angrily, and she began gathering up her fair tresses and thrusting them into their silken fillet with a petulant gesture. "Is not that enough? What is to keep me from evil and misfortune now?"

"Well, sister, perhaps I can help a little!" stretching out his long, massive arms, quite bare of covering, and bringing them back to an angle that made the muscles stand up like hillocks. "I think, possibly, I may have a word to say, or a move to make, provided misfortune comes in a visible form, eh?"

His persistent good-humor overcame her at last, and her pretty teeth gleamed in an irrepressible smile as she cried archly:

"Boaster! Do you think yourself even a match for the gods, then, because you have twice worn the Olympian crown? But indeed, dear Hector, it is a serious loss. It was of purest silver from the Cordovan mines, wrought by a silversmith of Ephesus, and delicately chased with one of the most favorable signs of the zodiac. Then it held a bit of the hair from a sacred white bull, and had been blessed by a Vestal. Think of its value, brother. Why, such an amulet is priceless!"

"But where did you lose it, child?"

"What a question!" laughing merrily now. "If I knew that, would I be crying here? It was hanging from a cord of silver wire about my neck but a day or two ago, and now it is gone—that is all I can tell you."

"Have you looked for it?"

"Yes, everywhere."

"Well, well! crying will not bring it back, and the gods hate tears. Besides, I am so hungry, Salome!"

He spoke in pleading tones, like a school-boy, for he knew this would conquer her; and it did.

"Very well," she said promptly, "light the brazier then, and I will steep you a cup from the chocolate beans you brought home yesterday. Then there are dates, oatcake, and fish. Will these serve you?"

"Excellently well, sister; only make haste."

And quite restored to good-humor now, Salome skipped away on light feet to bestir her one little slave, Persis, to these pleasant household tasks.

Left alone, Hector threw himself on the divan of sail-cloth, made in imitation of the rich couches draped in silk and gold stuffs much affected in the houses of the Roman nobles, and was soon in sad reflection, which plowed a deep line between his wide-set blue eyes. Because he was a Wrestler, and therefore used to sights of blood and suffering in the arena, did not seem, so far, to make his heart less tender to his own; and presently, as memory after memory of his lost brother, Herklas, rose before him, long sighs shook his close-knit figure from head to foot.

Herklas had been such a beautiful boy, and only six months in the toga virilis. which marked the Roman youth's coming into man's estate at fifteen. To be sure, he had never taken to the Olympic games, as had Hector, and had shrunk visibly from the often frightful spectacles which had been introduced into them since the Romans ruled; but he was no coward—he had proved that often enough in many an adventure of boyish daring and skill. It was only his instinctive good-heartedness that shrank from blows and bloodshed, not because he himself feared their hurt.

Then where could such a form be found in these degenerate days, outside the statues of the masters? Hector recalled him as he had

lain at meat, the last morning he was with them. He had been full of his fun and nonsense, selecting choice bits from the platter for Salome, and laughing gayly as she eagerly received them. He had never been selfish, never sullen nor severe—this well-loved brother. But there had been times when his whole nature seemed to revolt against the license and wickedness of the age, and he had dared sometimes even to criticise the gods, and wonder at the tyranny of emperor, prætors, and priests. Could spies have listened and reported these words, and was he in durance because of them? Certainly there could be no truth in the suspicion of his master's that he had been led away by the obscure and singular sect they called Christians!

Hector turned himself nervously about, the old couch creaking beneath his tall, sinewy frame, and just then Salome's welcome face appeared, as she drew aside an inner curtain and announced supper. He rose with a quick motion, as if thrusting sad thoughts far from him, and strode into the next room, where a modest board was laid in the shape of a crescent, with a broad divan surrounding it, except at the opening, which gave room for the servant to enter and pass the dishes inside the half circle. The brother and sister always ate together, for Hector loved and tenderly cherished his one female relative, who had indeed been half spoiled by her doting brothers.

By mutual consent the subject of the brother now gone for over a fortnight, was not resumed at first, nor that of the lost amulet. Instead, Hector told of a new throw he had been practicing at the gymnasium, and Salome grew cheerful chatting over a call from an old playmate not before seen for many moons. She had sketched in detail her looks, her dress, and all she said, when she suddenly broke off to cry:

"There! I know I had that amulet on when she came, for I saw it gleam on my neck as I glanced in the bit of steel mirror set into the wall of our vestibule when I hastened to admit her. Let me see!"

She buried her dimpled chin in her hand and thought a minute, then sprang to her feet. "I believe I have it! I followed dear Theta across the court to the very street entrance and peeped out through the wall gate, as we said farewell. Then I saw an escort of soldiers, with some of those gay courtiers from the Castle, coming close, and knew it was best not to let them see me, as I was unveiled, so I hastily shut the gate. And now I remember that I caught the silken tassel of my fillet in the latch, and had to jerk it away—perhaps it was then I dropped my charm. Come, Hector, if you have finished your supper let us go and see."

He rose good-naturedly. "If it fell outside it has been picked up long before this," he said, chewing complacently on his last date.

away the food, satisfying her own hunger with large mouthfuls as she did so.

Salome reached the wall door first, and shuffled her sandals with gay impatience on the smooth paving stones, as she awaited her brother's leisurely approach. Their little home was situated on one of the more quiet streets of Philippi, and this was unlighted, except by a pale thread of a moon,

Instantly Hector was upon them, and his arena training stood him in good stead.—See page 4.

"Yes, but it may be inside, you see, or caught in a cleft of the wall, or brushed into a corner. Bring a lantern, Persis, and let us try. If I can find it again I shall take it for a good omen."

The small iron censer, flat in shape and swung from three chains, was brought and lighted, Salome caught up a chlamys, or long wrap, tossed it picturesquely over her head, winding it about her chin and lips so that only the brow and eyes were visible, then crying impatiently, "Come!" started out first, Hector striding more slowly after, while Persis contented herself with clearing

low in the western sky. With the deliberate movements peculiar to him Hector inserted a clumsy key into the lock of the small portal, turned it, and let one wooden leaf fall inward upon its hinges. Then the two passed through the aperture, and, lifting high the lantern, began a search for the amulet, so precious to this heathen girl.

Both bent low, Hector fairly on his knees, searching the crevices of the stone pavement, and Salome, doubled under the long folds of her drapery, peering along the clear-running ditch of snow-water, brought from the mountains, which separated the sidewalk from the highway. They knew how unsafe were the streets at night in these lawless times, when the dissolute young officers from the Castle sometimes chose to steal out, disguised and masked, in search of adventure, to say nothing of thieves and rioters of lesser rank, who dared the galleys and terrible dungeons to ply their vocation.

But what could happen so near home? A step would place them behind the wall and locked door of their own little castle, which no one would dare to invade. So they continued to look about, oblivious of everything but their own exclamations and remarks, with which each spurred on the search.

Thus they failed to notice an outburst of song and laughter on a side street close by, or, perhaps, did not think it worth minding, and both were startled when suddenly at their very elbows appeared a tumultuous little crowd of well-muffled men, one or two bearing lanterns, and the rest reeling about with noisy talk and laughter.

"Quick!" cried Hector. "Run, Salome, run!"

But already the rioters had caught sight of the slender, white-draped figure, and with a loud laugh one tall young fellow leaped into the open gateway, barring her passage, while two more sprang to her sides, intercepting her movements.

Instantly Hector was upon them, and his arena training stood him in good stead now. At every swing of his powerful arms some one fell back with a howl of pain, and almost while one could tell it the whole party had dispersed, hastened thereto by the cry of one of the lantern-bearers:

"The bucket-men! The bucket-men!"

Breathing heavily, Hector looked about him. The crowd had melted like the dew. and Salome too was gone, having doubtless fled to the innermost recesses of the house.

Hector had no desire to be interviewed by the troublesome lictors, whom the populace called "men of the bucket" because they acted as a fire-patrol with tarred buckets of water in hand, as well as guardians of the streets. So he took advice of caution and, slipping quickly inside, locked his gate securely and hurried indoors, chuckling to think how surprised those young brawlers must have been to feel the weight of fists as hard as iron, and as heavy as a sledge-hammer.

The house was dark and still. As he stepped within from the moonlit court it struck a chill to his senses.

"Salome!" he called softly. "Salome!"

A frightened exclamation answered him, and the little slave girl, her eyes big with terror, confronted him.

"Oh!" she cried, "where is my mistress?"

"But do you not know?" he returned quickly. "She is here, of course—she must be. She is hidden somewhere, too scared to speak. Salome, dear! I am here. Your brother protects you. Oh, Salome, for Vesta's sake answer!"

But only the bare walls echoed his despairing cry. He ran to and fro, calling, searching, beseeching, groaning, cursing. He sent the little slave hither and yon, fierce as he had never been with her before, in his terrible anxiety. He ran to the roof, gazing out over the now silent street with great gasping breaths of despair. He sought in impossible nooks and crannies below, the tears gushing unashamed from his manly eyes. and then with a roar of rage and desperation, like a lion rushing upon its tormentors. he dashed out into the street, calling on the lictors for vengeance, utterly bereft of sense or caution.

Poor little Persis, frightened nearly out of her small wits, followed swiftly to the gate, and shook her head in perplexity as she slowly clanged it to behind him. Then throwing herself down in a dark corner of the wall, she crouched in a small heap, motionless with terror, and softly cried herself to sleep.

CHAPTER II.

IN AN UPPER CHAMBER.

DURING this turbulent scene, so common in all pagan cities as to cause no more than a passing thought to those who, safely locked within their own home walls, gladly turned a deaf ear to the brawls and crimes without, there was another scene taking place, as unlike this as the still lake of the mountains is unlike the sea in the fury of a storm. In a small room dimly lighted by flaring pine-knots, was gathered a little company, possibly twenty in number, who were noticeable only for their quiet manners, plain dress, and serene and lofty expression.

They were of all ages above young childhood, and they entered by twos and threes, stealing noiselessly to the barred outer door, there to give a peculiar knock which quickly gained them entrance. A password was spoken in a whisper, that most common being the Greek word "Ikthus," signifying "fish." This, universally given as the sign of the faith among believers, had a significance dear to them all, for its initials, taken in order, stood for "Jesus Christ, the Son of God, the Savior." It immediately admitted them, this night, and once inside, a spirit of delightful cordiality and brotherhood seemed to prevail.

They clasped hands like friends who meet after perils passed, and the gentle words, "Peace be with you!" seemed a favorite greeting. There was little laughter, or loud merriment, but smiles, serenity, and peace, seemed to pervade the whole assembly. For, strangely enough, here the patrician, the freedman and the slave met upon terms of seeming equality, and addressed each other as "brother" and "sister." All this, too, in a haughty Macedonian city that, in imitation of great Rome, of which it was a colony, disdained the rest of the world as conquered slaves, drawing the lines of rank so sharply that men had been thrown into dungeons—yes, even executed—for daring to presume upon certain privileges at banquet or in council chamber, in a simple matter of food, dress, or ornament, arrogated by those of higher rank.

The meeting was well under way, a hymn had been sung and a prayer offered, such as had never ascended to a heathen deity, when once more came the peculiar knock, this time louder, more imperative and startling than was customary.

The outer door having been opened, there was an unusual commotion in the small square vestibule, which caused the Presbyter, or leader, just beginning to address the assembly, to cease speaking and look intently that way. Every one's eyes followed his. In each face was expectation and something of anxiety, but neither fear nor cringing. They knew this might mean arrest, imprisonment, possibly death, for each and all, but they faced it steadily, as those who rest upon a Power stronger than their own.

The door opened wide and two women and a man entered, half leading, half carrying, the figure of another female, well muffled in white and apparently unconscious.

"Forgive our untimely interruption, brethren," said the man in deprecating tones, "but we found this woman lying in the deep angle of the doorway, and she seems badly hurt, or very ill. We cannot make her answer, so far, and she appears dazed and sick."

"Let the women care for her," said the Presbyter in tones that were instinctively commanding, though not with arrogance.

At once the women gathered about the figure, which had been laid on a divan, and putting back her chlamys, one said:

"Ah, but she is a girl only, and so fair!"

"Yes, and by her dress a modest one," put in another. "Poor child! how came she out at this hour?"

"See, she is hurt!" cried another, pointing to a swelling rising rapidly above the stranger's forehead. "She has had a heavy blow—there! her eyes are opening. Stand back a little and do not frighten her with so many strange faces."

Salome—for our readers have guessed it was she—did indeed open her eyes and gaze about. At first her expression was wild and unnatural, but presently it became more rational and only wondering in quality.

"Did they kill me?" she asked in a weak voice. "Is this the Realm of Shades? and you—surely you are not the cruel Eumenides come to harass me? You look too kind for that!"

"No, no, child! you are still upon earth and quite safe with those who mean you well," said one of the women who had assisted the girl in. "Are you feeling better now?"

"My head aches," raising her hand feebly to the swelled brow. "I remember—it was that blow! It must have knocked me senseless. Oh, did Hector get away? Were they too many for him? How he did fight! But I could not get inside the gate, there were so many in my way. Where is Hector?"

The women looked at each other, and one with a peculiarly sweet face answered gently:

"He is not here just now. Who gave you the blow, fair maiden?"

"I do not know, lady. I ran down the narrow court close by our house to get away, and soon I heard footsteps which I thought were Hector's. I turned to speak, and something came crashing down upon my head—that is all I can recall about it."

"Who is Hector?" asked the dame again, as she tenderly bathed the wound, and bound it up with her own kerchief.

"My brother. We were looking for my lost amulet. Alas! it is as I said—the gods have given us over to destruction."

"No, my child. God has protected and

spared you. You fell into the deep shadow of our doorway, where no one else could see you until our feet were guided hither by grace.''

"But Hector?"

"He too will be cared for—fear not! Our God is ' mighty to save.' ''

"You mean great Jupiter, because he is the protector of the Games? If only he will!"

"No, child, we mean—but wait! Her head is troubling her again. Let her rest.''

For even with the words Salome's eyes took on a wild look and she was soon tossing and muttering with fever. Finding she was to prove an all-night's care, at least, these kind Samaritans removed her to a pallet in a small room of the little house, and left one of their number to sit beside her, while the others reverently returned to the meeting. Here, quickly putting aside the interruption, they listened with rapture to the words of hope, comfort and encouragement spoken by their leader, and joined eagerly in such prayers and hymns as seemed to bring heaven into the plain little room, hidden by its humbleness from outer violence.

It was the middle of the next forenoon before Salome came to herself once more. All night she had tossed in the grip of fever, tenderly soothed and cared for by the sweet-faced woman, who proved to be the occupant of the house, and who was called Elizabeth. She was a young matron of a gentle cast of countenance, yet one versed in faces might have read in the brow, well developed above the eyes, and in the lips and chin, fine-grained but firm, a power of endurance and a force of will which the singularly quiet ways and speech scarce hinted at. The first impression she gave was entirely restful. In her eyes was a peace passing comprehension, Salome thought, as she curiously watched her, and she wondered what could give her that supreme content, for she was evidently very poor, and her garments were such as the pretty Greek girl would have scorned to wear. Besides, her pallor showed she was not well, and her husband seemed a gruff, silent man who spoke roughly, if at all.

Salome from her pallet watched every gentle movement and puzzled much to learn why, through all that was hard and trying, she seemed still to hug some secret consciousness of joy so close that no mere outward happening could affect it in the least.

"Perhaps," thought the little pagan after she had lain for an hour or two thus questioning, "perhaps she has received an oracle from the Priest of Apollo at the temple. Perhaps she feels sure that, no matter what may happen just now, she will have good fortune later on, and so bides her time, and scarcely knows anything is wrong. It looks that way. Ah! I was happy till I lost my amulet—that is," as memory came fully back, "I was as happy as people usually are in this world. Of course I wanted to be rich and noble, and it was a great trial to have to walk instead of being carried in a litter through the streets, but—I had my brothers."

She drew a long sigh, and Elizabeth came quickly to her side.

"You are weary?" she asked with her placid smile. "Shall I talk to you?"

"Please tell me about yourself, dear lady. I wonder about you as I lie here, and that tires me."

Elizabeth laughed brightly. "There is so little to tell! You have guessed from my dress that I am a Jewish woman, and I am proud to say I was born in our beautiful city—Jerusalem. But my husband, Junius, is a Roman, free born."

"Indeed?" questioned Salome with wonder, for the marriage of a free-born Roman to a Jew was extremely rare. Her hostess smiled a little and asked with gentle irony:

"Do you think that so unlikely? Yet why not, Salome? There is neither Jew, nor Greek, nor Roman either, in the sight of God—all are equal and his children." At which the girl, still too weak to argue, only stared dumbly, amazed at such strange ideas.

"But," thought she, "those Jews are all queer. I have even heard they claim to have a special god, who leads and cares for them. I suppose, too, they really were rich and powerful once, but now what miserable creatures they are!"

For, though one of an enslaved nation herself, being a conquered Thracian, Salome looked down upon the universally hated Jew. Yet this was only as a class; in individual cases she often liked and even honored them. So now she listened to Elizabeth, thinking how sweet her smile and soft her voice, until sleep closed her eyes in rest, which did much to restore her to perfect health.

Seeing how very weak she still was, her hostess left her to slumber and stepped outside into the narrow court of the humble dwelling. Here she called softly, "Nadab! Nadab!" and presently a little boy, who so closely resembled the fair Jewess that no one could have mistaken their relationship, came bounding in from the street.

"Well, mother?" he asked in a voice full of loving respect, "what is it you need me for now?"

"I will tell you, my son; but first, did you wet up the flags as I bade you?"

"Yes, mother."

"That is right. And now I want you to go to the second street south, and look along its length until you come to a low house close by a narrow walled court, and upon the corner of a paved and covered footway leading east. Inquire there for a man named Hector, and when he is found tell him his sister is here and safe, though ill, and that he may come and see her, if he please."

"Very well, mother." Then in a whisper, "But is she a Christian?" and he nodded his head toward the house to indicate the guest of a night.

"No, Nadab, she is a pagan."

"But, mother, why then—"

"My boy, have you not yet learned the true spirit of Christ? Does he make any distinction in his love and succor? Is not our great Paul, whom we are soon expecting here, constantly showing this to us in all his teachings? Surely, Nadab, you know this."

"Yes, yes, I was not meaning just that. I was thinking of—of our safety, mother."

"We can leave that with Jesus, child," she answered with a smile that made her pale face radiant.

The boy looked at her with a little wonder and much admiration in his eyes. Then he gave his head a wise shake.

"But father?" he asked archly.

Elizabeth's uplifted countenance clouded swiftly over for an instant, then as swiftly cleared.

"Let us trust he will be glad to have us do the right thing, Nadab—and until he speaks we will take his consent for granted. Now run along, my son, and raise no more objections, I beg."

Her sweet smile softened the reproof, and he waved his hand gayly to her as he started briskly off upon his errand. But his mother, left alone, stood a moment in thoughtful silence, then bent her head and clasped her hands. She was asking help for needs which only she and her God could under-stand. In a moment, cheered and strength-ened, she turned away, sought out from a little shed at the rear of the court a large bunch of flags, and seating herself on the stone pavement, was soon busily employed weaving them into a basket.

It was not a great while before Nadab re-turned, looking flushed from his run in the blazing sunshine. As soon as he could catch his breath he burst out with a long story. He had been everywhere in the near vicinity without finding any trace of the man, for the little house she had told him of was evi-dently deserted. He had knocked loud and long without making any one hear, and when some of the neighbors appeared, to ask what he wanted, they had told him that not one of the family had been seen this morning. One of these, who had been wake-ful last night, believed that Hector had been dragged off by the "bucket-men" to prison, and that Salome and her little maid had fled to some friends in another part of the city.

"And did you let them know where she really is?" asked Elizabeth quickly.

Nadab looked at her with a merry expres-sion on his face. "Do you think I am so foolish?" he laughed. "No, I told them noth-ing."

"It was not necessary," responded the mother with dignity. "Though we must al-ways be 'harmless as doves,' so must we be 'wise as serpents' also, in these hard times. We will do our best for the poor heathen girl, but we cannot let her friends know all the secrets of our home. Well, what next?"

"I had just finished talking with the man and was turning away to come home, he having gone inside, when a big boy with a splendid face and figure came swinging down the street. He passed me by and, as I looked back after him, I saw that he, too, had gone to the little wall gate, and was knocking as if he fully expected to get in. Finding nobody came, he stepped back and looked the house all over with surprise, then knocked again, this time in an odd way— three raps, a rest—two more, a rest—then one. But no one came. After a little he be-gan walking slowly towards me, still look-ing back as if he could not give it up. I thought this might be the one I was looking for, as he was a well-grown youth, so I stepped up to him and asked, 'Is your name Hector?' He looked at me in a queer way for a minute, then said, 'No; why do you ask me that?' But you have taught me caution, mother, so I only said, 'No matter,' and walked away."

"That was right, Nadab. Still—" His mother mused a moment. "No, she has spoken only of the one brother, Hector. And they really think he is in prison? Poor child! What will she do? She seems to have no other protector. I have talked with her a little and she says they are orphans. But come, while she sleeps we must hurry on the weaving, that we may earn the more to care for her. Sit right down here by me. You will soon grow cool in this shade."

For this Christian woman and her son eked out the scanty family purse by weaving baskets, and thus were enabled to carry on their charities without trenching upon what was required by the master of the house, the haughty Junius. He was, meantime, at his post as driver of a gang of street-cleaners, called police, mostly convicts or runaway slaves undergoing punishment, and thus condemned to serve at hard labor, chained together by twos, or fours, under a task-master who kept them to their labor with a whip of many thongs, called a scourge.

It was an employment to brutalize any man, and Elizabeth grieved in secret as she saw her once kind and loving husband grow daily more haughty, stern, and importunate of his own rights and comforts. Junius was not a Christian, nor in fact much of a pagan, either. He affected the hard philosophy of Seneca, Socrates, and lesser teachers, who bade men endure because they must, until endurance became impossible, when they were pointed to but one relief—the "open door."

This door of death by one's own hand was startlingly common. When a man lost heart or fortune, favor at court, or the preferment he had been hoping for, he fell upon his sword, or drank the poisoned cup, and really thought himself brave because he dared the dark unknown rather than suffer defeat in the present life. As if one could ever escape disgrace by added cowardice! As if such a death were not the loudest proclamation of utter defeat! As if it were not always a braver thing to meet a foe face to face than to turn the back and leap into a pit to escape him!

Yet Junius was but one of many who, disgusted with a religion which made the gods but a more powerful humanity, controlled by the every-day passions of every-day men, set himself up as his own only god to worship as long as he could stand erect, and to slay as soon as he was forced to yield to circumstances.

It was a dark, cold, and selfish belief, warping both heart and understanding, and Elizabeth's wifely heart yearned to bring him to a knowledge of the warm, living, loving faith in which she joyed and triumphed; but so far her efforts had been vain.

CHAPTER III.

WITH ELIZABETH.

BY and by Salome, waking from her long nap, heard soft strains stealing from the next room, apparently. She lay quite still, hardly awake yet, and dreamily listened. There were two voices, evidently—one a boy's, and the other, with its smooth, clear cadences, she felt certain belonged to her sweet-faced hostess.

Salome smiled in quiet enjoyment. She felt serenely comfortable; her head had ceased to throb, her fever to burn. A refreshing breeze blew across her from a window close by, bringing the faint perfume of jasmine blossoms, and the room in which she lay was fresh and cool from a recent wet sweeping and sanding. It was a tiny room, and plain to meagreness. Yet it gave her none of that repulsion she always felt in the homes of the very poor with which she was familiar, for its atmosphere was sweet with cleanliness.

The room, her own white pallet, the perfume, and the song, seemed somehow to melt and mingle in a perfect harmony, and she closed her eyes restfully, listening, while her body basked in calm repose. To this mood the music seemed to add its enjoyment, for it was of a gentle, peaceful character, and the voices, if untrained, were sincere and sweet. She listened to the words:

"But God, who is so rich in grace."

"How queer!" she thought. "That means kindness, good-will, generous giving. Not rich in great countries, luscious fruits, or beautiful garments and jewels—no, nor even in magnificent temples and many priests,"—as she had always imagined her gods to be rich.

"By His love, freely given."

"Oh, freely, indeed! No, no!" thought the little pagan, "that is not quite true. We must win great Apollo's or Diana's favors by gifts and sacrifices, and constant propitiation in processions and offerings."

But the song went on:

"E'en while we yet were dead in sin
Hath raised us up to heaven."

"Dead in sin!"—that struck her as a singular expression. It made her think of Pluto and the dark Nether World of helpless Shades and wicked Dæmons. But the next line was beautiful—"Hath raised us up to heaven!"

She knew about Olympus, where the gods dwelt in bliss, though, when hearing of all their quarrels and heart-burnings, it often occurred to her that they could not find it entirely delightful there! But these singers chanted as if fairly in heaven now and here, gladness thrilling all along the sweet, slow notes, as melody and merriment shake from the quivering roulades of the mavis in the loveliness of early morning. It made Salome's heart beat to a freer measure, also, and she rose up in bed, thinking:

"I must not lie here playing at illness when dear Hector may not know where I am. I will get up and put on my garments as soon as they cease that sweet singing."

But it stopped, even with her resolve, and in another instant the trim, small head of Elizabeth appeared at the door.

"Are you awake?" she asked gayly, and Salome noticed on her fair face a radiance brighter than smiles.

"Yes," was the reply, "and much better. Has my brother come for me yet?"

Her hostess stepped closer. "My dear," she said affectionately, "I am glad you are better; but you must keep quiet yet a little while," (seeing the girl about to rise) "or the fever may return and undo all the benefit of this long sleep."

"But my brother?"

Elizabeth dipped a soft cloth in a jar of water standing near, and placed it on the wounded head.

"Peace, child!" she murmured, pressing the eager little figure back upon her pallet. "My Nadab has been to look for your brother, but he is not at home, it seems, just now. Can you not wait patiently a few hours?"

"But it is so queer! Perhaps—where is Persis? Did he find her?"

"Your little slave girl? No, the door was locked. They may both be out seeking for you."

"Why, surely!" Salome caught at the idea with relief. "I never thought of that. Of course they would be. And how odd that I should be lying here, perfectly safe, so near home! Poor Hector! He will be in despair about me."

"You are fond of your brother?" remarked the gentle woman, bringing her weaving and sitting down sociably close by.

"Of my brothers, you mean. Oh, yes!"

Elizabeth looked up quickly. "Then you have more than one?"

"Yes, two—Hector and Herklas."

"But you did not mention the latter."

"No, alas! for I do not know where he is."

Tears came into her eyes, and Elizabeth, fearing new agitation, said quickly:

"I should not have asked—we will speak of other things."

"No, it will not hurt me to tell you. I have longed to talk about him, often, but Persis is so stupid, and Hector thinks it only makes me more unhappy. Herklas is my younger brother—I am between the two in age—not yet sixteen and the dearest boy in all the world."

"Dearer than Hector?" smiled the other, pleased with the girl's animation.

"Well, Hector is a great, strong man— more like a father, I often think, though a boy too in many ways. Besides, he is gone a great deal, for you must know he has twice won the wreath at the Olympics for wrestling. Thus he is ever thinking of his gymnasium, his new throws, and his plans for next year. But Herklas was almost like a girl in some ways—gentle and kind. He likes music better than fighting, and we used to sing together by the hour to the merry strains of his viol. He was in training for the temple choir. He was away most of the day at the shop, to be sure, but we always had our evenings together, and we were very happy."

"But you speak in the past, my child. Surely you do not believe him to be dead?"

"Oh, I hope not! Yet how can I tell? Madam," bending forward with an anxious look, and speaking almost in a whisper, "did you ever know any of those despised people called Christians?"

Elizabeth started and the blood flushed her whole face, then receded to pallor.

"Why do you ask?" she said sharply.

"Because I sometimes think Herklas has in some way been drawn into their hands. It is thus Vitellis, his master, hints, though he dare not come out boldly and say so. They tell me they are very sly and cunning, and that they stop at nothing."

"Who tells you so?" asked the woman in a muffled voice, bending closer over her work.

"Oh, the priests—and everybody. They say they take in Jew or Greek, Cyprian or Athenian, Persian or Cappadocian—all is fish that comes to their net."

A smile stole about the sweet, grave lips of Elizabeth. "And what do they do then, dear child, when thus they have become 'fishers of men'?"

"Ah, that is just what I do not know! Undoubtedly they are full of sorceries, and they may have changed my poor Herklas into an animal and sent him to wander dismally among the hills, for aught I know. Think! even should I meet him there I would never know him."

The other's laugh rang out merrily. "What nonsense! Do you actually believe such things, and you nearly a woman grown? Pooh, pooh, my dear! such superstitions are unworthy of you."

"But what so queer in that? Was not Narcissus turned into a flowering tree? And who, indeed, are the nymphs and naiads but wood and water clothed in human form? We hear of many being punished, or made immortal, by such transformations."

Elizabeth's answer was an arch glance and the words: "You give the Christians great power, Salome; as great as you ascribe to your own gods. Yet they pretend to nothing above other human beings, except a clearer idea of the Love that is divine."

Salome was silenced. She could but feel the force of this argument. Either she must give up her assumption that the Christians were a mean and despicable people, or else the other, that they could work such terrible changes as even the heathen gods, themselves, upon man. But before she could find an answer Elizabeth broke out again:

"Salome, it is only ignorance that makes people look upon us in this light—"

"'Us'?" interrupted the girl with a startled look. "What do you mean?"

"Just what I say, for I too am a Christian."

She turned a trifle pale as she made the bold assertion, and Salome drew back with an expression of alarm—indeed, almost horror. She had heard such terrible things of this new sect! In every oracle received, in every address given at the forum, in the private teachings of the priests, as well as

in their public ministry, she had listened repeatedly to warnings of the most austere nature leveled against this new worship. She had heard the Crucified One alternately named as a common criminal making uncommon claims, as a sorcerer whose arts could not save himself, as a lunatic and fanatic, as a common slave Jew, seditious and troublesome—as everything but the gentle teacher of a God of love. Is it any wonder she gazed upon her hostess as if she had suddenly turned into a monster? But the latter went on quickly, not giving her time to voice her astonishment:

"It is to Christians you are indebted for your escape, last night. Instead of doing harm we are commanded to be kind and loving, even to our enemies. This is the first example set us by Christ, and nobody can be truly one of His unless that rule of conduct is carried out. Have I ill-treated you? Did we show you insults, or neglect, last night? Yet one and all of us are proud to own ourselves followers of Christ."

Salome listened with almost breathless surprise.

"It is true!" she acknowledged half inaudibly. "It is all true, but—" She raised herself upon one elbow and bent her large dark eyes upon the fair woman beside her. "Tell me more!" she said with unconscious imperiousness. "Either they have lied to me, or else you are far better than your own God. Tell me more!"

A beautiful smile broke over Elizabeth's flushed face. "Indeed I should love to!" she answered heartily. "I always feel that if one really understands our lovely faith, he cannot help but embrace it. Yet alas! these are troublous times and we are few and feeble. Too often fear and self-interest tie our tongues when we should speak out boldly for the right. I risk something in thus talking to you, even, Salome, but I am resolved to think no more of that—only of your soul's happiness."

Then, beginning with Christ's beautiful life and continuing until His marvelous death, she told in plain and simple words the story of the Cross. Salome lay back on her pillow, but scarcely took her eyes from the speaking face opposite during the whole of the recital. Once or twice, she interrupted by a question or two, and Elizabeth noticed that these questions were shrewd and thoughtful. Not a word was lost upon her; not a thought came into the mind of the relator that did not seem instantly reflected in that of the listener. They were in perfect accord, except for the overwhelming sense of doubt and mystery that shadowed the girl's understanding.

Could it be true? Could the great and majestic God of all the universe come down to our needs, into our homes and our hearts, to heal, to work, to suffer, and to die, just for us? And all this for what? To teach us the better way of living; to make sacrifice and self-surrender divine, and self-seeking and worldly honors contemptible; to make us His friends instead of servants; to bring heaven to us here upon earth if we would but look, listen, and live as He taught us! Surely, no god, from great Zeus to the weakest Erynne of mischief, ever conceived of an idea so tender, and so filled with blessing to man. Salome drew a long sigh as Elizabeth ceased, then murmured in a faint voice:

"It is a marvelous legend, but do you expect me to believe it literally?"

"Assuredly," replied the other. "Am I not risking my own safety in telling you? And would I do that for a mere senseless tale?"

Salome lay very still. She was as white as the cover of sail-cloth on which she reclined. Strange, half-formed ideas, too great for her undeveloped intellect to grasp so quickly, surged through her brain. Elizabeth, glancing at her, saw the wistful, darkened eyes and the pallor, but only half guessed at the emotion they signified.

"Poor little girl!" she said pitifully. "You are harassed and troubled, and One is waiting to help. Cast all your care upon Him."

Suddenly Salome sat upright. "My care? It is anxiety for my brothers. How can He bear that for me?"

"Ah, do you not see? If you trusted Him as I do, you would not worry. You would know they were safe with Him, and that He cares for them even more than you do. So whatever came, in life or death, you could rest upon that knowledge and be at peace."

"Oh!" breathed the girl, sinking back once more, "it sounds so restful—if it is true. If only I could be certain!"

She nestled her head lower and closed her eyes. She wanted to think in quiet; but Elizabeth, looking at her, believed her wearied, and reproached herself for talking so much, and upon subjects so exciting. So she said softly:

"Well, then, rest now. And be sure it is all true. When you are stronger we will talk again." Then she left her guest to the

sleep or musings which she felt sure would follow.

Salome was a mere child, as yet, in wisdom and discretion, even if, by Oriental computation, a woman in years. She had been most tenderly cherished, having received a larger share of attention and petting than often fell to the lot of a girl among the lower classes. She was inclined to be petulant and vain, in consequence, but her heart was loving and faithful and there were capabilities in her nature which might develop stronger traits with time.

Just now, lonely, homesick and wounded, she longed only for consolation, and Elizabeth's sweet words had fallen upon her soul with tenfold power. Had they come when all was fortunate she might have overlooked them—now she clung to every sentence, repeating it again and again, longing to make this faith her very own.

CHAPTER IV.

IMPRISONED.

WHEN Hector rushed so madly into the street he knew well enough that he was risking his own safety. It was not for any common citizen to disturb the sleepers of Philippi, whatever the gay nobles at the Castle might do. As he went tearing along after those who, he felt sure, had carried his sister off to a slavery which, however gilded by wealth, was at best horrible and degrading, he did not cease to howl out threatenings and curses, not only loud but deep. Such high-handed deeds had been comparatively unknown in this beautiful mountain-walled town, except when a temporary residence of some of the dissolute Roman court brought the practices of that metropolis to its quiet streets, and Hector felt all the indignation of a man unused to oppression and tyranny.

For amid the industrious Philippians the Games, both Olympic and Isthmian, were held in high repute, and a well-trained participant such as Hector, was always treated with respect. Unlike the Roman gladiators, who were almost invariably criminals, or captives, condemned to death, and whipped on to their feats of valor by lictors in the pay of the government, the contestants in the Greek Games must be free-born, unsullied by crime, and of good reputation in the community. Their only reward was supposed to be the golden wreath bestowed by the judges, but in reality a successful runner, or wrestler, was scarcely ever in want of money. Many of the city's privileges were open to him, and the wealthier citizens were proud to make him the object of bounteous gifts and favors.

No wonder he felt himself in some sense superior to his neighbors. Thus, amid all Hector's rage to-night, was a strong feeling that, had these people known just who he was, they would not have dared thus to molest him, and this added an extra smart to his fears and doubts.

He did not cease his raging till he reached the very gates of the Castle, where he was promptly challenged by the sentinels.

" My sister!" cried Hector, the only password he could think of then. " Where is that mad party of drunken men? I saw their rich robes under the togas—I saw their link-bearers and forerunners—I know who they are well enough. Let the wretches give me back my sister or—"

" Peace!" muttered the outer sentinel, an honest fellow who did not care to see this venturesome young Thracian run his neck into certain trouble. " Peace! You will rouse the garrison, and what will they care for you and your sister?"

Even as he spoke came a ringing shout from one of the narrow slits of windows in the nearest tower.

" Arrest that brawler and fling him into prison! If that will not stop him, try the stocks or the scourge."

The tone was authoritative, and before Hector could make his escape, even had he tried to do so, he was seized by half a dozen soldiers, who soon beat him into tractability and dragged him down the hill to one of the loathsome dungeons of the prison in the forum, reserved for slaves and criminals of lowest rank. These dungeons were wet, cold, noisome, and rotting underground holes, full of pestilential odors, and with no windows except perhaps an inch-wide slit in the wall far above the head of the unhappy occupant. Here, chained to the moldy floor, with no bed, unless by special favor a heap of rotting straw, his condition was such as to kill all life and hope, if not the intellect, entirely.

Hector's manful resistance to his captors only increased his punishment, for finding him so lusty a fighter the keeper thought best to double-chain him—that is, secure

both feet instead of one, and have an extra chain run from foot to hand. He had been almost beside himself during his capture, and when his dazed senses returned he found himself unable to move and in utter darkness, a prey to the most anxious thoughts—anxious not only for himself, but for the sister he so fondly loved.

But in such a situation there was nothing to do but wait upon the will of others with a patience born of helplessness, and he lay back immovable and silent, though every heart-throb was a groan of wretchedness.

Meanwhile, a few days later, Salome found herself well enough to get about, and, begging the company of her hostess, the two sallied forth to see what had happened at the little house within the wall. It was hard for Salome to keep her steps down to a sober pace, so anxious was she to be at home again, and though she was still weak, and her head sore from the heavy bruise, she felt all the exhilaration of a convalescent out once more in the fresh air and sunshine.

It seemed to her that her adopted city had never been so beautiful since she had come to it, a tiny child, from the adjoining country of Thracia. And indeed there was ground for her raptures. Philippi, this fair city of Macedonia, seemed endowed with every gift of art and nature.

If not actually a seaport, it shared honors with Neapolis on the coast, and was scarcely ten miles inland, while the approach over a ridge of high land and across the wide historic plain, crossed and recrossed by numerous runlets of clear water, was really beautiful. To the west and north loomed the mountains forming the border line between Macedonia and Thracia, and from their pure snows came the precious water in such quantities it had once been called the " Place of Fountains." It was a garrisoned city, and the walls of the fort and castle rose massive and white against the south-western horizon, while its being a colonia of Rome gave it especial privileges, and freedom from most of the oppressions naturally expected in a conquered town.

When the two women reached the little house, somewhat aloof from the business portion, Salome knocked loud and long at the gate, but without response, and finally a neighbor appeared to say:

" The family have all gone away and— why, Salome, is that you?"

" Yes, indeed!" said the girl quickly. " But

what do you mean? Where is Hector? Where is our slave girl, Persis? Has no one been here since I left?"

"No one except your brother Herklas, and he could not gain entrance."

"Herklas? My brother Herklas—the younger—are you sure?"

"Certes! My daughter saw him from the roof and said he seemed much troubled because he could make no one hear."

"When was that?" interposed Elizabeth quickly.

He named the morning, and she felt sure it was this lost brother whom Nadab had seen when searching for Hector. Should she speak about it, or would it only add to the girl's regrets and sorrows? Salome interrupted her musings by asking sharply:

"But where is he now? Did he leave no word?"

"Not with any of my house. I know nothing more about him. Thirza told me he went away soon, as if in haste, and has not been seen again."

"Strange! And oh, how unfortunate that I was not here! I am fated to lose all I love." She caught Elizabeth's eyes fixed upon her in mild rebuke, and added more gently, "But let us hope all will yet come right. Can you tell me nothing of Hector, or Persis?"

By this time a group of women, many with water-jars upon their heads, just as they had come from filling them at the public fountains, had gathered around the two. One of these shook her head and muttered:

"I know what the men think, well enough."

The remark was not intended for Salome's ears, but she caught it and turned with the quick question:

"What, then?"

The woman hesitated; but another, bolder or perhaps less tender-hearted, blurted out:

"They all say he is in prison!"

"But why—why?" Salome's eyes were wild with terror. "What has my good Hector done? You all know his honesty, his high standing. Why, he is a twice-crowned Olympionic!"

Her voice rang with indignation and pride.

"We know," said one sorrowfully, "but you forget some of the Court are here."

"The Court? But what of that? A contestant is exempt from imprisonment for any cause for a month before the Games, and tomorrow the month begins."

"What do these Roman patricians care for that?" asked one young girl with the dark, spirited face of a Syrian Jew. "Little they stop for your sacred games and customs."

Salome turned from one to another, her face pallid.

She was trembling all over with the dreadful sense of outrage and helplessness.

"How have they dared!" she broke out in a deep voice as unlike the petulance of all former griefs as her present emotion, entirely for the dishonor done to another, was unlike her former selfish tears. "How have they dared to imprison my noble brother!" Then, turning swiftly towards the house, she added, "Wait! There is a locksmith near by whom I know. I will have him open this door, and see for myself what is within."

She was off on swift feet, for anxiety lent her wings and lost her all sense of weakness, and the women stood looking after her, their sun-browned faces full of consternation and pity. Very soon she appeared once more, accompanied by a man whose loose tunic was gathered up in a bag-form and thrust beneath his girdle to hold a lot of small jingling tools. As soon as the door was open Salome rushed inside, followed by the whole group, whose curiosity would not be balked by any sense of delicacy.

Salome, running on ahead, was confronted only by the silent rooms, and suddenly her heart failed her. She turned back and grasped Elizabeth's hand, her own cold as ice. "Come with me," she whispered. "I am afraid of what I may see. Oh, pray to your Christ to spare me now!"

"He is with us even here," whispered the Christian woman, her face growing bright with inner radiance. "He knows your grief, dear, and will give you strength to bear it."

Salome looked at her and caught something of her divine faith. She ceased to tremble, a warmer rush of blood set her heart to more natural beating, and, stilled to endurance, she led her companion forward.

After all there was nothing to see. It was at once apparent that no one had occupied these rooms since the strange night of so many happenings. The table, but half cleared of that late supper, was now given over to flies and odors, and upon the stone floor of the apartment, where Salome had been lying when Hector came in, a yellowed rose, which her friend had dropped upon her afternoon visit, lay crumbled into dust.

Could it be she had ever thought herself unhappy here? In the shadow of these darker griefs those seemed but summer clouds, almost transparent to the glory behind.

As she looked around her she gave a sob and turned to Elizabeth, who seemed at that moment her only friend.

"What shall I do? Where shall I go?" she cried bitterly. "The gods of my fathers have abandoned me."

"The blessed Christ, who is yours as well as mine, Salome, will never leave us nor forsake us. Come to Him, poor tired heart, and come with me. Until your brother is found you shall share my home."

"But you are not rich," objected Salome, "and I am a useless girl."

"You need not be. You shall help me with the basket-weaving, and we who follow Christ always share with each other. Be one of us in every way, and you shall not want."

They were quite alone by this time, the others having fully satisfied their curiosity and returned to their neglected tasks. Salome stood in thoughtful silence a moment.

"Does this mean I must abandon all hope of finding my brothers?" she asked.

"No, I trust not. My husband, Junius, sometimes has opportunities to learn who are in the prison, though the keeper has no right to tell. Let us go to the market-place and see if we can find him there."

It seemed indeed the only thing to do. With quivering lips Salome turned away from the deserted place which had once been warm with the feeling of love and home, but was now like the tomb of hopes departed, and sadly followed her guide into the street. The locksmith, who had stopped for a chat with one of the men living near, responded to her signal to come and fasten up the gate once more, and paying him out of the few silver pieces she had in her possession, the two women at length left the now gloomy precinct, to turn into a wider street beyond, leading directly to the forum, or market-place.

Like the more imposing forum of Rome, this was built in the shape of a parallelogram, the stone wall surrounding it being fashioned into massive arches. Within the unroofed space were the booths of the market gardeners, the shambles of the butchers and the pretty stalls of the flower-and-herb sellers. Near the center was a raised dais

for public speakers, often occupied by traveling showmen or jugglers, surrounded by stone benches always plentifully filled with loungers and lookers-on. At one end was the court of justice, roofed with tent-cloth, with a raised divan for the judges' seats, and beyond it, well walled and with gates of bronze, was the prison court, beneath which were the dungeons and off from which were the keeper's living apartments. At the further end of the forum were the religious houses—namely, the various temples, the homes of the priests, the blocks of sacrifice and the votive offerings. In close connection, though outside its many arches, were the palaces of the Duumvirs, the two mayors of Philippi, who received their authority direct from Rome, and were almost kingly in their pride and state.

Thus in this great oblong space centered all the civil and religious life of the city, to say nothing of its business. Here honest traders bought and sold; here dishonest magicians, fakirs and sorcerers plied their low arts, and sought to draw the idle crowd; here rich brokers in purple togas talked of finance, or borrowed and lent their money; here poets sang their songs, and philosophers told their new systems of belief which were to revolutionize the world; here beggars displayed their sores; here the camel-trains from Damascus halted with their rich goods, while the air was filled with spices as they rested, and bits of gold stuffs gleamed from their wrappings; here were gold-workers from Thessaly, silversmiths from Ephesus, and dyers from Thyatira. Among these last there was great emulation to see how many shades of purple or crimson each could show, without trenching upon the sixteen shades reserved for royalty, and one who commanded great admiration for her exquisite tints was, as Elizabeth informed Salome, a friend of her own, and a woman.

As the two approached this great hive of industry to-day they saw it, as usual, teeming with a lively crowd of every nationality, while its babel of cries, laughter, and loud-voiced gabble came to their ears long before they reached its first open archway. Just as they entered this a large group appeared, surrounding some figure off at the right, whose child-like voice, strained to an unnatural pitch, was chanting out long sentences with the measured cadence of an oracle in the temple. These sometimes called forth laughter, again sudden silences, thrilled with shudders of dread.

The voice was a girl's, and pressing closer to her companion Salome whispered:

"Oh, who is it? I had just a glimpse of her through the crowd, and she seems no older than I! But she looked so strange! Her eyes were glassy and set, and her black hair tossed about in wild disorder. Who can she be?"

"A poor slave girl," returned Elizabeth in a low voice, hastening her steps. "Let us not get into the crowd. Her masters call her a prophetess, and say she is possessed by Python, the serpent of Apollo; but alas! I fear it is only an evil spirit that holds her mind in subjection. What brutal-looking men those are who own her! I have heard they make several denarii a day from her utterances—poor degraded creature!"

Salome turned upon her quickly. "What! When she is instructed by the sacred Python? Surely you do not understand, Elizabeth."

The latter's sweet lips curled with scorn. "Does your god, Apollo, think it then a noble thing to inspire a half-crazed girl to make a spectacle of herself, that her brutal masters may carouse upon her gains? Surely I would worship a purer, higher Deity than that!"

Salome looked astonished at her expression, but had no answer ready for her argument. Like most of her sex and rank, she knew little of her own mythology, outside the customary rites and ceremonies, so she could not reply to the higher learning and better sense of this well-instructed Christian.

──────◆──────

CHAPTER V.

MARKET-DAY IN PHILIPPI.

THEY hurried to the other side where were the buildings devoted to justice, and here they timidly stood about for some time, hoping to catch a glimpse of Junius, or to see some one of whom they could make inquiries as to his whereabouts. His wife knew he was not apt to be out with his chain gang of street workers at this hour, it being near the close of the afternoon, but it would not have been seemly for these veiled women to address upon the street any man who was not a near relative. They fortunately, however, came upon Nadab, who, with a beaming face, was minding a fruit stall while its owner was off on some errand, and who greeted his mother's well-known figure with a boyish shout of pleasure.

"Ah! mother," he exclaimed joyously, "you see I am selling fruit for Æbulus, and he is to give me a penny if I sell anything, and a quadrans if I do not. Do buy some dates for supper!"

"Indeed I shall have to!" laughed his mother, pleased at her boy's pleasure; "and meanwhile you run on swift feet and find your father while we in turn mind your stall. Do you know where he is?"

"Yes, indeed! See, he is over there by the wine-stall talking with two Romans from the Castle. Look! He is just raising the gourd to his lips."

Elizabeth looked, and a shadow fell upon her placid brow.

"Go, call him to come to me," she said gently.

Nadab went on the run, and the two women, watching, saw that Junius turned somewhat impatiently as the boy caught at his tunic, and motioned him away. But Nadab persisted, and after listening to him a moment, the father at length put down his empty gourd and reluctantly followed.

"Well?" He greeted his wife churlishly, as he approached with a stiff and dignified air. "What would you with me?"

"Junius," she returned, dropping her veil a trifle that she might smile up into his rugged face, "I would not have disturbed you, but this poor damsel has lost all track of her brother, and the neighbors think he has been arrested and flung into prison. Could you find out for her what prisoners are now in the dungeons?"

He gave a short, hard laugh. "How little women know! The only prisoners I have to do with are those of the chain gang. I am not a jailer, but a keeper of the streets."

"I know." Elizabeth's voice was quite unruffled. "Yet you are such friends with all these men in power, that I felt sure you would have some way of finding out this matter, if you chose."

The implied compliment pleased the man. Nothing so delights a petty tyrant as to feel that his women-folk think him of great influence in the community.

"Oh, I could, to be sure," he returned pompously, "only you know how it is with prisoners of the lower ranks—they are put down deep!" chuckling amusedly. "Most likely, though, they will have him in my gang before long."

Salome shuddered visibly. She recalled the miserable wretches she had sometimes seen whipped along to their tasks and nearly doubled under their heavy chains. Could her bright, brave Hector ever come to that!

Junius noticed the movement. "And glad he will be to exchange his cell for the free air, even in that way," he proceeded oracularly, without one touch of feeling. "You know not what those pits are, you women!"

"But my brother has done no wrong," spoke up Salome from behind her veil. "Besides, how can he be in order for the Games if he is left to grow weak and flabby of muscle in prison? And to-morrow begins the month of exemption."

This was quite a masterly stroke of the girl's. Junius cast an approving glance in her direction. Certainly, contestants must be looked after better than this. Every citizen had an interest in an Olympionic and should see that his rights were not interfered with, nor (what was more to the purpose in the mind of Junius) his strength weakened. So the man nodded his head once or twice with grave complacency.

"Very true," he said, "most correct! I will see what can be done. And now you would both better go home out of this crowded place. It is not just the spot for modest women."

Salome felt indignant and longed to reply, but left that for Elizabeth, who simply murmured, "Thank you!" in her soft voice, and drew the girl along beside her at a rapid pace. When they were well outside the forum, and still speechless with engrossing thoughts, the matron suddenly asked in a low voice:

"Salome, can I fully trust you? You would not do anything to harm one who is doing her best to be kind to you?"

"Certainly not, Elizabeth! Why do you ask such a question?"

"Because I would like to take you to a place I think might be blessed to you. But you must promise you will go as a friend, never as a spy and informer."

"I promise," said the girl readily enough, for she felt certain this meant being admitted to a religious gathering, and she was longing to hear more of these ideas which seemed to her so marvelous. "Where is it you would take me?"

"Come and see," said the other, with a smile so full of happiness that it shone even through her veil; and she hurried on with footsteps so rapid that it was difficult for the semi-invalid to keep up with her.

They quickly passed from the clamor of the more public streets to a long and quiet thoroughfare leading to one of the city gates, and, passing through this to the plain beyond the wall, they turned to the left, and soon came to a shady grove on the banks of one of the many small streams abounding there. Close by the bank was a light structure, roofed only with tent-cloth, about which clustered a few people, principally women, whose manners were too quiet to suggest that they came for amusement. In fact, the pavilion was a Jewish synagogue, and the usual market-day congregation had gathered for the second service of the day. This consisted largely of women of the lower class, and as the services had not begun they were at present somewhat excitedly discussing an expected event, which had just been announced to them. They pressed forward to greet Elizabeth, who seemed a favorite, and upon her presenting Salome as a friend and guest, she too was welcomed in kindly fashion. Then one said eagerly:

"Have you heard the news, Elizabeth? Two Apostles of Christ are to visit us—the great Paul and his companion, Silas. Even now they may be landing at Neapolis, and some of our company have gone there to meet and welcome them."

The speaker wore the picturesque dress of a Jewess of means, and was evidently a woman of importance in the assembly. She added:

"Now we shall hear more of this new Gospel which has brought peace and joy to so many. What say you, Elizabeth? They tell me you, too, have found joy in these teachings."

The young woman smiled. "I was in Jerusalem when Stephen died," she answered in a voice of joyous emotion. "I was also at the Pentecost after the death and resurrection of our Christ."

The other looked at her thoughtfully. "I have heard of that wonderful Pentecostal day, but I do not know about Stephen, except that he is talked of as the first Christian martyr. One thing is certain, though—those people do know how to die."

"And I hope how to live, too," smiled Elizabeth.

"If they were all like you!" returned the woman affectionately. "But have I not heard that this very Paul, your greatest

Apostle, was one who helped put Stephen to death?"

"He did," said Elizabeth, "but in ignorance. He was Saul of Tarsus, then, a devout Pharisee, and he felt it right to hate the very name of the Lord Jesus."

"Yet now he is the friend of that crucified man, and the teacher of his doctrines!--what a turn-coat!"

The woman smiled ironically, but Elizabeth gently answered:

"He has learned to know Jesus as the Christ, and his sole desire now is to prove how sincere is his love of Him."

"Well, we have had many prophets," mused the other, "but only one God."

"Yet we were all looking for the Messiah," put in Elizabeth quickly.

"Yes, he is long delayed." The well-to-do woman smoothed down her rich-hued robe complacently. She too was a Pharisee, and therefore not easily set right. There was a stir and the group began turning toward the synagogue. "Come," she said, "the services are beginning."

They gathered about the reader, who, as usual, was seated before them, and listened while he explained a portion of the Scriptures. He was a Jewish rabbi, and this was the regular service of that church, which Elizabeth still attended with reverence, though she felt they had not yet attained unto the higher life, as taught by Christ. Yet she longed to have Salome imbibe the idea of one sovereign and spiritual God, all-powerful, all-loving, and with no lesser deities surrounding Him. This once thoroughly understood, the new Gospel would soon make its blessings felt in her young heart. The Christians at Philippi were still few and feeble and had no place of meeting except in private houses, and most of them, if Jews, still worshiped, on stated occasions, with the mother church. Nor did they, as Elizabeth knew when she took Salome with her, like to have their pagan neighbors present at the services. The presence of a worshiper of Apollo would make them "unclean," according to their rabbinical doctrines, and might do them harm in other ways. Elizabeth, in her emancipated common sense, knew the heathen girl could not harm them, unless by tale-bearing, and would doubtless receive good, so she took the bold step of bringing her upon her own authority.

Salome was greatly interested in it all. She thought the ceremonial extremely sim-

ple, and wondered that there was no oracle, no procession of priests, no offerings, no prostration of the worshipers. When they came away she was silent and thoughtful. It seemed to her that life meant more than it had before. There were deeper things to think of than the buying of a new tunic, the watching of a heathen game, or even the loss of a special amulet.

Then she remembered that, but for that loss, she might still be with Hector, free from care and happy—but was she happy? Even before the sad breaking-up of their home—yes, even before Herklas went away—had she not been often discontented, dissatisfied, and ill at ease?

They were turning into the little court now, and she looked around at Elizabeth, who had dropped her veil for a breath of the sweet air before entering the house. How untroubled she was! Again Salome had the feeling that she hugged to her bosom some secret consciousness of joy, but now she knew what it was. Not an oracle of future good fortune, just as she had thought it out, but an assurance of peace in this world, and in that to come life everlasting.

As they reached the house door she stopped and said timidly:

"Elizabeth?"

"Yes, my child."

"Do you ever pray in secret to your Christ?"

"Often, child."

"Then next time ask him something for me, please. Ask him to give me your kind of joy. Will you?"

Elizabeth suddenly bent and kissed her, her eyes wet with a grateful rush of tears. "Will I? My dear, I have been praying ever since you came to me, and He is already letting me know that He has heard. Listen, Salome!" She stopped in the doorway and laid her hand upon the girl's shoulder, while she looked down into her eyes. "Listen: 'As the Father hath loved me, so have I loved you. If ye keep my commandments ye shall abide in my love; even as I have kept my Father's commandments and abide in his love. These things have I spoken unto you that my joy might remain in you, and that your joy might be full.'"

"Oh, who said those beautiful words?" breathed the girl in an agitated whisper.

"Our Christ—yours and mine, Salome! He is the Source of our joy, our hope, our love."

"Ah! if only He will be mine!" the girl

cried wistfully, and passing quickly indoors, shut herself away in her bit of a room.

CHAPTER VI.

LYDIA'S VISIT.

IT transpired that the woman who had talked with Elizabeth at the meeting was the one whom she had mentioned as a successful dyer, with a good business of her own. She had formerly lived at Thyatira, where she belonged to the ancient guild of dyers, but her business had grown until she felt it best to come to the larger town of Philippi.

She had a comfortable home, and her employés were mostly slaves, quartered upon her own premises. She had made a specialty of dyeing in purple, having succeeded in producing some new tints that were much admired, and was a thoroughly successful woman. But she had her griefs and troubles, and she never ceased to mourn the loss of a husband who had been very dear to her. Her reputation for good works was of the best, but she was slightly exclusive in her friendships, and, some thought, felt her consequence more than was agreeable. Elizabeth was not of those who said so. Between her and the good woman was a strong attachment, and she knew that often a certain air of hauteur in Lydia was simply a shutting of herself away in closer communion with her own heart. Elizabeth loved and respected her, and the sad, successful woman often sought the joyful, unsuccessful one to pour out her griefs and troubles, and to receive of that sweet faith and 'peace which made the other so blessed. What Elizabeth had said of Stephen—or more properly the tone in which she had said it—stayed by Lydia all that evening, and made her resolve that she would try to hear the new Apostles who were soon coming. Being a Pharisee of the strictest sect, she found it difficult to believe that any Messiah could be other than a great King and Deliverer, who would restore Jerusalem, and make the Jewish nation once more a power among men.

In all these respects Jesus of Nazareth had seemed to fail. Yet, when Lydia's sweet-faced friend talked to her of His greater mission to elevate and save all men, be they of whatever nation, and to establish a king-dom "not made with hands," certainly, yet "eternal in the heavens," it appealed to something high and pure in her own nature, though it could not quite bring her into full accord with Him.

She felt restless the next day, however, and suddenly resolved to go to Elizabeth and ask her to relate the story of Stephen's death, and explain why it had affected her so deeply. So she left her shop in the care of a trusted overseer, took a last look at her bubbling vats, each stirred continuously by a nearly naked slave, then started to cross the forum toward the same gate at which our two friends had entered the day before. It was not so crowded now, this not being a regular market-day, but within the gate was quite a concourse of people around a young girl, who seemed chanting something in imitation of the oracles in the temple, while her evil-looking companions greedily gathered up the mites and quadrans that were thrown into their uplifted tunics by the astonished listeners to whom she had promised some exceptional fortune.

Presently, as Lydia lingered, curiously watching the proceedings, she saw, crossing the forum, two men whose dress showed them to be traveling Jews. They carried themselves with a certain free dignity which at once attracted the noble woman, and she observed upon their enkindled countenances that same serenity which had always attracted her in Elizabeth. The older of the two men held her gaze longest. He was not tall, though his dignified presence made him seem so, but his brow was broad and clear, and the eyes below were keen, bright, searching, and above all kindly. As they turned casually upon her for an instant, they seemed to flash new life and hope into her heart.

"Who can they be?" thought she, and almost with the question came its answer: "They must be the expected Apostles!" Still more eagerly, then, she watched them. As they approached the slave girl she, too, stopped her chanting and turned towards them. Her eyes were set in the glassy stare of a sleep-walker, and her hands were clinched nervously at her sides. She stood quite still, the people about watching her intently, while the two strangers passed by in such earnest conversation that they did not seem to notice the excitement in the least. All at once her face flushed warmly, and a new light came into her eyes. Wheeling quickly, she followed after and began to cry aloud, but not in her high-pitched sing-song —rather in the sincere accent of assured belief:

"These men are the servants of the Most

ignorant of great religious truths as she must be? No wonder everyone looked after her with astonishment, and followed to see what she would do, or say, next. But the men whom she had thus designated kept upon their way, taking little note of the matter, apparently. Lydia, debating all this in her mind, started on at a rapid gait, which brought her abreast of the girl's two masters, who had so suddenly found their occu-

"Who can they be?" thought she; and almost with the question came the answer, "They must be the expected Apostles."—See page 18.

High God, who show unto us the way of salvation."

The words thrilled Lydia. How did this pagan know, if indeed she spoke the truth? Who had revealed it to a poor demented girl,

pation gone. They were scowling fiercely after the girl, yet seemed held back by some impulse stronger than their greed of gain. They did not beg of these she had so strangely singled out; they rather slunk back as if to avoid them, though evidently all their evil passions were roused at having their dupes so summarily dispersed by this singular interruption. Lydia threw them but a glance, then hurried out and up the street, to her friend's.

She found the Christian woman sitting in the shade in her little court, busy with her weaving. She greeted Lydia with cordiality, calling her to a seat on the mat at her side, and presently Salome appeared from an inner room, carrying another bundle of damp osiers for which she had just been sent, and with which she joined the two. Lydia began by relating the incident of the morning, which Salome heard with eyes grown large and wondering.

"Surely," she remarked, "it must be true if the soothsayer has declared it."

Elizabeth laughed in her sensible fashion. "It is true," she said, "but not because this possessed girl says it. No doubt, though, even the evil spirits recognize God's elect—but who could fail to note that these men are better and higher than most? I, too, saw them this morning, Lydia, when I was at the market. Does not the love of Christ shine from their souls through their faces? They reminded me of Stephen," she added softly.

"Stephen? He is the very one I came to ask about. You mentioned him so reverently the other day that I long to hear all about him. Was he not stoned because of this new faith?"

Elizabeth nodded, then said in a far-away tone: "I was young, but I have never forgotten it. Such eloquence, such sweetness, one can hope to hear but once! That day I was with my father in the market-place when some excited men of his acquaintance came along and touched his shoulder, saying, 'Come, quick, to the council chamber! They have arrested a man of Christ and are going to try him for blasphemy.'

"Now, my mother had been greatly interested in the new doctrines, and was anxious to hear and see all she could of the followers of Christ. This, however, my father had opposed up to that time, and as she was obedient and true, she had said little, while perhaps thinking the more. So, this day, father laughed lightly as the men called him, saying, 'What! Has another king of the Jews arisen?' and started after them, entirely forgetting me. But, child-fashion, I followed close at his heels. We pressed as near as possible to the judges' seats, where the San-

hedrim was convened, and my father, suddenly perceiving me, began to chide me for following; but when I begged and cried, saying I was afraid to go back through the crowd alone, he laughed good-naturedly, and bade me be quiet then, kindly lifting me to a jutting bit of stonework close by the steps, that I might see better.

"There was a man standing in the prisoner's place, talking, and young as I was, I listened to every word, for I thought I had never heard the story of our nation told so plainly and so well, even by my mother's tender lips. Besides, the man's voice and presence were full of power and spirit. His eyes kindled with enthusiasm, his lips grew sweet with love and pity, and though he said some severe words to the scowling rabbis glowering upon him, his own countenance was so lighted by love to the Christ that it shone like the face of an angel.

"As he closed with words that accused the priests of killing the prophets and rejecting God's Holy Spirit, they grew so angry that they gnashed their teeth and snarled at him like a pack of unclean dogs; yet still he stood there in perfect peace, calm, smiling, serene as a messenger from heaven.

"I remember how my father's arm gripped me as he held me on the stone balustrade, and how his face worked with admiration and doubt. For my father was a strict Pharisee and had come here in perfect sympathy with the Sanhedrim, yet he could not listen to these words, spoken with such serene conviction and heavenly wisdom, without being impressed. Even I, a child, felt tears rolling down my cheeks, and I longed to cry out to the angry Doctors of the Law to wait and listen, for there could be no wrong in this man.

"Even at that moment, while the tumult about him was loudest, I saw him raise his eyes heavenward, where the canvas roof was rolled back, and fix his gaze on the deep blue sky. A great and glorious light came into his face, he reached up his right hand, and cried in a voice that thrilled me through and through:

"'Behold! I see the heavens opened, and Jesus standing on the right hand of God.'

"Instinctively I, too, gazed up, as did all that multitude who had been gathering through the long discourse, and it has always seemed to me that through the deep, clear blue I also could faintly see forms of light and whiteness floating in glory. But who can tell? The imaginings of the young are great, and surely such a wondrous vision would not be granted to a simple child.

"Certainly those rabbis saw nothing, for in their anger they began a tumult so outrageous that I stopped my ears, and cowered close to my father in terror. And then—oh! then I saw them fall upon the speaker, fairly struggling with each other in their haste to seize him and drag him away. He made no resistance, nor answered a word to their curses and imprecations, but as they surged by us I peeped out from behind my father and caught one more glimpse of Stephen's face—pale, still, and peaceful, not at all as if he were in the grasp of a furious mob bent on his destruction.

"Then father caught me up in his arms, muttering, 'What are they going to do? Will they kill that just man?' and ran after as fast as he could go. It was to the place of execution in the ravine of Joshaphat, just without the gates, that they hustled him by a short way back of the Temple, and we had to take a longer way around. All the crowd went with us. Some cried, 'Stone the blasphemer—stone him!' and others urged, 'Wait! wait! Let him have a word for himself. He has done nothing worthy of death!' And among the latter I was glad to hear my father's lusty voice, for my whole child's heart had gone out to this 'just man,' as father rightly named him.

"When we reached the ravine we saw they had already thrown him from the wall, as was the custom when a man was condemned to be stoned to death. But the fall had not mercifully killed him, as it sometimes did; and already the fiercest of his accusers were throwing off their abbas, and piling them in a heap at the feet of a young man whom I scarcely noticed then, I was so intent on the martyr; but now I know it was—who do you think, Lydia? The very Paul you and I saw this morning."

"Ah!" cried the other. "It is passing strange. But go on—they threw off their upper garments, you say—"

"Yes. His adverse witnesses, you understand, for they were privileged to cast the first stone. Each sought out the largest he could find—oh! friends, one bore a red stain already, as if it had been an instrument of death in that dreadful place before—and though I shrank and hid my eyes, I had to look again, and then my gaze seemed riveted upon that man in the midst, fallen, bruised, torn, and despised, yet who still bore in his face the look of a conqueror.

"For even as I gazed he feebly raised himself to his knees and fixed his eyes upon the sky above, which was not more peaceful than his own expression then. I thought he had forgotten us all and had thoughts only for the Holy One he loved and was dying for, but that was all I knew. Because he did love the blessed Christ he must have had thoughts for all of us. One cry he gave for his own soul, 'Lord Jesus, receive my spirit!' then, as the stones began to hail about and upon him, he looked with love even upon his tormentors, and cried aloud in a voice so sweet that it thrills me yet:

"'Lord, lay not this sin to their charge.'

"Oh, the wonder of it! the wonder of it, Lydia! He could forgive those murderers in his dying agony! I had heard that this was true of Christ and had felt that He was God, or He could not have done it. Now I saw that for love of Him a poor weak man might die like Himself.

"As the words ended, a great stone crashed against Stephen's breast, and he sank gently back and seemed to fall asleep, with a smile like that of a child in its mother's arms. And as we looked on, almost wistfully, at one who had overcome death with faith, a man close by whispered solemnly, 'He sleeps in Jesus.'

"I did not fully understand his meaning, but my father reverently bowed his head in prayer, and I did likewise.

"Even those fierce rabbis grew still, and moved away in sullen self-disgust. Then father turned to the whisperer and asked hoarsely, 'Who was this man?' 'Stephen,' answered the other, lingering on the syllables as if he loved them. Father gazed at him. 'The word means a crown,' he said in a reverent tone. 'Yes,' was the reply. 'His is the martyr's crown, most glorious of all.' And father nodded, consentingly.

"Still holding me close, father then turned homeward in silence, and when there told my mother all, while great tears ran down his rough brown cheeks. Ah! how I loved him then! Nothing makes a father so dear to a child as the display of deep and pure emotion. I could not let go his hand, and, taking my mother's also, he said earnestly, 'I can no longer doubt that Jesus of Nazareth was the promised Deliverer.' So the day of Stephen's glorious death was the beginning of our new life."

She stopped, half choked with emotion, while both Salome's and Lydia's tears flowed freely. The woman was thinking, "If these things be so, is not this Jesus indeed the Messiah?" while the pagan girl mused:

"Our gods do not make their followers like this. Surely this is the strangest of all religions, yet the most beautiful, too. And I have feared Herklas was drawn away by the Christians! Now I could almost wish he had been!"

<hr/>

CHAPTER VII.

LIGHT IN THE DUNGEON.

A DAY or two later was the Sabbath, and Salome, whose interest was thoroughly aroused, gladly accompanied her hostess to the river-side synagogue, hoping to hear and see something more of this new faith. Nor was she disappointed. Paul and Silas were both there, and, being courteously treated, sat among the rabbis, and were requested to address the assembly. This was a small one, mostly women, and they heard the good message which was presented with eloquence and power, as a call from God to "come up higher."

Elizabeth, strengthened and confirmed in faith, listened with a shining countenance; Salome with eager, wide-open eyes, wondering, hoping, yet still half doubting because it seemed too good to believe; and Lydia with powerful conviction and trust. But the Greek girl was almost as glad as Elizabeth, herself, to see this proud, yet sincere, woman rise modestly in her place to profess belief in this beautiful doctrine, and to ask baptism for herself and household. The little congregation had partly dispersed, afterwards, when Lydia came towards them, her head bowed in thoughtful humility. Elizabeth stepped quickly to her side, saying in a glad voice:

"Dear sister Lydia, welcome! I am so glad—so glad!"

Lydia took her hand and pressed it. Her eyes were moist with tears and her lips tremulous.

"Not so glad as I!" she whispered back. "Nobody can tell the peace and joy I feel."

"Will you not come home with us and talk more of this?" asked Elizabeth, much moved.

"I would, but I am waiting for these good men. They have promised to honor me by lodging at my house while they remain here. I will see you soon, however."

She left them, but, lingering to watch her, they soon saw her start towards her pleas-

ant home with the two Apostles, and Elizabeth turned to Salome with the words:

"I am glad they will be so comfortably housed. They looked weary this morning, and indeed their lives are very often hard and fatiguing."

"Have they ever suffered persecution?" asked the girl.

"Oh, many and many a time. Paul has been even stoned, like Stephen, and left for dead, though in fact he was only senseless for a while; and from many places they have had to flee because of their persecutors."

"Yet they never think of giving it all up and settling down to a quiet life?"

Elizabeth looked at her with a singular expression. "You do not understand," she said. "When your heart has opened to the truth you will not ask such a question."

"But does your God command these things, Elizabeth? We believe our gods like us to enjoy, and escape hardships if possible. All they ask of us is to give them due honor and listen to the oracles."

"Then why do hardships come?" asked the older woman quickly. "Are not your gods powerful enough to make you happy, if that is their desire for you?"

Salome hesitated for an answer, and Elizabeth continued rapidly:

"Our Creator does mean us to be happy, and Christ came to show us the right way. But, my child, happiness is a state of mind, not a possession. One who truly loves God is happy anywhere if feeling His presence. It is only alienation from Him that is wretchedness."

"But, dear friend, could you be happy, say, in prison—in those dreadful dungeons that your husband tells us of, where there is no light, and scarcely any air?"

"If Christ were with me—yes."

"Ah, that is too much to believe!" cried the girl emphatically. "They are such horrible places—and there are the tortures too! If you had to suffer those?"

"I cannot tell," shuddering a little. "My flesh creeps to think of such things, but the Christ will not let me be tried beyond my strength. I rest on that assurance, and do not worry. The one thing I could not do would be to deny Him!"

Salome glanced at her. They had just entered the home court and Elizabeth had dropped her veil. Upon her serene face was a joyous smile of confidence, and in her eyes an expression of perfect peace.

Salome's young heart went out towards

her in affectionate appeal. She wished, whimsically, that there were some way of absorbing from her a little of that lovely personality which made her so winning and so enjoyable to herself. The girl put out her hand and touched the other's long robe.

"Dear Elizabeth," she said wistfully, "I wish I were like you!"

"Nay, Salome," answered the other, clasping the hand warmly, "rather wish you were like Christ, the One 'altogether lovely.'"

Meanwhile, poor Hector was learning more of the dungeons that haunted his sister's mind, than she could even imagine of them. So dark was the pit in which he lay that he could scarcely distinguish the bare walls around him, and the only alleviation of his fate was the healthy power to sleep long and often. Then, for a time, he forgot his sufferings, and again wrestled in the arena, strolled outside the gates by the pretty brook-sides with Herklas and Salome, or romped through some game in the court, a little boy again.

When the soldiers delivered him over to the keeper of the prison he had made one more effort to defend himself, though not with fists this time. But before he could tell who he was, and how guiltless of offence, a sudden blow from the knotted scourge had silenced him.

"Hold your peace, fellow!" cried the keeper shortly, as he turned with an imprecation. "It is nothing to me whether you are guilty or not. On with you there!" and he drove Hector before him with the relentlessness of fate. The latter saw it was of no use to remonstrate, but his whole soul rose up in rebellion against such undeserved treatment, and he could have cursed all the gods in turn when the surly keeper left him chained to the moldy stone floor of his fetid cell.

Hector was brave in his own way, and in the arena dared to stand up in the wrestling matches with any one who might be pitted against him. But his strength was physical, not moral, and he had no religion, no philosophy even, to sustain him now. For a time he howled with rage and despair, beating his head against the cruel stones until its dull ache but added to his misery, and sent him into a sort of stupor, which was but the sullen quietude born of despair. He had no way of counting time except by the intervals between his wretched meals. When this interval was doubled he knew it

must be night, when halved it must be day, and he thus managed to keep a tolerably correct idea of the flight of time.

In this manner he calculated that the sixth night had arrived, and was feeling indignant that precious sleep did not, as usual, come with it, when a sound unlike any he had heard here before fell upon his ears. He had been several times aroused by the clanking of heavy chains outside his door, or by loud voices in strife or ribaldry, and he had twice been sickened by the shrieks of those under torture. But this was none of these.

It was the voice of music, peaceful, joyous, and swelling from the deep throats of men who sang with all the heart in an absorption of enjoyment. He raised himself upon his elbow and listened breathlessly. This could not be the song of those too far gone in liquor to care for their surroundings! No, these steady, sustained cadences meant controlled joy, triumphant worship. Astonished, cheered, and longing to hear more, he crept to the thick door and placed his ear close against its smooth surface.

The singing came, evidently, from the next cell, where he had become convinced were kept the stocks and other instruments of torture. Could these men be in those fiendish wooden things which held the limbs distended and the head and neck contracted, until every muscle was like a tortured nerve with its agony? It seemed incredible! So men might burst out into swelling strains on a triumphal march after some great victory. But what could prisoners in such a hole know of victory?

He soon assured himself that they were in the stocks, however, which were placed almost against his door, and presently the singing ceased, and he heard a voice speaking in the Greek tongue, with which he was so familiar. Straining his attention, he caught words of praise and devotion mingled with supplication, all seemingly addressed to one great God who was powerful over all others.

"How they believe in Him!" was Hector's thought, as he held his breath to hear. "How certain they seem of His presence and care! When I call upon great Zeus, or Apollo, they are so far away my cry seems lost in air; but these men appear to think their God is with them in this very prison."

Presently the tones sank to lower murmurs, in which he could distinguish no words. Disappointed at hearing no more, and wearied with confinement and grief, he finally sank into a deep sleep just where he was, his head against the heavy door.

How long he had slept he did not know, but he awoke instantly and completely, with the knowledge that the door had given way, letting him fall outward into the other cell, which was heaving, trembling, rocking, and cracking around him. Terrified, he raised himself amid the falling stones and mortar, to find, with amazement, that he was freed from his shackles, and to see, in a sudden glare of lightning, that the doors were all wide open, even that into the outer court, while the stars, half concealed by turbulent clouds, were shining in.

All around were other prisoners, their eyes wild with affright, for the building was rocking to its foundations, and the rending walls gave out sharp sounds with horrible meaning. All were indeed too paralyzed to move for an instant, during which the keeper, who had been asleep, suddenly appeared in the outer door, and at one glance saw that his captives were all at liberty. With a cry of fright and despair he drew his sword, not for defense or punishment, but for self-destruction. This was the universal resort of the desperate. The lack of all justice among those in power led such philosophers as Seneca, such generals as Brutus and Cassius, to prefer what they believed the oblivion of death to the debasements of tyranny.

But something stayed this man's rash hand, and also held back the lawless prisoners, who might easily have fled—held even Hector, who felt himself so unjustly imprisoned here. A voice cried loudly through the gloom:

"Do thyself no harm, for we are all here!"

Calling loudly for assistance, the keeper soon had re-inforcements and light, though he did not seem to have needed them. All were present, and the two men still sat in the stocks, though the heavy beams had split apart from the great screws and left them at perfect liberty. The keeper, shaking with excitement and terror, now threw himself before these strange prisoners and cried in anguish, "What must I do to be saved?" He felt that here was some Power before which his petty tyranny was impotent, and if the cry was selfish it was certainly sincere.

He had always bowed before his masters, and exacted every concession from those over whom he ruled. Yet here were two, who had meekly submitted themselves to his scourgings and tortures since early yesterday, whose power was evidently beyond that of most men. It must then be from some Being who could control earthquakes to His own purposes. It must be from God!

He was ready to acknowledge His power and to worship at His feet. He could fear and respect Him now; perhaps later he would learn to love Him. At all events he was anxious to become His follower without delay.

One of the men answered with prompt decision: "Believe on the Lord Jesus Christ, and thou shalt be saved."

Hector listened in astonishment. He could not yet quite understand what had kept him from rushing outside to certain freedom in that one moment when all was open and unguarded. But, strangely enough, he had not cared to go; all thought of safety seemed merged into a desire to see and hear more of these wonderful men, whom even chains, stocks, and prison doors could not affect in body, or in spirit!

He listened breathlessly to the talk that now followed. First one, then the other, in an emulation of eagerness, told of a love, a hope, a joy, so great that no prison walls could damp them. The time fled swiftly. All the prisoners were gathered close about the two, and their unkempt, haggard faces softened into wistfulness as they listened. As for the keeper, his manner was transformed. Consideration and sympathy took the place of cold indifference and sullen cruelty. He said presently in a voice subdued to gentleness, "Come with me, please," then turning his eyes from one to another of the remaining prisoners, he called to Hector, "Here, boy, I need your help."

Hector went at once.

"I want you to help me care for these holy men," he said with reverence; and the Greek was glad to obey.

He led the two into the inner, walled court where was a well, and while the young man drew water, the keeper with his own hands softly washed their stripes, cleansing the raised welts from the coagulated blood, which added so greatly to the smart and fever of the wounds. His family stood around, thoroughly roused by these strange happenings, and when this act of mercy, the first fruit of the new Gospel in that hardened jailer's heart, was ended, one of these "holy men" baptized both him and his whole family.

Hector looked on, greatly impressed by the solemn ordinance, though secretly longing to hear the men speak again of the Christ they so dearly loved. But the ceremony was no sooner over than the keeper, bowing reverently before them, begged they would honor him by coming into his own apartments, and led them away. Hector, being conducted into the large common room of the prison by an attendant, was left there unchained until the morning. Throwing himself upon the bare floor, he leaned against the wall in a state of mind far different from that of yesterday.

What words were these he had heard tonight? There was but one God, and He had been lately living upon earth in the form of man! This was a part of what he had gathered, and the idea was not wholly strange to him, as he had been taught that the deities used to come down from Olympus to live among men, and he had always believed it. But this God came for but one purpose— only one! Not for His amusement; not to witness the fairness of the daughters of earth; not to disport Himself in sylvan groves, nor enjoy the triumphs of great processions, but to redeem man from his sins. To teach him His own grace and love, until sin became hateful to him, and the beauty of holiness desirable. To show him the glory of self-sacrifice and the might of love. To be to him a Friend, an Elder Brother!

In these surprising thoughts Hector forgot he was a prisoner, did not notice that he had no bed but the bare stones, and finally dropped to sleep in a blissful calm that made patience a thing of course, and happiness, even here, more than a possibility.

He was wakened by a dazzling light, and looked up to see the keeper and several other men walking about in earnest conversation, while they examined the damaged walls. The brilliant light was caused by a large crack at his side, into which he could easily thrust his hand, and through which one ray of blessed sunshine fell directly upon his face, as if with a morning greeting. It cheered him inexpressibly, and he sat up with a smiling face, ready to meet the day's troubles in a new spirit.

The earthquake had done considerable damage to the prison, but the inmates seemed like other beings under the influence of last night's events and this morning's light. They were all gathered in this large common room, and the question of their further disposal was now agitating these magnates, whose purple togas showed their high rank and dignity. One came and looked down at Hector, as he sat upon the floor. Instantly the youth bounded to his feet, and bowed with the grace of a well-knit figure and courteous training.

"Ah, my fine fellow, and what are you in here for?" asked the magnate, smiling a little, as he slowly measured Hector with his eyes.

The latter looked at him frankly. He saw a tall, handsome young man with the clustering curls which the royal boy, Nero, was making the fashion, and with a dress richer even than that of the Duumvirs, who had given Hector his ideas of royalty up to this time. He saw also a carelessly kind expression, a rather bored droop to the handsome mouth, and crow's-feet about the eyes, that spoke of dissipation rather than of age.

The keeper took the answer from Hector's lips: "For a night brawl, sire. Then he was violent, and had to be double-chained."

The young patrician glanced down at Hector's feet, and the other men turned to look, also.

"But he is unchained now, I see."

"Yes, sire, as all the rest. The fetters were all broken by the earthquake."

"Yes, so I heard. Rather remarkable, that!"

He turned and began talking with the others of something which had seemingly just occurred that Hector found himself deeply interested in.

Evidently those strange prisoners of last night had turned out to be free Romans, therefore exempt from scourgings and torture, unless by the decree of royalty itself. In their fright at what might result from this insult to the strangers, the magistrates had sent word at dawn to release them. But when the keeper gladly brought the word he was amazed at the dignified answer of the two prisoners, that having been openly disgraced they would not accept of secret pardon! The magistrates must themselves come and set them free. And they had been obliged to do it—that was evident. Hector wanted to chuckle as he heard their low talk, half chagrined, half amused at their own mortification, and saw their annoyed faces. He only wished he had been awake to see it all! The young man who had spoken to him seemed to be enjoying the situation greatly, and did not cease his raillery at the discomfited officers.

Presently, however, the others passed on and he turned back to Hector.

"A night brawler, eh?" said he with a laugh. "I thought we of the Castle reserved all such sport to ourselves in quiet Philippi. You must have been very drunk, though, or you could have held your own, my man!" running his eyes admiringly over Hector's well-developed figure. "There are not many with such muscles as those;" and his fingers closed over Hector's massive biceps.

"They are flabby now from disuse, sire," the latter spoke up quickly with professional pride, making them as tense as possible. "But indeed I was neither drunk nor quarrelsome until goaded to madness. I defended my sister from a crowd of your own castle people, sire, and supposed she was safe in the house when they dispersed. Then I found they had carried her away, and what could I do but run after them with cries of fury and revenge?"

"'They'? You don't mean our Roman bacchanals?"

"Yes, sire, I do."

"No, no! I should have heard—how long since?"

"By my reckoning, which is uncertain in these holes, six nights ago, sire."

"Six?" The patrician mused a second, then looked up with a start. "Why, I—" Then he stopped. "Who arrested you?" he asked next.

"The Guards of the Castle. Some one called from a turret window and they at once surrounded me. I felled three with my bare fists, but they tripped me up and fell upon me, so that I was overpowered and nearly senseless."

"I should think so! Jove! it was a feat! Felled three full-armed guards, and you half-naked, while they had spears and breastplates! Pretty well, pretty well! But tell me more. Why did you think your sister was carried off to the Castle, my youthful fighter?"

Hector now told the story in detail, and the young lord listened with evident interest, waving off the Duumvirs when they approached, with the words:

"Presently, presently! Go on and wait for me in the hall of justice. I think I have found another case of misguided zeal, and you are not the victims this time;" ending with a taunting laugh.

They hurried out, red and warm, but did not answer the arrogant young lord as he

deserved, and this convinced Hector that his rank must be greater even than he had at first supposed. The noble turned to the interesting prisoner again.

"Your tale is true—of that I am certain—but in some way you have made a great mistake. Your sister was not carried away, nor is she at the Castle. She escaped into the darkness somewhere, and is doubtless awaiting you, safe and well, at home."

"Oh, would I could go to her!" sighed poor Hector from his very heart.

"You shall!" was the quick response. "I know who ordered—that is, I have an idea of the manner of your arrest, and am sure you have been simply forgotten. But you have suffered enough. In a few moments you shall be free. And here,"—the young patrician drew from his finger a ring of peculiar workmanship—"when you have found and comforted your pretty sister, come to the Castle, show that ring, and ask for its owner. It will admit you. Will you remember?"

"Certainly, O gracious prince. Accept the thanks of one who has twice won the Olympic crown, and therefore is perhaps not entirely unworthy of your clemency."

"Hah! Is that true? I thought you were no common prisoner the moment my eyes lighted on you. Well, well!" smiling with easy kindness, "put this upon your finger and mope no longer. You will soon be free, and there may come a time when you will not regret this short imprisonment. I will see you again."

He turned quickly, waved his hand in return to Hector's deep salaam, and hurried on after the magistrates. The delighted young Greek gazed after him, wondering if he were really awake, or if this whole strange night were not some bright and vivid dream from which he must awaken to his dismal inner dungeon once more.

CHAPTER VIII.

THE SOOTHSAYER AT HOME.

NEAR the outer wall of Philippi was a quarter given over to the very poor. It was squalid and dirty beyond description. The low, mud-walled houses, crowded together and running over with human life, were set flat on the ground, guiltless of drainage or paving. Here garbage collected until the hot air was reeking and poisonous. Here starving curs wandered in bands and fought for a seldom-found bone; here women cooked over their tiny braziers, and scolded their crying children; here men sold and squabbled over their small, unclean stocks of goods; here they all ate and drank, dressed and slept, lounged and worked, in the open street, or on the flat roofs of the hovels they called home.

A group of men of evil aspect and in the ragged garb of traveling mendicants was squatted in front of one of the vilest of these hovels, busy at some game in which dice were thrown and mites and quadrans changed hands frequently, and with heads close together in consultation at every pause in the gaming. Whenever they stopped to talk they ate of a sort of cake, made of a hash of mixed ingredients highly spiced and flavored, and drank largely from a common gourd of fermented liquor, sour and stinging in taste, but with strong intoxicating properties.

"I tell you," said one, whose features spoke of Roman descent, "she must go if we have to carry her! She has been the best speculation we ever handled, and if I had had any luck at play, and you had not been so greedy, Alois, we could have called ourselves rich by now."

"What aileth her, anyhow?" asked one of the group, quickly, with intent to divert a quarrel, for the "greedy Alois" had started up with clenched fists; but he slowly dropped to his place again, and leaned back indolently as the Roman explained:

"Oh, she is feigning some ailment only. Since that affair with those two would-be priests, the other day, she has been as weak as water, and as clear in her brain as you are—to our hurt!"

"She looks it rightly enough," put in another, taking a long draught of the rank-smelling liquor.

"Oh, she is always white as the snow up on the range," returned the Roman, pointing carelessly to the mountains beyond the city, "but that is nothing. I wist she is sullen only. She declares she can not prophesy any more. She bewails her 'wickedness,' the jade! and begs just to be let alone. She ought to have a good beating, but—"

He hesitated, and Alois, who wore a Phœnician's headgear, added coolly:

"Peradventure that would end the business. It would be poor policy, Flavius. Better glut your temper some other way.

Your little plan did not seem to work very well with the prophets, though!" and he laughed tauntingly.

The two men glowered at each other, but Alois grew more cheerful. He had avenged his partner's insulting epithet, and felt better. Indeed, the two men never ceased to snarl and bicker; yet while each feared and hated the other, they were so bound by mutual infamies and mutual distrust, that they clung together the more closely the greater their longing to pull asunder. It was a vile and terrible bond, which indeed had become a very chain of fret and turmoil, wearing into their sin-laden souls.

Flavius, once a seaman and more likely than not of the galleys—at any rate an off-scouring of Rome—was cruel, unscrupulous and brazen, a coward at heart, though capable of hardships almost incredible; Alois, the Phœnician, his junior by many years, was brave in action and had generous instincts, but self-indulgence had buried these better qualities till he was little more than a glutton and wine-bibber, getting the means to satisfy his appetite where and as he could. Yet, beneath his bloated exterior beat a heart which might even yet be stirred to pity, if the brain were not too stupefied to control it.

The helpless victim of these two wretches now lay upon her mat on the roof of the house, a bit of soiled tent-cloth stretched between her and the sun, which beat down hot and relentless at this hour. Yet it was better here than in the small furnace-like rooms below, always close and odorous, for an occasional breath of air touched her white cheek and lifted the dark locks from her burning brow. She was a young girl of delicate form and features, but so pinched with famine and worn with travel and ill-usage that little beauty remained to her. Yet her eyes, large, soft, and heavily shaded by the black lashes, could never be less than beautiful.

Presently a woman, deformed and hag-like, came up the outer stair, and, stepping to the side of the girl on the mat, bent over her. The great dark eyes opened and looked up with a troubled gaze.

"Well, Agistha," said the woman in a high, cracked voice, "how do you feel now?"

"No better," said the girl faintly, shutting her eyes again, while her brows contracted in a frown. "Why can't I be left in peace?"

"'Peace'! She talks of peace!" cackled the crone, apparently to the sky. "And that when she has been lying here a stretch of thirty-six hours, at least! But who is to earn the mites while she is taking her peace, I want to know?"

Agistha made an uneasy movement on her hard bed. "I am too ill," she muttered. "Oh, for rest, rest, rest!"

Tears began to ooze out beneath her white eyelids and fall over her sunken cheeks, while her lips, already lined by misery, quivered like a child's.

The woman muttered something and turned quickly away. She had had a daughter years ago, she had a grand-daughter now, and a mother cannot be quite dead to feeling. She turned back, and with a sudden, half-shamed movement caught up her girdle and wiped Agistha's face with a not ungentle touch. "There, rest!" she said. "Sleep! I'll keep those wolves at bay. Sleep, I tell you, and fear not." Then, before the dazed girl had fully caught her meaning, she was slipping down the rotten old steps, her face set and stern.

The men were still throwing dice outside in the street, their voices raised and rapid in their ceaseless quarreling. But the woman only threw them a contemptuous glance, and shrugged her shoulders as she went about her work.

By and by Flavius peered in at the door and called out:

"Say, Phryne, where lyeth the girl? Did you arouse her, as I bade you, and tell her to be ready for the evening hour when the rich idlers gather at the forum, waiting to be amused?"

"Oh, I told her—yes."

"You told her—well, is she up? She must have some food, I suppose, and by that time—"

The old woman looked at him, showing two long fangs of teeth in a horrible smile. "What a fool you are, Flavius!" she remarked in an abstracted fashion. "Know you not the creature is dying? Why cannot you let her go in peace?"

He started and stared at her. Alois, too, set down his dice box and came forward, while the other men glanced up from their gambling to peer through the open door, their throws suspended in air.

"Dying? Who says so? How do you know?" shouted Flavius, hoarsely.

"Hush! I would not tell her of it were I you—though, Pluto knows, she must be glad to go! Yes, she has one chance in twenty, perhaps, to live."

"One chance! You're lying, witch!"

She chuckled. "That is a bit of foolishness I lay no claim to—lying just for the sake of lying. I keep it for occasions when it will serve. Usually it is quicker to tell the truth. It is now. She is dying, unless something I do not expect turns up to save her. Go see for yourself, go ask the best leech in Philippi, go consult any soothsayer—they will tell you the same. It is written on her face—it looks out of her eyes; but there is always a chance."

Flavius scowled fiercely, seeing his easy gains about to desert him forever; for though Agistha had not been able to prophesy since the two strange men, whom she had persisted in following to designate them as "servants of God," had commanded the evil spirit to come out of her, yet he had fully expected the power would return as soon as she was well enough for him to once more subdue her by famine, fright, and the force of his own will. Could it be that death was to steal her from him, and leave him bankrupt?

As he stood thus, filled with evil musings, Alois asked with a touch of real concern in his voice:

"But the one chance in twenty, Phryne; what is that?"

She looked from Flavius to him, and laughed maliciously. "What an interest you have in her—you two! Why should I help keep her alive to make a living for you two lazy louts? She does not care to get well, I will warrant you."

"Do you not share our gains, you old imp from Tartarus?" cried Flavius in a fury. "Do we not buy your rotten fruit and spoiled wine, you old cheat and usurer? Do we not—"

Phryne burst into a louder laugh, and shook a long, bony finger in his face. "Who asks you to buy my wares, you galley slave? Take your trade elsewhere, if you like—there are plenty to buy—and next time you come whining around for credit, just remember my fruits are rotten, will you?"

She turned her back on him and spoke to Alois. "Her one chance?" she repeated, as calmly as if she had not just been screaming at the top of her voice. "It is this—that she be left to sleep undisturbed till the moon is full. That is all that will save her. She is literally worn out."

"And it is but a crescent now!" cried Alois. "What will we do meanwhile?"

"Work, you dogs!" said the woman in a fierce tone, "and I will keep the girl. She will not eat while her fever is on, and my little Persis can sit by her at times."

"I will have a look at her myself!" said the man suddenly, and stepped to the stairway.

Flavius instantly followed him. Nobody could tell what plan this precious partner might have in mind to defraud him. Perhaps he and the old woman were in conspiracy together.

Alois reached the roof first. The sun was setting and the low housetop, overhung by higher walls beyond, was quite in shadow. In his bare feet he stepped across the rough flooring of dried sticks and mud, to the reclining figure on the mat under the tentcloth. She must be asleep, for she was very still. He bent over her, gave a startled cry, and touched her cheek—then sprang back and turned to see his partner close behind.

"She is dead already!" he said in an awe-struck tone. "And look! See how she smiles. She is glad to go, poor little thing! Flavius, we have been hard with her."

He watched her with a softening expression for an instant, while the other man, after one look, turned away with a curse.

"Peace!" said Alois. "She was a meek, docile creature. I am glad she can smile now—I thought she had forgotten how. Why, she is really comely, Flavius!"

He looked around, to see his partner's brows met in a black frown.

"She was worth a half-dozen denarii a week!" he muttered, setting his teeth together with a curse. "That was beauty enough for me. And it will cost at least one to bury her. I thought the omens bad enough when I heard those wretched priests had got out of prison in such a strange way, and in high feather, but this is worse! Cover her face, Alois; she looks as if she was laughing at us—curse her!" and, turning hastily away, he flung himself down the stairway in the blackest of even his black moods.

Alois lifted the end of the girl's ragged girdle and laid it gently over the white face, stopping another instant to place the hands together on her breast.

"I wish we had been a bit kinder to you, little one!" he muttered, then turned and followed his partner, leaving the poor girlish soothsayer to sleep in peace.

Burials were never long delayed, especially among the very poor, who had no money for embalming cloths and spices. That evening, not two hours later, Phryne wrapped the child—she was little more—in an old white chlamys made into a grave-cloth and wound about over her chiton of roughly-woven cotton, then with the help of Alois, carried her below.

Flavius had left the house immediately, and did not return for a day or two. A rough bier was procured, and a few neighbors gathered with torches. Some one had secured a permit to allow of their going without the walls to the place reserved for the pauper dead, and amid a procession of not more than half a dozen, four of whom bore the light burden and two the blazing torches, Agistha was borne to her tomb. Some one with a charitable heart slipped between her stiffened lips the obolus, or silver bit of coin for the payment of Charon when he should tow her over the Styx, and as they set down the bier before the rude cave, one sang a wailing chant in lieu of a flute. The tomb was poor and shallow. As the men rolled away the entrance stone, a cloud of bats flew out and circled about the flaring torches, startled by their smoky glare.

The men had just turned to take up the bier, and stood to repeat an incantation before shoving it into the tomb as a baker shoves a tin of loaves into his brick oven, when there came an interruption. A band of marauders, who lived in the fastnesses of the mountains, had stolen down into the plain just without the gates, in order to pick up whatever spoil in the shape of stray sheep, goats, or unprotected travelers they might come across. Seeing the lonely little funeral train, they, in pure wantonness, came dashing down upon it, yelling in their savage manner, and ripe for plunder.

As with one accord the bier was dropped, the torches thrown down and extinguished, and the frightened mourners—who were in no real sense mourners at all—hastened to hide amid the thickets close by, thence to creep tremblingly back by varying routes. Thus slinking and crawling between clumps of weeds and outcropping rocks, they gradually drew nearer the walls, until they dared make a dash for the gates, leaving the laughing raiders to ride away.

But the body of Agistha lay on the bier out under the pale stars, in the dark shadow of her tomb, unprotected by even its rude stone from prowling beast or unclean bird.

CHAPTER IX.

SOME MEMORABLE MEETINGS.

IT had been a hot day, but the night was cool, and by midnight the condensed vapors fell in a brisk shower, sudden and drenching, though brief. A small party of travelers, hastening across country, made a quick rush for the bluff off to their right, hoping to find an empty cave among the tombs therein, and at any rate a partial shelter from the driving storm, amid its rocks and bushes.

It had grown intensely dark, and as they stumbled along, their footsteps and voices drowned in the roar of the heavy rainfall, one of the young men became separated from the others and groped his way in an opposite direction, as he followed the bend of the cliff. Here he was glad to find that by squeezing between two tall boulders, fallen together in tent shape, he could secure shelter.

As we have said, the storm was brief though severe, and presently the driving sheets of rain grew thin, as if torn into strips, then fluttered into mere rags of vapor, and finally cleared entirely away, as though blown quite out of existence.

Almost immediately the moon broke forth, bright as a golden crown still unjeweled. Seeing the storm was entirely past, the youth was about to crawl out from his cramped quarters, when, with a thrill of superstitious terror, he noted that just beyond him, quite close to the honeycombed bluff, was a rude bier, and that the white-enshrouded body upon it, which should have lain motionless, was sitting up, eerie and solemn against the moonlight.

As he watched it, awe-stricken and chilled at the ghostly sight, he saw its head turn slowly like a child's just wakened from deep sleep, and then, still slowly, as if from weakness or cumbering garments, it rose to its feet, and looking in every direction, with hastier and more confused motions, it broke into a pitiful little cry:

"Oh, where am I? Help! help!"

The youth, being of better sense than some of the superstitious multitude, saw at once that the child (the voice sounded like a child's) had not been dead, as supposed when hastily borne to the tomb, and had been roused by the stinging rain to full life and consciousness, only to suffer an agony of terror in that gruesome place.

He quickly answered the sharp, feeble wail by the brisk words: "Do not be frightened—I am here. I will help you—wait!" For he knew that her feet must be bound together with the grave-cloths, and that if she should stumble in that rough place, it might injure her seriously.

Still thinking her a mere child, he hurried to the trembling figure, telling himself that it looked so tall only because of the clinging white garments and the moonlight at its back, which set it out like a picture never to be forgotten by the beholder.

"Wait!" he kept urging as he clambered across the boulder-strewn space to her side.

And she answered: "Oh, who are you, and where am I? Have I waked in Hades, and are you sent from Pluto to bear me into the Eternal Shades?"

"No! no!" cried the youth cheerily, yet half shrinking from the spirit-like figure too, "no, indeed! Do you not see the moon? This is good old earth yet, and I am a traveler who happened along just in time. When did you die—go to sleep like this? Do you know?"

Agistha looked at the stranger wonderingly, for the bright light, falling full upon his face, made it quite plain to her. He was ruddy and fair to look upon, like David of old, and from his blue eyes beamed a kindliness not so common but that Agistha noted it at once. She watched him silently, without attempting to answer a question she had not yet fully comprehended, as he loosed her feet and hands. Then a long shiver went over her—she was beginning to remember.

"Where is this?" she whispered. "Are Flavius and Alois near by? Did they do it to punish me? Am I outside the city gates? Where is Phryne—oh! is this the place of tombs?"

These rapid questions were poured forth so eagerly that the youth really caught but one name which was in any sort familiar.

"Phryne?" he repeated. "I know a woman—but then, it is a common name. Yes, this is near the tombs. You have been in a deep sleep that they took for death. But no one else is here, and the city gates are now locked for the night. Be patient, however, and I will conduct you hence in the dawning. Look! Already the moon is near its setting, and it will soon be quite dark. I have friends near by who will help me care for you. Come!"

The girl looked at his outstretched hand a

minute, as if slow of comprehension or reluctant of friendliness. But soon she slipped her own into it with a gesture of trust that pleased the youth.

"It is a good child, but hardly a bright

"Thallus, is that you?"

An eager voice answered at once: "What, Herklas? We were frightened about you. We thought—but whom have you there?"

"It is a child, brought here while still

He quickly answered the sharp, feeble wail by the brisk words, "Don't be frightened—I am here. I will help you."—See page 30.

one," he thought, as he led her carefully amid the roughnesses. He refrained from calling aloud for his friends, however, as he had no desire to attract the notice of lurking thieves, or animals.

Presently, as they stumbled along in the dimming light, he saw a body moving beyond him in the thicket and, after a sharp look, ventured to call out restrainedly:

alive, for burial, and left, for some reason, outside on her bier. A fortunate thing for her, too, as the rain evidently revived her."

"Dreadful! This smacks of crime. How she shivers, poor thing! She must be wet to the bone, and frightened into the bargain. Come, we have found a dry and empty cavern. The others are kindling a fire, and we will have something warming before we go farther. Let the child come in and dry herself."

Still clinging closely to the hand of Herklas, Agistha was led into the cavern, and as they stooped to enter the low door-way a bright tongue of flame shot up against its inner concave wall. Some one glanced up from blowing it, to ask:

"Did you find him, Thallus? Ah!" He looked hard at Agistha, while the two other men who were crouched near by, talking in low tones together, stopped and turned to gaze.

In a low tone Thallus explained, and at once the other three became gentle and attentive in manner. They made room for the girl close by the fire, and one laid his abba on the rough stone floor for her to sit upon, while another wrapped his, freshly warmed, around her shoulders.

All this was so unusual that Agistha was speechless from sheer astonishment. When, presently, they passed her plain hot food and drink, she took it in silence, eating and drinking ravenously, but speaking never a word of thanks or acknowledgment.

She felt that she must, somehow, have got into another world, or country, even if she had not died. She noticed that, before the others ate, one spread his hands above the food and begged of God to bless it. He did not speak the name of one of the Penates, either, but seemed to address some great and glorious Being for whom his heart was filled with love. Agistha gazed and wondered, but she felt strangely weak and sharply hungry, so she attended closely to her meal. She was on the lookout, however, for what might come next, and marveled to see that these men neither quarreled nor threw dice, but only talked in gentle tones of some dear and lost Companion whom they seemed to think God-like in all his attributes.

Enjoying it all with a restful sense of safety and comfort, basking in the warmth of the firelight, and feeling without knowing it the first effects of that broad, Heaven-born love-light which was to flood the world in beauty, she soon fell asleep once more and "rested"—poor, weary maiden!—as she had not for years.

It was indeed a haven for the little slave girl. Three of those with whom she found herself were Christian Jews from the mother church at Jerusalem: the fourth and youngest was, as we have seen. Herklas, the lost brother of Salome and Hector. The

reasons for his continued disappearance were as follows:

One day the old worker in metals, Vitellis, to whom he was apprenticed, sent the boy to Neapolis to inquire for a consignment of gold, which he had ordered shipped from the island of Thasos some time before, and over the delay of which he was growing thoroughly uneasy.

Herklas had no time to let the home friends know of this jaunt, but thinking he would of course be back by evening, he set off briskly on foot for the seaport, between eight and ten miles away. The well-built Roman road, leading to Neapolis, first crossed a plain thickly traversed with rivu-lets and larger streams, and famous as the battle-ground where Antony and Octavius defeated Brutus and Cassius, after which the two latter, despairing of restoring "honor to Rome," both committed suicide. Beyond this, Herklas came to a ridge of highlands from which fine views of city and coast broke upon his view. But to-day he was thinking neither of the historic battle plain, nor of beautiful scenery, as he trudged lightly along, whistling in boyish fashion. He was reflecting, as he often did, that this might be a much brighter and better world if only a few things were different. He looked about on the green and beautiful country, then up at the blue sky, and mused:

"It would not need any prettier world than this to make an Aiden, if we who live in it were different. There are days when I feel like being kind and helpful to everyone, and then everything about me looks fairly radiant; even my master unbends and ceases to growl at me. Then there are other days—oh, how they drag! I feel dissatisfied with everything. My work all goes wrong, my graving tools slip and work mischief, I feel almost like murdering old Vitellis, and will not even praise the nice dish Salome has helped prepare for my supper! Yet everything is just the same as it was the day before, only I am different. So it is plain enough to see that when I feel right all is right. I must consult the oracle about that and see if there is nothing—no charm or talisman I can use—to keep me feeling so. But alas!"—he ceased whistling, to sigh, —"those oracles are so vague I cannot half the time make out just what they mean. They tell me to ask the gods, and so I do— but there are so many! I sometimes think I have never really hit upon my special patron, because they do not seem to hear when I call. I suppose, if I had gone into the priesthood, as I once thought of doing, I should know more about all these things, but they do puzzle me now."

He reached Neapolis some time before noon, and found that the galley which was to bring the gold had been detained off Samothracia by a pestilence that had broken out among the slaves at the oars, and had just been permitted to enter the bay and discharge its freight by means of lighters, this very morning. So, until the small barges had accomplished their work of unloading, he had nothing to do but lounge about, and secure a porter to help him carry the gold and protect it, in its conveyance to Philippi.

For a long time he stood on the high promontory overlooking the sea, and watched the busy harbor—a brilliant sight to see on a fair summer's morning. But, at last, hunger called him back into the town, and he was soon munching his bread and fruit at an open booth, on the lookout for a certain Nubian porter whom he knew.

He had not long to wait before the tall, massively-built fellow came down the street, his white turban towering above all those he met, his good-natured face like an ebony carving below it.

"Salve! Welcome!" cried the boy, running to meet him. "Come, Aram, I have business for you, and we can get about it soon now, I think."

"'Tis well," said the black slave, showing a set of perfect teeth in his broad smile. "It has been a dull time, Master Herklas, and I am glad to earn a stater. What will there be to carry?"

"Gold in the nugget," said the boy.

"Ha! Then let us hasten, that we may have full daylight for the journey, for they say the mountain brigands have been out in force lately, and I want no meetings with them."

"Well, come on then," said Herklas carelessly. "We will see if the freight is all in by this time. As for the brigands, if they know anything they will keep in the shade, for there is a fresh troop of guards at our Castle, just brought by some Roman general, and they will give sharp chase to those marauders some day."

Still talking, they returned to the pier, where, after an hour or two of delay, they were enabled to secure the gold and start out for Philippi, with the treasure well hidden in their loose girdles, beneath which they also carried dirks of tempered edge.

It was late afternoon when they left the seaport town. As usual, at that hour, the broad Roman highway close to the city gates was well filled. Merchant traders carrying their goods up into the interior, or agriculturists bringing their products for shipment to south and west; soldiers who had been on a furlough of a day, hastening back to the fort before evening roll call; pagan priests in perpetual journeyings to and fro, looking well after their offerings; workmen seeking employment; pleasure parties; and always the ragged, filthy, traveling mendicants, begging or stealing their way.

As they trudged along over the rising ground, Herklas fell into conversation with two other young men whose looks pleased him. They were from Jerusalem, and talked intelligently of their magnificent home city, while Herklas listened with open ears, being a youth who was glad to pick up information whenever and wherever he could. He soon found they were of the sect called of late, for brevity's sake, "Christians," the name having been first used at Antioch, whence it rapidly spread in all directions. He had heard such distorted accounts of them hitherto, that he was surprised to find these men exceptionally courteous, well-informed, and friendly, and he began to ask some questions concerning their faith.

He soon learned they were of the number who had been "scattered abroad upon the persecutions that arose about Stephen," and who, after Barnabas had taken charge of the growing church in Antioch, determined to press on farther, carrying wares to sell through the upper country, and telling the glad tidings as opportunity offered by the way. They were not Apostles, nor ordained Evangelists, like their more learned brethren soon to arrive at this port, but humble followers of their beloved Christ, who could find no happier task than telling the story of the Cross to any who would listen.

Herklas heard it this day, as they kept pace together, their long shadows stretching at their sides where they kept the northerly direction, with the fresh sea breeze at their backs, while they crossed the ridge and entered the famed battle-field of nearly a century before, rich in its running streams. He listened and his boyish heart received an impression such as had never reached it before.

To think that God should take upon Himself the form of man! And for what? To prove He could feel for the poorest, the humblest, the most sinful!—for did not these men say that Jesus confessed to being "tempted like as we are"? To show us there is no glory like that of giving, no power like that of loving; to save us—not from the wrath of gods like Vulcan or Pluto, but from our own wretched, torturing selves! To bear our burdens, to heal our infirmities, to understand our sore trials and temptations.

"Why, we need not fear such a God as that! We—yes, we could be real friends with Him, even!" cried Herklas suddenly, in a tone of wondering awe.

The young men smiled, and one whom his companion called Amasa, said gently:

"'Henceforth I call you not servants; I have called you friends.'"

"Who said that?" asked Herklas quickly.

"Christ, our Lord," was the reverent answer.

To some, belief comes slowly and painfully, born of the throes of doubt and difficulty; to some in despair and shrinking, with Fear whipping the reason into subjection; to some instantly, fully, and with joy, like the sunburst through a gray cloud. In this way it came to Herklas. He had long questioned of his own gods, his heart hungry after truth, and now he threw his soul wide to the welcome Light, and cried:

"Oh, may I be His friend? May I love Him, walk with Him, help Him do for men as He did when here in the body? May I, Amasa?"

The young man turned and looked into the enraptured face of the youthful questioner, glowing in the pink glory of the sunset radiance. The thought thrilled through him that here was one who had not come, like so many, dragged by pains and infirmities, but rather bringing treasures of youth, hope, work, and life to offer. The boy must fully know what he was doing, so Amasa slowly, gravely, told him what would be expected of Christ's friends—that they must even drink the cup that He drank of—the cup of sacrifice, loneliness, poverty not only, but of persecution and possibly death itself. Was he ready? "Could you endure all these for the sake of the Christ?" asked the man in a deep voice. "Remember He said, Himself, 'He that loveth father or mother, brother or sister, more than me, is not worthy of me.' And again, 'He that taketh not up his cross and followeth after me, is

not worthy of me.' Can you forsake all—business opportunities, pleasures, family, home, and perhaps life, for Christ?"

Herklas did not answer at first. Truly these considerations were weighty with a lad happily surrounded, well loved, and with brightest prospects for the future. Gravely he paced along with his now silent companions, the Nubian toiling after, well loaded with the gold, and some rich stuffs from Damascus, consigned to a Philippian merchant.

But the love that had so suddenly sprung into life within the boy's soul was no feeble plant, to die with the first breath of cold air. He felt it grow stronger, surer, more steady, and pure, with every step he took. They were now on the plain, and here Herklas met the tide in his affairs for time and eternity which would lead to God.

He turned presently, stopping in his walk, and the others stopped also, listening for what he might say. His ruddy cheek had paled a little, but in his eyes shone a clear and steady light.

"I am young," he said, "and not very bold, nor strong, but"—he drew in a long breath—"for such a Friend I can risk all. Yes, I accept the work. I will be His!"

———◆———

CHAPTER X.

HERKLAS AND HIS COMPANIONS.

THE little company had lingered as they talked, and the Nubian was growing impatient.

"I want to get by the place of tombs before darkness falls," he said, "for that is a favorite lurking-ground for these hill folk, and we are but a small party, Master Herklas."

"We are stronger than you think for, Aram," was the boy's significant answer to this low-spoken warning.

"Yes, with these two—but will they fight?" asked the practical Nubian.

Herklas smiled. "I was not thinking of them," he said, "but I believe they would help us defend life and property, surely."

Even as he spoke the silent Jew, whom they called Thallus, suddenly raised a hand.

"Listen!" he said; and responsive to his gesture, each one stopped and stood intent and watchful. "You hear it?" he asked in a quick, low tone, "the thud of horses' feet on a run? It is no caravan train. Come into this clump of willows and wait."

He led them down the sloping bank of the stream they were still following, into the little thicket of half-grown trees, all yellow-green in their spring livery, which had not as yet deepened into summer's hue. They had scarcely entered its soft twilight shade when the thunder of hoofs grew louder, and in another instant a swarthy band, armed with lance and spear, went dashing by on the run. They looked neither to the right nor left, but were making straight for the highlands, where, protected by the ridge, they could work their way in roundabout fashion to their home caverns in the mountains.

Their faces were stern and set, but among them Herklas saw one that made him shudder, for he was a captive and young. His long hair swept back from a face gray as ashes, and his teeth glittered between lips tense and parted. He was bound to his horse, which was led by a fierce-looking brigand, and he swayed to and fro in the saddle, rigid as a corpse, held only by the thongs, for pain and fright seemed to have bereft him of his senses.

It was but a glimpse and they were gone!

"They are pursued!" whispered Thallus, as soon as the fleeing riders had been swallowed up in the twilight shadows; "but let us keep still until we see what it all means."

A moment later came a second troupe, all agleam with bronze and steel, as could still be noted in the fading light—evidently a portion of the Roman guard from the Castle. They too had been pressing straight forward, but just here made a detour to the right, across plain and intersecting streams, evidently with the intention of cutting off the robber band at some opening in the hills, as it was manifestly impossible to overtake the daring riders on level ground.

When both troupes had disappeared in a cloud of dust, our four travelers emerged from their retreat and proceeded in security, but not a quarter of a mile beyond they came upon a scene which made even the Nubian cry:

"Well for us we were detained!"

A small party, like themselves, had evidently been lately plundered. The ground was strewn with fragments of their merchandise, and the proofs of a fierce struggle were many. No doubt some of this company had escaped to rouse the garrison, but one, at least, had been taken, and their goods destroyed, or plundered. It was certain now, however, that all danger was over for that night, and our friends soon entered the welcome gates of Philippi, without further adventure.

Here Herklas dismissed the Nubian, paying his price, and bade his new friends a brief good-by, for he felt that before joining his fortunes with theirs, he must report to his master, Vitellis, deliver the gold, and inform him of his intention to leave his service. This, somewhat to the boy's surprise, proved a rather difficult task, for Vitellis, who was old and deliberate, could not seem at once to comprehend, and was very loth to let him go. Herklas had not supposed he would care—for the goldsmith had often censured, but seldom praised his work—and was now both gratified and troubled to see that he really clung to his late apprentice.

"What would you?" he cried sharply, as he eyed the youth with an astonished gaze. "You have your holidays, one suit a year, and your wage, do you not? You are not bound to me by law, so I never beat you; and at the meal you eat with my family—are you not one with them? Do you think yourself called and chosen of the gods, that you give this up so easily?"

The eyes of Herklas lit up at this expression. It was common enough, to be sure, but it meant a great deal to him this day.

"Yes," he said gravely, "I am called of God."

Vitellis started. "Would you be a priest? 'Tis foolish!" The old man spoke with warmth. "You have no learning—no money. You would be but a mendicant, footsore, weary, and homeless. It is not a comfortable lot, and there are many. Let those go who will not work. Good tradesmen are always needed to keep their scrips supplied. I never refuse my offering to the wandering priests, but I—I do not envy them."

Herklas shook his head. "You do not understand me, master. I shall be no priest. I am going with honest traders, and I too shall work as they do; but I have a message to take—a message for Jesus the Christ."

He brought out the name boldly, and his master fairly jumped.

"For Christus? For that sorcerer of Jerusalem, who was crucified with thieves? Are you mad? Know you not our great Claudius Cæsar has a horror of these new sects and their pretensions? Do you court imprisonment, torture—perhaps death, my son?"

Herklas felt he was making his first stand in the new life. "I do not court them—no, master—but if they come I shall be ready. I love Christ. He lived for me—He died for me. I wish to follow the example He set, and give all in return; for in giving all, do I not receive all? Let me go, master, with your blessing."

The old man gazed at him. He was no enthusiast in his pagan belief. He was a hard-headed business man, not given to fine words or deep thoughts, but with a simple creed of minding his own affairs and letting the rest of the world mind theirs. It never occurred to him that these might be in one sense his affairs, also. Such an idea as resigning his shop, his home, his daily round of narrow duties and pleasures, for the mere purpose of winning people to better ways of thinking and living, could never occur to him. But in the face of this young proselyte he saw something that awed him and kept back the ironical laughter which Herklas had expected to hear.

"Well, well!" he muttered at last, "the world progresses! If, at your age, I had had your chance, not all the religions on earth could have drawn me away. But you are different."

"Good-by, then," said Herklas gently, making a salaam full of reverent affection.

"Farewell," said the old man gravely. Then raising his hands above the bowed head, he murmured:

"The gods—your God counsel you, boy!" and turning abruptly, walked away into his own apartments behind the smithy, leaving Herklas free to depart forever.

From thence the boy expected to go directly home, but as he sped through a narrow street near by, he met Thallus and Amasa again, also hurrying along, with anxiety upon their faces.

"Ah, here he is!" cried the latter, adding quickly and joyfully, "Well met, Herklas! We must depart at once for Amphipolis, we find, and we were about seeking you to ask if you would join us."

"Now—this minute?" cried Herklas. "I have not told my brother and sister yet."

"It must be now," said Amasa; "the merchant train is ready to start, and we must travel with it this night for safety."

"But—" began the boy again, when Thallus sternly interrupted:

"Jesus said, 'No man, having put his hand to the plow, and looking back, is fit for the kingdom of God.'"

Herklas bowed to the rebuke. "I go," he said briefly; "lead on." And after a moment he added, "I have neither a change of raiment, nor have I money."

"Fear not," said Amasa, in his bright way; "we Christians always share with each other. 'The earth is the Lord's, and the fullness thereof.' Will He not see that your body is cared for, when your heart and life are given to Him? Come with us and fear nothing."

So Herklas went, consoling himself with the thought that Hector would inquire for him of Vitellis, who would let his brother know that he was alive and well, at least.

"And Amphipolis is only thirty miles away," he murmured. "I shall soon return."

But it was over a fortnight that Herklas spent wandering along that populous seacoast with his new friends, the trio being soon joined by a fourth, a Syrian named Cyrus, who was as unlike Thallus and Amasa as they were unlike each other.

He was between them in age, small, keen, brave, and ardent, yet with a vein of shrewdness which made him resent imposture, or oppression. He had been slow to believe, but having given himself, the surrender was complete; even Herklas had no greater zeal. Yet in many ways the lad far surpassed his companions. He had an indefinable charm of manner, which, added to a face and figure such as even the usual Greek—famed the world over for perfection of form—might envy, gave him a subtle power to attract and win friends. Then he was a natural orator. All untrained though he was, the street crowds listened eagerly to his every word, and the slow, stern Thallus and plain, good-natured Amasa—even the keen, witty Cyrus—watched with wonder his compelling power and resistless energy.

But while recognizing this, they felt no envy. Each gave his all to Christ. If his endowments were not so great as another's, that was not for him to worry over. God had created him as he was for some wise purpose, and if he could not do one thing, he could another. When one's life becomes in its possessor's eyes but a part of a great plan, conceived by Wisdom far surpassing his own, such trifles as envy, disappointed ambition, and failing powers are as nothing.

The time slipped by quickly enough to the youth—more so than to his friends at home, who could get little information out of the taciturn old Vitellis, except that Herklas had left his service, and was well when he did so, always ending his gruff answers to anxious questions by the words, which they could not rightly understand at that time: " Ask the Christians—not me. Perhaps they have bewitched him!" after which he would turn back to his work, and refuse to speak further.

Amid a roving people, in an equable climate, where private correspondence is almost unknown, family bonds are readily made and easily broken. The poor have little to anchor them, and when work fails in one locality, it is no trouble to drift to another. Herklas had often been sent up-country for days at a time, and he had no thought that his dear ones would feel anxious; nor did they until Salome conceived the idea of his being bewitched, as we have seen. Still, the affectionate boy was glad when word was passed to return to Neapolis for a time, in order to meet Paul and Silas there, and he took the occasion to hurry away at the break of dawn to his own beloved Philippi, bounding with light steps over the few intervening miles, because he was once again to see his dear Salome and brave Hector, and beg their sanction of his new plans. But it was while Salome lay ill and poor Hector was in prison that he thus hastily returned and could find no one to tell him a word of either, though little Nadab, had he but spoken, might have enlightened him concerning his sister, at least.

For the few hours he had to spare he wandered about, vainly seeking them, to leave word with a neighbor, finally, as to his own whereabouts before he returned to his new friends. This neighbor, however, had also left the city when Salome was seeking her brothers, and so it was that a series of petty accidents, apparently, kept the three apart.

Herklas and his companions were in the surrounding country several days, and it was as they were returning to Neapolis, after a short tour amid the farmers of the foothills, that they were overtaken by the storm and sought shelter in the cave, just in time for Herklas to come to poor, shivering, scared Agistha's aid.

When, the next morning, the girl awoke from her sound, sweet sleep it was to find herself alone, with the bright sunlight shining into the low opening of the cave. She sat up and looked about her in the strange daze that one feels on awakening in an unaccustomed spot. But slowly memory returned, and bit by bit she recalled the chain of incidents which had terminated in this cavern.

It seemed to her as if for years she had been wandering in a sort of evil dream, in which impure influences made her say and do things she neither desired nor understood. She felt she had been sadly abused and that always worse when she tried to resist the influence and be her better self. When her masters told her she was losing her power, they beat and starved her until the strange trances enwrapped her again and she was ready to shout her crazy utterances as they desired. It had been a dreadful time! All the more dreadful because away back—ages, it seemed to her,—she could vaguely remember such different things—a garden, a cool court with a fountain, and a little child—was it herself?—playing happily about its marble basin.

No, that part must be either a dream or something she had once seen in those wearisome journeys they were always taking from place to place. How wretched they were!

But worse than all, was that trouble in her head; those long, dazed spaces when she was not herself, but some one else, yet when by snatches she realized that everything was wrong. Before she could right herself, however, she would again lose the thread she had barely caught, and sink off into chaos once more. Now, for the first time her head was clear and cool, and had been growing so for many hours; in fact, ever since the day—she could not place the date—when, as she was ranting at the top of her voice, two men had passed by on the street, and she had seen them in a flash of sense and reason and been impelled to cry out: " These men are the servants of the Most High God."

She had thus followed them more than once until—was it yesterday, or the day before, or a week ago?—one had turned, and in a stern voice commanded the evil spirit to come out of her. She only knew that something seemed to snap and rend in her brain, after which she had, as it were, awakened, her head and sight clear, her understanding bright, while a great loathing of her former state took possession of her. From that minute she could not " prophesy," no matter how her masters might coax, or scold. Her understanding was too clear, she saw realities too plainly for visions or lunacies, and they were left to lament her lost power. But she was like a new creature, though weary—oh, weary unto death, it seemed! "Rest I must have," was all she could say. "Rest!" And she had sought the roof of their miserable lodging-house to lie down and sleep, too ill to mind threats or kicks, in that utter exhaustion of body and spirit.

She could remember no more until that dreary awakening on the bier, in the moonlight. He fatigue must have thrown her into a sleep so near like death that no one could tell the difference, and—what had it brought her to?

She looked around again, and her eyes, accustomed now to the dim light, saw there was food close at her side, spread neatly on a bit of scrip-cloth. She partook with relish of the wafer-like bread, dried fish, and fruit, and felt the better for the meal, which was abundant and satisfying. "But," thought she, gaining courage with strength, "I am thirsty now. I will go outside and see if water can be found near by; learn too, if possible, where I am and what next I must do. One thing—I will not return to my wicked masters if I can help it, for some great Spirit stronger than the Python, even, has broken their evil dominion over me, and given me clear sight and sense again."

She rose, crawled to the cave opening, and looked timidly around. It was a glorious morning, and the blue sky was scarcely broken by a cloud. Directly before her lay a plain, stretching away into gently rising ground at her right. At her left were the city walls, no long distance off, rising sturdily against the soft background of an undulating range of mountains, and close about her was a rough bit of ground, bushy and boulder-strewn, leveled from the cliff-like hill in which these tombs and caves were excavated.

A little spring issued from the hillside near by, and trickled away in a tiny rill into a larger stream crossing the plain. But no person was near. Even the highway built by Rome, which gleamed white in the near distance, was quite deserted at this minute. She was all alone.

———

CHAPTER XI.

AT THERMÆ AND CASTLE.

WHEN Hector found himself free once more he could have leaped for joy, though his limbs were stiff from long confinement, and sore from the rusty fetters. As he drew in long breaths of the outer air and blinked his half-blinded eyes in the glorious sunshine, his heart bounded in gratitude, and half involuntarily he said to himself, as he looked upward:

"For this I could thank the great God who loosed my fetters and those of the two men of Christ, last night. I could even thank the Christ who seems to be their Friend. He must be greater than our gods, and certainly He is nearer and dearer to their hearts than any god has been to mine."

Hector walked away from the busy forum full of these thoughts, his feet making straight for home, where, ever since his talk with the young lord in the prison, he had fondly hoped to find Salome. But when he reached the tiny house within the wall he found it empty and chill. Salome was not there. Upon investigation, however, he found that her clothing was gone, which was proof positive that she had been back since that dreadful night, unless—a surmise occurred to him which darkened his face again —unless Persis, the slave girl, had taken the garments and fled. If so, that young patrician had not been right about Salome's escape, after all. And indeed how should he be so certain? Could he know everything that went on inside those garrisoned walls? Of course not!

There seemed but one thing left him, and that was to go, as directed, to the Castle, show his signet ring, and see what good or ill fortune awaited him there. But before doing that, he must remove the marks of the dungeon; he must visit the baths and provide himself with fresh raiment.

He found his own clothing undisturbed, and, selecting his best sleeveless undervest, the loin cloth, toga, and buskins, which formed the street attire of one of his station, he betook himself to a great building adjoining the forum, in which were the public baths of Philippi. These were under the same roof with the gymnasium in which Hector was a pupil, and he therefore had the privilege of private baths, with an attendant free, while ordinarily the poorer classes must content themselves with the great swimming pool, or natatorium, and depend upon their own exertions for the showerings, rubbings, and scrapings, which accompanied, or followed, the immersion. Even the smaller towns boasted fine baths, and that at Philippi was modeled upon those at Rome, though far smaller, less pretentious, and freer from ornamentation.

As Hector reached the large stone structure he entered first an open court, fitted with long stone benches at either side, which were shaded from the hot sun by a portico supported on Doric columns. Here were always groups of men lounging and gossiping as they awaited their turn to enter the thermæ. Hector recognized several of them, this morning, but feeling ashamed to be seen in his present woeful condition, he hurried by with bent head through a vestibule and short corridor, into a small room beyond, called the frigidarium. Here pegs in the wall offered a convenient place for hanging one's garments, but as it was only for the use of those going into the natatorium, or large common bath, Hector hurried through into an apartment close by, serving the same purpose for a private bather who wished the hot tank, with an attendant's service, for which a small fee was demanded.

Here a young page was in charge who, after saluting Hector with a wondering look, hurried off at once to summon the attendant he knew was desired, for the gymnast being an almost daily frequenter of the baths, the boy needed no directions in his service.

Hector hurriedly disrobed, kicking his stained and ill-smelling garments into a corner for the boy to burn, then passed into the next apartment. Soon his attendant appeared, smiling and ready. He wore nothing but a breech-cloth, and over his arm hung the great rough towels used by all bathers.

"Ah, Hermes!" said Hector pleasantly, "hurry with your ointments, for I am stiff and sore."

"Indeed!" cried the other briskly, beginning to set out a row of tiny phials, pots, and pestles, with thin, crescent-shaped articles of shell, upon the marble slab jutting from the wall. "Indeed! Been wrestling again, have you? I hope you were not thro—hah! What's this?"

He looked up keenly. Those red welts on wrists and ankles never came from wrestling.

Hector flushed warmly. "Be gentle, boy! Your lightest touch is painful. I see you understand. Yes, I have been in prison."

"But why? I cannot understand that! Hector, the Olympionic, in a dungeon! That is passing strange."

Our friend briefly explained, and the youth, while tenderly anointing the raw parts, looked the sympathy and indignation he felt, for he was fond of this bather, and greatly admired his splendid strength and courage. As the narration ended he broke out bitterly:

"It is of no use to be honest in these days—that does not serve! Let one try all his life and yet by ever so little offend some patrician, and click!—the dark doors shut you in, and there you lie to rot, forgotten. 'The gods have memory only for the great, and the great have memory only for those who can serve them,'—that's the truest thing Seneca has said yet."

Hector was silent. Should he tell about this God of whom he had heard so lately, who sought out the poor and walked with them—who chose them out of all the world for His friends? But just then Hermes rose to his feet, his task accomplished, and Hector was ready for the caldarium.

This long and narrow apartment was entirely of marble, its walls being laid double, that the space between might serve as flues, to conduct the hot air from the furnace beneath to every inch of the chamber. At its further end was the bath-tub, a shallow cistern twice as long as a man, and about four feet wide. It was raised above the floor so that Hector had to mount two steps to reach it, the top step forming a seat, while all around the inside ran a ledge, which also served as a resting-place.

Upon this the young man placed himself, while Hermes poured over his head and shoulders large vases of the warm water from the great cauldrons opposite, which were placed directly over the furnace.

"There, that's enough!" cried Hector at last, as he plunged gayly into the now well-filled tub. "Oh, this makes me feel like a new man! It has taken all the smart out of my body, and the stiffness too. Be prepared, Hermes; I must have such a scraping and pounding as you do not often give me, I tell you!"

The attendant laughed. "I am ready for you," he said, as Hector stepped from the tub, or alveus, into the labrum, a huge saucer-like receptacle of white marble into which led a pipe which threw up a forceful stream of cold water that descended in a spray upon his shoulders. Its cold dash was allowed but for an instant, then Hermes caught up his great towel and quickly dried the bather, afterwards placing him upon a marble slab at full length. Here he first plied the horn or shell scrapers, thin half-rounds that left the flesh smooth as ivory, and then added the poundings, punchings, slappings, and rubbings, which gave both flesh and muscle the pliancy and perfection of an infant's, with the hard endurance of the man's.

Thoroughly refreshed, and clean in every pore, his hair cut short in gymnast fashion and daintily perfumed, Hector finally issued from the great building feeling that the prison taint was removed from body, if not from soul, and stepped off at a brisk pace, prepared to push his fortunes with energy.

It was something of a walk to the Castle, which connected with the fort that guarded the south-western wall, but he enjoyed every step of the way, feeling as never before the beauty of earth and sky, and the blessing of simple freedom, with pure air to breathe, and sunshine to bask in.

He climbed the ascent and reached the outer gate, guarded by two stalwart soldiers, whose helmets and spears glistened in the sunlight. As he approached they crossed spears before the gate, and awaited him. He made known his somewhat vague errand:

"I was bidden by a young lord to call here this morning. Here is his signet ring that I was to show."

He handed it to one of the guards, who gave it a glance, nodded, and passed it over to his fellow.

"Aulus Clotius!" said he, and rang a sudden call by striking spear and breastplate sharply together, even as the other threw one leaf of the bronze gate wide open and, returning the ring, bade Hector pass in.

A page now stood before him who examined the ring, said briefly, "Follow me!" and conducted the visitor across a broad court to an outer stair leading to an entrance in one of the many turrets of the Castle.

Up these marble steps the richly-clad page lightly tripped, then opened a heavy door into a tiled vestibule. Across this Hector followed him into a large apartment with a raised, richly-covered dais nearly surrounding it, and a small fountain playing in the center. Several curtains of Tyrian purple, heavy with embroidery of gold thread, indicated entrances into adjoining rooms, while between gleamed exquisite marble statuary, shown off the better by pedestals of malachite and ebony. All the light there was filtered through many-tinted sheets of mica in the great dome above, and surrounding this tower-room at a goodly height was a gallery guarded by a balustrade of richly-carved cedar, from which like apartments seemed to open.

Hector, who had been bidden to wait in the large, round room, decided these must be small, probably mere alcoves serving for private apartments, and lighted by the slits of windows he had observed without. Was it from one of these the voice had ordered him to prison? He was just considering the rather startling suggestion. when one of the curtains on the gallery was flung aside and the young man of the prison came out and leisurely descended the stairs, which began in two flights, to meet in a few broad steps at the base. He was carelessly dressed and his long curls were tumbled, as if he had been lying down. In fact, he looked sleepy still. Hector concluded he had been making up for an unusually early rising by a forenoon nap. And he was right.

"Well, my man, you are prompt!" said the patrician, half pettishly, as if not relishing the disturbance. "But"—looking him over with critical admiration—"you can never be the prisoner with whom I left my ring?"

"I am he, sire," said Hector, salaaming.

The other laughed. "To be sure it was too dark to see plainly there, but—well. well! who would believe that mere externals could make such a difference? I thought you a big, strong fellow; now you look like a statue by Phidias—but there! I must not make you vain. And now tell me, you found your sister safe at home, of course?"

"No, sire, she was not there."

"What? Really, this surprises me! She certainly is not here, and never has been. I have made diligent inquiries, and no one has seen her since that night."

"Her clothing is gone," said Hector, looking thoughtful, "though that might have been stolen by the slave girl. I believe she was none too honest. But I begin to hope Salome has found protection somewhere. I will make inquiries among the neighbors."

"Yes, that will be best. I understand you are a Wrestler, and have twice won the Olympic crown."

"It is true."

"And is this glory so much to you that you could never exchange it for any other?"

"What other?" asked Hector quickly.

"That of a soldier."

Hector's eyes flashed. "This has served me, sire, so long as I could down all who were pitted against me," showing his white teeth in a broad smile; "but the soldier's glory—that is lasting! And Rome is liberal to her brave men on the field."

"True! 'Tis pity, though, you were not Roman born, for you would make a soldier to delight Mars, I wager. You are a Macedonian by birth?"

" A Thracian, sire."

" Of Greek parentage?"

Hector bowed, while the other looked him over with a lingering glance. " I should hate to spoil you by making a mere courtier of you," he finally remarked, as if he were speaking about his guest to some one else. " And yet, I like you. I would gladly attach you to my household—by the way, do you know who I am, boy?"

" I overheard the guard at the gate mutter ' Aulus Clotius,' and I hoped you might indeed be that gallant young officer of whom the people say, ' He is bright, but he never knows when he is beaten.' "

The other laughed and flushed, well pleased at the rough compliment. " The people know something, if I do not!" he cried, gayly. " But that is only one side of the tale. Do they not also say this foolish soldier is rusting in inaction and becoming simply a weak favorite of his master, Claudius?"

It was Hector's turn to flush, now. He hesitated an instant, then answered: " They say, sire, your talent for music is as great as for fighting, and that pleases the young Nero so well that he would keep your sword rusting if he could. Yet Aulus Clotius is again the soldier, is he not?" glancing about the Castle chamber significantly.

" Ah, you'll make a courtier after all!" laughed the other. " But be not too ready, my boy; the real warrior has no fine phrases, you know. And, bah! do these look like soldier trappings?" waving a hand over the rich apartment. " No, no! Nowadays luxury creeps even into garrisons like this, and the days go by idly enough when Rome has nothing to do but count her kingly prisoners and celebrate her too easy triumphs." He gave a quick sigh, shook back his disordered locks, frowned a little, then burst into a gay laugh. " But come! we will make the most of it all wherever we may be. Say, boy, will you go with me to Rome?"

To Rome! Hector's eyes grew large. It was the dream of his life to visit that magnificent capital—a dream he had never expected to realize. He thought of Salome, of Herklas—both apparently lost to him; then he let his thoughts center on self. To go to Rome with Aulus Clotius!—to see its wealth, grandeur, gayety! To be one of a patrician household—perhaps a favorite! To be at Court and a part of that regal, luxurious existence!

" Will I go, sire?" he cried with a laugh of delight. " But give me the chance and see!"

" It pleases you so?"—eying him with a sort of scornful surprise. " Is it the thought of its luxury or its glory, I wonder? Well, both are myths to a great extent. But why should I moralize over the foolish boy, when I am as like him as one javelin is like another? Yes, Rome is a great city—and a wicked one. No wonder the idea delights you! What is your name, boy? I forget."

" Hector."

" That promises well for a hero, anyhow; but nobody ever does live up to a heroic name, more's the pity! I am to start tomorrow with a large escort. Be ready, and meanwhile—but have you breakfasted?"

" In the prison, sire;" making a rueful face.

The patrician laughed amusedly. " Its memory is not enchanting, I see. But we can mend all that. My favorites do not starve on lentils and dried fish, I promise you!"

He clapped his hands, and the page entered, bowing low before his master.

" See that this man is well fed and lodged," he said briefly; then carelessly waving them away, he departed into one of the adjoining rooms.

Hector followed the page down the outer stair and around the tower, to a court in the rear, where a row of shed-like buildings bespoke the quarters of the men. At the end of the row was the kitchen, a large open place, covered only with tent-cloth, its sides entirely open to the breeze. He was sharply hungry, and the smell of the pottage steaming in a great kettle over a fire built in the depression made in the hard paving, came with most agreeable sensations to his nostrils. He was about to stop and take a seat on the stone bench near by, where two guards, just relieved from duty, were enjoying a gourd full of the soup, sipping it in great gulps, when the page called him onward.

" Is that a place for one of Aulus Clotius' favorites to eat?" he asked disdainfully, and, turning through a narrow door in an intervening wall, finally stopped before the fine bronze door of a long building well arched and windowed. It was two stories in height, and above it was a dome-like skylight similar to that in the tower. It was, in fact, the banqueting hall reserved for special suites from imperial Rome, its second story being a gallery for dancing and music, or for spectacles and athletic games, if desired.

Hector took in at a glance the noble apartment, finished in carved woods highly polished, with a raised dais at one end, where the half-round table was surrounded by rich couches, and the longer, plainer board below, with benches at the sides.

"Sit here," said the page, placing him a short distance below the dais, "and I will call some one to serve you."

Hector obeyed in a sort of daze. Soon the page returned with a white-capped attendant, who, in an obsequious voice, began naming over the dishes at the new-comer's disposal. The somewhat bewildered young man modestly mentioned a few which had always seemed great luxuries to him, and soon found them smoking before him. The page meanwhile lolled indolently near by, and asked questions, which Hector managed to answer between mouthfuls with the good-humor engendered by satisfaction.

"Have you finished at last?" he cried saucily, as Hector swallowed the final crumbs of his repast, and wiped his lips. "If you have, I will show you where the men of our company sleep. It is in the left wing."

He hurried Hector along from this building to another, which joined the Castle itself. It was a long wing divided into small apartments.

"Here," said he, "is where my master's special suite lies. You will of course have a bed-fellow—may he prove a pleasant one! Make yourself at home, and keep your own counsel. That is the rule at Court."

Still laughing, he turned, and, throwing up his hand in the fashion of the Bedouin who meets a friend in the desert, he sped briskly away to his light but often galling duties in the tower.

CHAPTER XII.

THE HOME OF A ROMAN PATRICIAN.

HECTOR'S day passed rapidly, and but a short time was left for making his inquiries about Salome, which, not being rightly directed, proved futile. As he came back towards the Castle he again saw the two Christians of the prison. They were across the street, walking rapidly towards one of the city gates, being on their way to the little synagogue beyond the walls, for the second service of the market day. Had he seen them in the early morning nothing could have kept him from their side, but since then, all-engrossing worldly plans had stepped in, and while he stood hesitating they disappeared.

Had he spoken to them they would doubtless have invited him to the service, and had he gone he would have met his sister there, and his whole after-life might have been different. But his new ambitions held him captive, and he was led by them and not by God.

Early the next morning Aulus Clotius and his train started on the long journey to Rome. They made the short march to Neapolis, and there took ship for the remainder of the distance. Hector found himself hastily fitted out with a uniform and horse, and he was proud to see that he formed one of the special body-guard of ten who rode in close proximity to the young chief, at the head of the train.

Just behind this gleaming cohort of spearsmen were two or three litters, also specially guarded, in which Hector learned there were ladies, and behind them marched a large band of slaves, porters, and attendants, to the number of perhaps a hundred, while still beyond trailed a miscellaneous company of laden asses, camels, and pedestrians, merchant traders or mendicants, who gladly joined the cavalcade for sociability and protection.

The garrison band accompanied them for a mile or so, waking the echoes with its stirring strains, and as Hector rode leisurely along, carried so easily by his trained animal that he almost forgot he did not know how to ride, he felt that life was opening most brilliantly before him, and his pulses bounded in time with the stirring beat of drum and blast of trumpet.

Every one they met on the broad highway stopped to gaze at the brilliant sight, and many a cheer greeted the brave young leader who rode so proudly at their head.

In this pride Hector participated. If he was not the sun he was certainly close to it, and as a satellite he absorbed some of the adulation, and swelled with pride and vainglory. Thus they rode into Neapolis, the town turning out to view the brave sight, and took their way directly to the pier, where lay the galleys in readiness to convey them to Rome. Hector had never taken a sea voyage, and the very sight and smell of the blue, billowing waves stretching far as sight could reach, filled him with delight. The wide harbor, glittering in the morning sunshine, was filled with every sort of craft, from the blunt-prowed junks of the fishermen to the graceful Roman ships, with their great gilded figure-heads and pointed bows.

"This is to live!" the youth thought, as, at a quickly-spoken order, he brought his horse around alongside several others to help form the double line through which the company were to pass as they embarked.

But after he had sat motionless as a statue in the blazing heat for nearly an hour, his raptures were modified. In fact, he concluded that so much ceremony was monotonous and unnecessary! First, the ladies were embarked. There were several of these—the young wife of Aulus, Julia by name, his mother, Pamphylia, and their ladies-in-waiting—who were led across the gang-plank into a finely-appointed galley which floated the imperial colors. Next the house slaves and stores were placed in a second less pretentious boat, and lastly the guards were divided between the two, Hector being among those consigned to the royal galley.

It was a relief to quit the saddle and take his place in the stern, on a level with a bank of oarsmen, where he could watch their every motion. Yet often during the journey he turned away, sick at heart, from this sight, for their broad bare backs were scored with the lash, and down their haggard faces the sweat of their arduous toil poured like rain.

"It is a hard world for them," he muttered often, "even if they deserve their punishment. I wonder what they are thinking behind those brown, sullen faces all these long hours of labor, when they bend to the oars like machines rather than men. Does hope still beckon them on, and do they count the days till they are released? But if the release comes only with death—"

Then sometimes came the flashing memory of those two Apostles in prison. Under scourging and torture they were not only brave and patient—they were triumphantly glad! It was a puzzle beyond his solving. He wished now he had sought them out and talked with them. There were so many things he would like to ask in these long, lazy hours when there was little to do but speculate and dream.

But when he reached the great metropolis, such musings vanished in the wonder and delight of looking and living at this center of the world. As he once more rode by his master's side and gazed out over the teeming streets, with their magnificent buildings, giving every evidence of unlimited wealth and power, he again swelled with exultation at being one of the gorgeous mass, and cared little for the sufferings of other atoms.

The stately palace reserved for the use of Aulus Clotius and his household formed a part of that great agglomeration of buildings known as the "royal mansions," and was directly guarded and officered by the Emperor himself. It was now 52 A. D., and Claudius had been eleven years upon the throne, a welcome successor of the detested Caligula, who during his short reign managed to make himself hated by all sects, but especially by the Jews, whom he had persecuted from Jerusalem to Joppa, with every form of indignity his evil mind could conjure up. If Claudius was not much more of a man, in many particulars, he was at least not a monster, and his faults were those of weakness rather than tyranny. Indeed, he was entirely under the control of his wife, Agrippina, the beautiful but unscrupulous daughter of the brave old general, Germanicus, and she was already plotting to make Nero, her son by her former husband, his successor, rather than Claudius' own boy, Brittanicus, who was a few years younger than his step-brother.

Nero was fifteen, a fair, curly-haired youth of a seemingly amiable disposition, and with some talent and great taste for music and poetry. He had been well taught by his tutor, the wise Seneca, and was the idol of his mother, for in him she thought she saw the docile instrument of her most daring ambitions.

For a few days Hector found little to do beyond settling himself in his new surroundings. He was not lodged with the other guards in the barracks, but had a room in the palace which was comfortably fitted up, and ate at the table in the great hall, where he, with several other favorites, among whom were the page Lucian, the secretary Theophilus, a poet or two, and a centurion, occupied the raised dais at one end of the long table, surrounded by couches, the rest of the household being accommodated a step below, upon stone benches. Occasionally their young lord condescended to eat with them, but not often. He was, indeed, frequently a guest at the Emperor's table, and when at home liked best to sit at meat in a smaller room, most luxuriously fitted up, where only his immediate family and friends were present. It was a special mark of favor to be invited to join him at these informal but exquisitely served meals, and one thus singled out was puffed up with pride for a week, at least.

In order to introduce Hector into his household, Aulus had appointed him to an office similar to that of groom of the chambers, which really meant, in this case, that the young Greek daily trained his ambitious lord in athletics, and wrestled with him till the latter was fain to cry, "Enough!" In the two or three hours thus spent Hector always felt that he well earned all these favors, for while the brave Aulus was constantly crying to him to "Lay on!" and come at him harder, the Greek knew that he must not leave so much as a small bump on that fair flesh, and the effort to "seem" and yet not to "do" became a real penance, beside which the hearty blows he received in return were as nothing.

In fact, these words might fitly describe all Hector's life, now, and that of most of those around him. It was brave seeming, but alas, such feeble doing! Even Seneca, the grave and reverend philosopher, soon began to show himself insincere in the youth's keen eyes, or else how could he so constantly write and talk of the doctrine of extreme simplicity, extolling its delights by the hour, and yet revel in every attainable luxury? Did he not own those much-prized tables of citron wood ending in ivory feet, not by the dozen or score, but by the hundreds? and was not his villa set down amid gardens which on one occasion had even excited the envy of an Emperor? Then there was Nero, the young aspirant to the purple. It was the fashion everywhere to praise his beauty, his voice, his poems, his good judgment, and his amiable disposition. Yet Hector soon discovered that his talents were but mediocre; and as for his disposition, it happened one day that a slave was being whipped in the court-yard just as the young prince started to cross it, before mounting his horse.

Hector, watching, saw Nero follow the movements of the lictor and his whimpering charge, a mere child, then stop to watch with a look of intense satisfaction the prep-

arations at the stake. Hector turned away, then, for the first scream of the poor creature was enough for him, but a moment later he was startled by a laugh, and glanced around to see the "amiable" young prince laughing and clapping his hands at every blow of the cruel lash, in a perfect ecstasy of evil enjoyment.

From that day the boy's softly-colored face, though wreathed in smiles, was to Hector but a mask for a cruel heart, and no one could convince him that the idol of Rome and the toast of the poets was not pitiless to the core. More: he was certain that Aulus Clotius felt the same, though self-interest closed his lips. For, like all the others, Aulus was brave only upon the surface. He could fight like a tiger, but in this courtly atmosphere he was weak and cowardly where he should have been strong, effeminate where he should have been bold and manly, silent where he should have spoken out in thunder tones. All these things the Greek felt keenly, and they often made his easy life a burden of discontent and self-disgust.

Ere long he had so completely won the confidence of his master that he was given the honorable post of special knight to the women of the household, whenever they went abroad. At the head of from two to four guards he attended their chariot, or basterna, and in this office the faces of Pamphylia and Julia soon became familiar to him.

The first-named was a dignified, grayhaired matron with dark, sad eyes, but a beautiful smile, and her voice was plaintively sweet. She was always gentle, and it was evident that the gay, bright Julia, the bride of a year, loved her well. They were constantly together, and usually accompanied by Julia's nurse, a little woman full of chatter, and Pamphylia's companion. This latter was a young captive maid from Gaul, slender, dark-eyed and agile, with the grace and also the timidity of a fawn. Something about her vaguely suggested Salome to Hector, and this made him watch her more closely than he might otherwise have done, and as he soon became a great favorite with all the ladies, he often found opportunity to exchange a word or two with her.

One day, after a boxing contest with his lord, which had been unusually exhausting, Aulus threw himself, panting, upon the couch and, after watching Hector, still fresh and full-winded, for a long minute, said:

"Well, my boy, that was pretty well! Dost note how much stronger I am getting? I shall make you puff too before many days."

Hector only smiled slightly at the banter, which he was used to, and the other, seeing

was naturally kind-hearted—when kindness was no trouble—so he said gently:

"You miss her, I see."

"Yes, I do," breathed Hector under his keen eyes.

"I know—I understand!" spoke up his

"No, sire; I was thinking—one does sometimes, you know."

his absent manner, went on: "Why, what megrim have you now? Are you regretting the Olympic games?"

"No, sire; I was thinking—one does sometimes, you know—of my old home and friends."

"Ah, of that sister, eh? Verily, it is strange where she hath gone; is it not, lad?"

Hector nodded. The homesick tears were so close that he could not speak. Aulus saw his emotion and respected it. The patrician

master quickly. "You need not be ashamed. Did you never hear about my sister, Hector?"

"Yours, my lord? I did not know you ever had one."

"Yes, it was years ago." Aulus threw his arms above his head and gazed up at the ceiling. "I can just remember her. She was three years my junior, and I thought her my special charge, for she was a tiny creature, dainty as a bird. It nearly killed my mother when she—"

"Died?" cried Hector compassionately.

"No, no! I think that would have been easier to bear. She disappeared. That is all we know. One day we were playing in the court, and I ran into the house for a toy boat I wished to sail in the fountain's basin. When I came back she was gone, and though we sought her high and low, spending money freely, we could never find a trace of her. Perhaps, if my father had been living, he could have done better at the search, but we had been orphans nearly a year, and my mother was young and inexperienced. Her hair turned gray that twelvemonth, though she was not yet twenty-five."

"Such are terrible griefs!" said Hector feelingly. "How old was the child?"

"Barely four," responded Aulus sadly. "The sweetest baby in the world. We called her Cleone."

Hector, looking sympathetically at his young master, thought no less of him because he suddenly brushed the back of his hand across his eyes, and their common grief seemed to draw them more closely together. He stepped to his side and said feelingly:

"The brave and favored must have their troubles as well as the humble, my master. And this accounts for the young face and white locks of your beautiful mother."

Aulus turned and looked at him affectionately. "Is't not a dear woman, Hector? I am glad you admire her, for she likes and trusts you. So, too, does my merry Julia."

"Ah! she should make your heart sing for joy, my lord. Her very glance is sunshine."

"True, true! I hope I shall never sadden her with my wild ways."

At this moment Lucian the page appeared with a message for the master. "Sire, if you are ready, Prince Nero wishes to consult you in regard to the musicians' stand they are erecting for the spectacle. Can you attend him at once?"

CHAPTER XIII.

JUNIUS FAR ASTRAY.

SALOME was now thoroughly domesticated with the family of Junius and Elizabeth. She had no more hope of seeing her brothers, for though Junius finally exerted himself enough to make some inquiries as to the occupants of the prison,

the keeper knew no one there answering to his description. This was not strange, for the summary manner in which Hector had been assigned to him, without name or complaint, had given him the impression that this unruly prisoner was a slave, an impression confirmed by his abrupt release without trial, all at the command of one man—for, as the reader has possibly divined, it was Aulus Clotius who had sentenced as well as released him. To the jailer, therefore, Hector was simply the Roman slave undergoing punishment. Thus the inquiries of Junius were answered most decidedly in the negative—the more so because this man was no favorite with the official.

After a time Salome decided to give up the rental of the little house and remove her few belongings to her new home, where the addition made a bright and pleasant change. At first Junius had demurred at taking in a new member, but as days passed and Salome proved helpful and quick to learn the trade, he made no further objection, and the maiden, having never known of his hostile attitude, was as unconscious of his favorable one, for Elizabeth from the first treated her as a dear and welcome sister.

The visit of Paul and his companions, with the exciting circumstances attending it, had greatly strengthened the little church of Philippi, and nearly doubled its membership. The converted jailer and Lydia proved active and influential members, bringing fresh means and renown into the assembly, and Elizabeth, though so quiet and humble, made her beautiful beliefs real in her calm, consistent life.

Almost insensibly Salome imbibed her ideas and began to rule her conduct by them, and as in their frequent talks the real meaning of Christ's life and death became instilled into her brain, so did its divine spirit and power take possession of her heart, until she was almost startled, one day, to find that her gods had become mere myths to her, and that Jesus was all-in-all.

The summer was nearly over when she started out with Nadab one afternoon, to help him carry a lot of broad and shallow baskets to Lydia, she having ordered them for the bestowal of her various cloths after dyeing, pressing, and rolling into bales. Almost daily there were processions and offerings in acknowledgment of the bountiful harvests, and one of these blocked their way for some time, not at all to their regret, for, though neither of the two felt any religious interest in it, they liked to watch it simply as a spectacle.

"See, Nadab! There come the Vestals all in white and wreathed with wheat-ears—are they not pretty!" cried Salome.

"Yes—and look! Is not that a fine car all covered over with corn and grain? Is that Ceres sitting under the canopy?"

"Of course. And that figure with the up-lifted horn is Fortuna, and that on the opposite corner with the fruit is Pomona, while Dionysus has the grapes and wine cask, and—"

"Oh! there, there! Is not that Pan with the horns and goat's beard and hoofs? What a noise he makes! And who are those, Salome?"

"They are Nymphs and Dryads. They look lovely in their sea-green and grass-green robes. What a pretty contrast to those rosy Hours!"

As the procession moved by, there was a constant din of pipe and timbrel, with the ringing of tambourines and the clashing of cymbals. Into the midst of this somewhat irregular music the grotesque Pan broke, occasionally, with a hideous bellow, partly from his own strong lungs, partly from an oddly-shaped wind-instrument of several reeds fastened together, which he held to his lips, meanwhile cutting some clumsy capers on his hoofs that sent all the children lining the way into shrieks of laughter.

He who represented Dionysus (or Bacchus, as the Romans called him,) had also a part to play in this strange religious ceremony, for every little while he drew from his well-filled wine cask a gourd full, either for himself or some favored one in the shouting, surging crowd, and then he would reel, and leer, and drivel, in the disgusting semblance of an intoxicated man.

Salome grew thoughtful as she watched the long line file by, beginning with the gay group of the Hours, dressed all in rose color, and ending with a dancing trio of Graces, weaving long gayly-colored sashes in and about themselves as they kept up a sort of swaying movement, in time to the music. These constantly changed places to form new groupings, bewildering the eye with their airy postures and kaleidoscopic hues. When the last of the brilliant pageant had vanished in the dust-cloud kicked up by their many dancing feet, she walked silently along with Nadab.

"What is there in all that to help one in the real cares and sorrows of life?" she was

thinking, for loss and disappointment were aging the girl rapidly. "It is a pretty show, it amuses for a moment—at least some of it—but that Dionysus made me shudder! I am glad Elizabeth did not see him. I fear it would bring back the look I saw on her face the other night, when Junius reeled home so queer and cross. How can people laugh at anything so sad and low! How can they make a god of drunkenness! Oh, what did you say, Nadab? I was not paying attention."

"I was saying that your people seem to think it is cunning to be overcome with wine, but mother does not. She thinks it is a sinful, dreadful thing!"

"Do not say 'my people,'" said Salome quickly. "I belong to you now."

"That is well, sister! You are ours to keep, art not? And I will be both brothers in one. But I hope father will not see that procession, Salome."

"I fear he will, Nadab; how can he help it? It will pass around and through the forum, and you know he is there so much."

"Yes, of course. And I know how it will be. He will look on and laugh, and then he and the other men will think they want some wine, too, and they will go to old Ænan's shop and drink till they are not themselves at all. It is too bad, Salome!"

"It is too bad! I see that plainly enough, child. How can anybody think such practices are right? Yet a few months ago I firmly believed in them, myself. But once having known of Christ, such impurities revolt me."

They found Lydia seated in the large, cool family room of her house. Its latticed windows in front overhung the street, and in the rear opened upon a terrace leading down into the garden. Its floor was tiled, but a few rich rugs were laid about, on which cushions were piled invitingly, while, following the outward curve of each overhanging window, was a broad, well-cushioned divan. A marble slab, resting upon bending figures cut in bronze, was in the center and held a rose jar of East Indian workmanship, well filled with blossoms. The two or three oddly-shaped chairs were straight and trim, with a quantity of carving, but evidently more for show than use, as the cushions, couches, and low curving ottomans invited to easier positions, while the stately throne-like chairs were seldom used except in entertaining with greatest ceremony persons of exalted rank.

Lydia, who was seated among a heap of cushions near an open terrace window, spinning fine wool with a small distaff and wheel, looked up with a pleasant greeting, as the two were ushered in by a tiny slave boy.

"Ah!" she cried, beckoning Salome to a seat close by, "I was just thinking of you. First, because we need the baskets at once; and second, because I need you."

"I am at your disposal," laughed the maiden, dropping easily into a nest of cushions by the other window. "But first let me tell you my errand. Elizabeth says you are to keep out two denarii of the money for the baskets, to send to our Apostles, Paul and Silas, at Thessalonica. It is all we can possibly afford this time, for trade is dull, and—" She did not finish her sentence, but with a hasty glance at Nadab changed confusedly to something else.

"And what, Salome?" asked the boy curiously.

"Oh, nothing much. It will soon be winter, and then there is fuel to buy, and Nadab here needs another tallith, naughty fellow!" shaking her finger at him merrily.

The answer satisfied him, but Lydia, looking keenly at the girl, read between the lines. She too turned gayly to Nadab.

"I see you are getting restless indoors, like all boys," she observed with a laugh. "Go down the terrace, my son, till you find my pretty Persian cat, Alanna, and have a play with her. She will chase a ball and bring it back in her teeth, or lie flat on her back and pretend to be dead."

Nadab was off before the sentence was fairly out, and the woman nodded with satisfaction.

"I thought that would dispose of him. He sees too much!" Then more gravely, "Salome, what is the trouble at your house? You know I ask from friendship, not idle curiosity. Is it anything I can help about?"

"It is the same thing, Lydia, only growing worse all the time."

"You mean Junius? Has he been already discharged, then?"

"Discharged?" The girl started. "What do you mean?"

"Then it has not come yet. I am glad for that! But it will, Salome. He is certainly going to lose his position."

"Oh, oh! Who told you?"

"Our friend, the jailer. He says it will have to be. Junius neglects his chain-gang for the wine shop, and leaves them to do poor work, or none at all. The street commissioners are full of complaints. Then, of course, the poor wretches are likely to escape, when they comprehend his constant condition, and that menaces public safety. I should not be surprised any day to learn they had risen up and overpowered him."

Salome shivered. "Poor, poor Elizabeth! But does he know he is to lose his place, Lydia? Would he not do differently if he was warned?"

"He has been warned and threatened, but I do not think he fully understands just how much is implied. Remember, I am telling you in confidence, that together we may do something in the matter. I do not want Elizabeth to know, yet. She is deeply troubled as it is—or would be but for her perfect trust in the wisdom of Christ, who would not willingly afflict her—and I would spare her further worry."

"But what can we do?"

"I intend to talk to him, to begin with," said Lydia with decision. "It is not a common thing for a woman to admonish a man, I know, but for that very reason it may prove effectual. As for you, simply be good to her—relieve her of all you can in work and care, and keep up her spirits by constantly recalling the one subject she so dearly loves. I see nothing else, only,"—she rose and stepped to a tiny cabinet of ebony upon the wall, and, unlocking its wee door, drew forth a silken purse. "Here," she said, "is the money for the baskets—all of it. Tell her I ask as a favor to send her contribution this time."

"Oh, she will object!" said the girl.

"She ought not. Are we not one in Christ? I have been prospered of God, only that I may assist those who have heavier burdens to bear. Surely you remember Christ's command—'Bear ye one another's burdens'? That is binding upon her as well as me, for how can I share her burden if she will not let me so much as touch a corner of it?"

"Ah, Lydia, if she could hear you she must submit! I will tell her, at any rate, just what you say. But alas! I fear I am but an extra burden upon her."

"Nay, I do not think so. You have not failed to make yourself useful, and she loves you. But be more, even, now. Be cheerful, be gay, be constant in kindness and affection. Help her to live so close to the loving Christ that she will forget her cares, or hide them in His breast. It is the only way for the Christian. Each morning should be a new birth into God's good world, with the soul rising like a lark to sing His praise and learn His will. Thus trouble will catch the sun's rays and become a shining thing, and peace will be where we had thought was care."

Salome gazed at Lydia with astonishment. It was a new thing for the often sorrowful woman to speak like this, and her face seemed to shine with the uplifting thoughts within. The girl resolved to be worthy of such friends and to stand by Elizabeth through good and evil report.

A burst of laughter from Nadab, who had found the cat, and was racing up and down the paths with the pretty yellow fluff of fur, floated in to them on the soft air.

"He has noticed, too," said Salome in a low voice. "He sees his father at the wine shop, and it distresses him."

"I thought so, poor child! I misdoubt hard times are coming. But we will not borrow trouble—that is distrusting God. While we keep close to Him we are safe, whatever comes."

Salome went home with a new sense of her responsibilities, and grew daily more womanly with the sweet desire to shield and serve her friend, so that Elizabeth often thought, "Dear girl! What would I do without her?"

For her heart was sore over her husband, who grew cold and cruel as the strong drink gained more and more complete mastery over him. She listened to Lydia's arguments in regard to the donation, and after a moment's pondering bowed her head.

"She is right," she said gently. "It would be only pride in me to refuse;" and felt that the loving gift sent by the growing church was partly her own, while all were one, and God looked only at the heart.

Yet another month slipped by before the blow fell. Several times during these few weeks Junius had lain all day upon his mat, too besotted to leave the house, and then the trembling wife was obliged to send word by Nadab that he was unable to attend to his duties. At length, one day, the boy came home almost crying.

"I wish you would not send me with that message again!" he whimpered to his mother. "The men in the forum gates laugh and nudge each other, and father's captain looks grave and stern. He turned and muttered something to the jailer to-day that sounded like 'This cannot go on!' but I am not sure. What did he mean?"

Elizabeth's face blanched, and Salome, who was passing through the court where they stood, stopped at the word and stepped hastily to her side.

"Never mind, Nadab!" she said, cheerily. "I will go along next time the father is ill, and if they laugh at us we will laugh back—laughing hurts nobody. Dear Elizabeth, let us sing while we weave. There is that lovely air you taught me the other day. When I sing that it seems as if nothing mattered here. To be 'forever with the Lord'—just think of it! He who comforts everybody, who helps everybody, and who knows exactly how to do it. Come, you start it, dear."

The other smiled, and the color crept back to her cheek. She began with a faltering note or two, then gained strength and steadiness, until presently the two were singing with well-blended voices, their souls far above all earthly sorrow.

Junius awoke from his deep, bestial slumber and at first wondered what paradise he had been transported to. Then he recognized the voices and began to feel his own aching head, furred tongue, and general wretchedness.

"I wonder what is the hour?" he thought. "Probably I shall be late at my post again, and get another rating from the captain—surly wretch! Elizabeth! Elizabeth!"

The singing ceased suddenly, and a moment later she appeared in the doorway, her face still shining with its inward light.

"Oh, you heard at last, did you?" he grumbled. "I never knew such people to keep up a noise as you are! How can anybody sleep in such a hubbub? What are you doing?"

"Weaving," answered his wife in her low, sweet voice.

"And why are you not getting breakfast?" he snarled.

She hesitated, glanced at the outer open door an instant, then pointed to a narrow sunbeam that lay upon the floor. He followed her glance and caught its meaning. The sun ray had passed the noon mark by many minutes. He raised himself hastily, then dropped back so giddy and sick that he could not sit up.

"It is past midday?" he questioned falteringly. "Did—did you send word to my superior?"

His wife nodded slowly. "I did, Junius. I tried to rouse you first, but—" She shook her head to show the hopelessness of the attempt, and he muttered an oath.

"You ought to have made me get up, woman! They told me if it happened again —Well, get me something to eat, will you? Do not stand there staring like an image of Hecate! I must hasten, I tell you, before the working hours are quite over. Perhaps then all will be right."

At his first angry call Salome had run to prepare food, and in a trice Junius was off; but he did not come home for the evening meal, and the two women, listening and longing, felt with a sickening dread that all was not right, and might never be again.

It was nearing midnight when he returned, so noisy and beside himself that Elizabeth hastily and imperiously ordered Salome away to her couch.

"No, no," she said as the girl tried to insist upon remaining. "This is my trouble. You must not bear it more than is necessary. Go quickly! I can manage him best."

How she did it the frightened girl, listening for abuse, perhaps blows, never knew, but in a short time all was quiet in the little home, and for one night more they might sleep in peace. But the next morning when Nadab, accompanied by Salome, went to make his excuses to his superior, they found it was unnecessary.

"He is discharged," said the captain bluntly. "We have no need for such as he."

Then his eyes met Salome's, above her veil, and their sadness softened him.

"I am sorry," he said more leniently, "but the place has been given to another. Junius might have retained it if he had kept himself in order, but he would not. Let Dionysus look after him now!" And turning on his buskined heel, he left them.

"Oh, Salome, what shall we do?" said the boy, half-crying. "Winter is coming on and we have nothing ahead, for you know father has not helped at all lately. Mother and you have been doing everything. What will we do?"

The girl sighed. "I must learn to be still more of a help," she said musingly. "But what is there beside the weaving—hark, Nadab! Who is calling us?"

They looked around and saw the captain hastening towards them. He was a young man of a good disposition, and his pity had been touched by their evident distress. He hurried to their side and said hastily:

"Fair maiden, would you like to earn a gold-piece?"

Salome looked up, startled. "Why, yes, sir," she said quickly. "How?"

"We want one or two more beautiful Bacchantes for the Lenæa, or Feast of Wine-pressing," he explained, "and you would do well. Each is furnished her gauzy costume, her flower wreath, a measure of wine, and the gold-piece."

During this speech Salome stood perfectly still, and the young man could see, even beneath her veil, the color surging into and out of her expressive face, as the thoughts surged to and fro in her awakened soul. Once she would have considered this a compliment, if not an honor, for only beautiful girls were chosen for this service, and though Hector might not have allowed his orphaned sister to join in the mad revel, which all the better class of pagans looked upon with doubt, yet he would have been pleased that she was given the chance to refuse. Now, however, the very thought of its lewd songs and dances sickened her. But just as she was about to utter an emphatic "No!" came another suggestion:

"Here is an opportunity to earn more money than I can make in many days at the weaving. Ought I not to put my personal feelings by and do this for Elizabeth?"

Seeing the agitation and hesitation of the maiden, the young pagan began gently urging her.

"You need not join the closing revels if they offend you. Only show yourself in the procession, the libations, and first dance to the gods; then you can slip away before the wine has begun to work and the crowd grow mad with gayety. Come, think of it!"

Salome did think of it, and recoiled more and more. She had not yet fully learned the horror of these unholy rites that all Christians felt, but his last words called up a scene which banished her unselfish wish to help her friend. Even her good motive could not condone such an act! Why, what would she be doing but countenancing Junius in his sin—but uplifting his degradation into a religious ceremony? How inconsistent! How hideous!

She drew herself up proudly and looked straight into the captain's eyes, her own flashing with indignant feeling.

"Be a Bacchante!" she cried scornfully. "I, a Christian maiden? Sir, you greatly mistake me if you think I could do such a thing, even to keep us from starvation. And, furthermore, it seems to me singular enough that an officer of your rank and judgment should discharge a man for too fond worship of Bacchus in one minute, and in the next try to win a pure maiden to his service. Such inconsistencies may belong to the gods you serve, but not to the Holy One whom I love."

She bowed low, gathered her veil closer, and turned proudly away. The captain watched her graceful figure till it was hidden behind one of the booths in the forum, an almost dazed expression on his face. Then he slowly turned, gathered himself together, and strolled thoughtfully back to the hall of justice.

" A doctor of laws could not have put it better!" he muttered. " I never should have looked at it in that way, certes—and what glorious eyes she has! I have a great mind not to join the procession myself, now. Something in her look made it suddenly seem horrible to me—and it does leave a bad taste behind, 'tis true. But to think that little girl should have reasoned it all out so quickly!" And, laughing inwardly, he returned to his duties, the first Christian suggestion of his life having found lodgment where it must remain, until it could grow into something—either a stunted plant, or a spreading, all-embracing tree.

CHAPTER XIV.

THE WANDERINGS OF AGISTHA.

WHEN, a few months before this, Herklas and his three Jewish companions left the cave at the first glimmer of daylight, they hastened on their way to Amphipolis, from whence, by leisurely stages, they meant to pass on to Thessalonica, nearly a hundred miles southwest of Philippi; a free city governed by its own politarchs, or magistrates, without interference from Rome.

It was a populous seaport and quite a Jewish center, a large share of its population being of that nationality. The wise Paul had quickly discovered its advantages for spreading the truth abroad, as upon its streets could be seen representatives from every country, consequently the gospel told in this market-place was likely to be carried to all parts of the known world.

Our four friends had news that Paul intended to be there shortly, so they desired to make it their own headquarters during their daily journeys .among the agricultural people back from the coast. For, as traveling

traders, they visited the remotest farms along their route, bringing to them not only needed goods, but spiritual help and gladness.

It was a busy yet happy life in many ways. Each morning they rose at early dawn, and after a cold lunch from their scrips, tramped for two hours or so in the cool of the day, to eat a hearty meal with some family who was glad to exchange food for merchandise. Then, during the noonday heats, they sought shade and rest. Sometimes they slept in a welcome grove; oftener they gathered a few farmers also taking the noon rest, in vineyard or orchard, and conversed with them upon the subject close to their hearts, starting on their way once more as soon as the fresh afternoon breezes began to blow in from the sea; and from thence till late in the summer evening they journeyed, sold, and taught.

They had a common purse, and Herklas, being a good accountant, soon became their purser. Nor was it a troublesome position, for money really meant almost nothing to them. Their lives were already "bought with a price," and they cared only to supply each day's needs, that they might not become public burdens in a strange country. Thus casting all care upon their Lord, and walking in the constant glow of love, hope, and consecration, the little worries and hardships of a day were swallowed up in a lofty purpose and a holy joy, which gave their homely lives dignity and peace.

They had supposed that the girl, Agistha, would upon waking return to her people within the city walls, so dismissed her from their minds when they had supplied her with a good breakfast, and stole softly out, leaving her in a sound, refreshing sleep. She, however, had no such intention. Starting out with only the vaguest idea of distances or directions, she determined to go to Neapolis, in hope of finding some work to do there, but took the wrong road, and presently found she was in a part of the country quite strange to her.

She was not specially troubled by this, however, for so long as she kept to the Roman highway she knew she must in time reach some populous town. She had, indeed, taken the route to Amphipolis, thirty miles distant, and long before the day ended was glad to stop at a small hamlet on the way, and seek food and counsel.

It was not an inviting spot—a few low, dirty-looking huts of mud, with outlying fields and orchards poorly kept. But seeing a girl coming from one of these, with a water jar upon her head, the traveler ventured to accost her. The girly stared at her a moment. Agistha was but scantly clothed, and had no veil except the linen grave-cloth, which she had managed to wind about her head and shoulders for a chlamys, while her pale, sad face, visible above the eyes, lacked the deep sun tan of a professional beggar.

"What do you want?" asked the girl finally, when she had gazed her fill.

"Food," said Agistha, "if you will be so kind. I am starving, and I have lost my way. I started for Neapolis, but—"

The girl laughed. "You are far from the road, then! This is the direct route to Amphipolis."

"Oh!" cried poor Agistha. "But that is far away, is't not?"

"About eighteen miles from here, yes. How far have you come?"

"From Philippi."

The girl's heavy face brightened with sudden interest. Evidently she had heard of Philippi before; perhaps she knew some one there.

"You have had a long walk, and must be warm and tired."

"I am," said Agistha.

"You look as if you had been sick, too."

"Yes, I have."

"Well, sit down there in the shade, and I will see what I can do for you."

The girl placed her tall jar on the ground and went into the house, from which she presently brought some coarse food to the weary traveler, who was so hungry and so unused to better fare that she received it eagerly. While she ate the girl lingered, and began to talk again.

"If you live at Philippi you must have heard about the two Christians whose chains were loosed by the earthquake a few nights ago; have you not?"

Agistha looked up listlessly, and shook her head. "No," she said, "I have been ill. I heard nothing."

"It is a strange tale," continued the girl, "and I wonder you did not hear it. Some traders came along this morning and told us—one was such a handsome young Greek, but the others were Jews, and they were Christians, too."

At this Agistha looked up quickly. Could they be her helpful friends of last night? The girl babbled on, detailing, with some variations, the story of Paul and Silas, and

as the escaped slave girl began to comprehend that it was her own story she was listening to in this remote hamlet, she forgot to eat and sat with parted lips, taking it all in. It was the first she had known of the imprisonment of Paul and his companions. She had been hurried away after the solemn adjuration of the former, and had been so ill subsequently that she knew nothing of the tumult her masters stirred up later, nor the suffering which came upon those good men in consequence.

For they must be good! Else how had their God loosed their chains in so wonderful a manner? And these kind men of the cavern were their friends and of the same faith, also! How she wished she had known it when with them! How she would have forced herself to keep awake and glean from their conversation some bits of knowledge about all these mysteries!

She began asking the girl questions as to the direction they had taken, and learned with joy that it was the same as her own.

"I will follow them!" she said to herself, with a quick resolve, the vague intentions of the morning having now crystallized into a definite plan and undertaking.

She said nothing to the girl, however. She would not have dared let her know how closely she had been associated with those events, lest by this her former masters might be able to track her.

She warmly thanked the girl, bade her farewell, and hastened onward, her goal Amphipolis, and her wish to know more of the followers of Christ. Yet try her best, she could not reach there that night, but again sought rest and shelter by the way. The next day, as it was nearing the noon hour, she entered the city, weary, footsore, and almost despairing, where, dragging herself to the market-place, she sank down in the shade of one of the booths, wondering what she was to do next.

At present she was too exhausted to do anything but rest. She huddled herself up under her once white mantle, now dingy with the dust of the road, and simply watched and waited. One or two compassionate passers-by threw her a mite or two, which she treasured securely until food should become necessary again. So the long day slid into evening, with nothing accomplished. She had just risen to her feet, finally, faint with her long fast, and was about to buy a small oat-cake with her bits of money, when she started to see coming towards her at a brisk pace the youth who had been in her thoughts all day—Herklas. He was about to pass her by unobserved, when the desperate feeling that she might again lose sight of her only friend gave her courage to address him.

"Sir," she said, "I beg you will pardon my boldness, but are you not the young man who rescued a frightened girl from the place of tombs but lately?"

Herklas looked at her with astonishment. She had her face well muffled, but the slender figure and weak, childish voice were the same.

"Yes," he answered quickly, "the maiden of Philippi. But surely you are not she! How came you here so far away?"

"Oh, sir, I have escaped from cruel persecutors to whom I could not return. I am hunting for work—for something to keep me that shall be honest—and you were all so kind to me before, I thought perhaps—"

She stopped, for Herklas began to knit his brows in perplexity. Coming and going as they did, how could they stop to find employment for this poor girl? Even now he was hurrying to purchase supplies for the morrow, that they might be off that night. But Herklas had learned much of Christ's spirit in these last few weeks, and the words which had been so often repeated to him, "Inasmuch as ye have done it unto one of the least of these, ye have done it unto me," had a literal meaning for him. To have passed this poor girl by unassisted would have been to neglect his Lord.

"If only you were in Thessalonica now!" he said with a smile. "We have friends there, and are ourselves going soon, but—"

"Oh, I will go there!" said Agistha quickly. "It is a large, busy city, is it not? I could surely find something to do."

"But it is nearly seventy miles away, and—wait! let me think. I have it. I believe we can arrange for you. Wait here a few minutes till I go to see about it."

Herklas had walked many miles that day in the hot sun, burdened by his pack of goods, and still had much to do before the morning, but this was "for Christ," and those magic words dispelled fatigue. As the good soldier, weary with a hard march, is aroused to fresh zeal by his captain's call "To arms!" so Christ's follower held his personal feelings in abeyance whenever there was a special call for his service. Not only his soul, but his body also, was the Lord's; if it must be taxed unduly, that was His matter and He would make it right.

Herklas hurried to the lodging-place of the four and sought out Thallus, who, as the oldest and most sedate, was the acknowledged leader of the group. To him he rapidly described his late interview, and the idea which had occurred to him for the girl's assistance, and Thallus, after some reflection, answered:

"I think it will do. Go and speak to the steward of the noble lady, while I return to the maiden and see if she be fed sufficiently. It is more fitting that a man of my age conduct her to the lady's presence."

Herklas acquiesced and hastened away to a large caravansary some squares distant, where, crossing the court, which was well filled with a motley collection of men and beasts making ready for their start in the cool of the day, he sought out the host and asked for a certain man.

Upon being conducted to his presence, Herklas bowed low before the somewhat gorgeously-attired individual, and said:

"Sir, your proclamation for a female servant, to take the place of one fallen ill in your lady's train, was called early this morning in the market-place. Did you find one to your liking?"

"No, but we ceased the proclamation because the slave, Lucilla, seemed better, and we hoped would be ready to attend her mistress by night."

"Then you no longer wish a maid?"

"Yes, because she is suddenly worse again, and must be left behind while my lady presses onward. She wishes to reach Thessalonica by the day after to-morrow."

"Then, sir, I have in mind a young maiden who would be glad to go with her. She is docile in speech and manners, but not overstrong, yet—"

"Her duties will be light. Where is the girl?"

"My friend, Thallus, will soon bring her, I think. She has been sadly neglected and is so poor her clothing is in rags."

"Oh, well, my mistress can supply clothing. What is her native tongue?"

"Greek."

"Very good! And you say she is of gentle manners?"

"Yes, sir."

While they were talking together, Thallus was announced, and behind him, well wrapped in her chlamys, appeared the slave girl, shrinking timidly in his shadow. The steward questioned her a few minutes, learning that she was from further east, and had been abandoned when very ill and left to die; that she wished to leave the old life behind and earn a respectable living; that she was willing and—as he saw for himself—modest and soft of speech. Presently, then, he led her to the apartments of his lady, who was of exalted rank, and whose name was Ænone.

She was hastening home to Thessalonica after a visit among friends at a mountain resort, and was hurrying in order to see her husband before his departure for Rome upon official business. She traveled with a long train of guards and slaves, as did all of high rank, but her special maid, upon whom she depended for personal attentions, had fallen seriously ill.

The steward, Cleophas by name, formally presented Agistha as an applicant for the situation, then at a sign from his mistress withdrew, leaving the two together.

Ænone was a young matron of fine presence and keen, bright eyes. She was lounging upon a couch playing with a beautiful boy of perhaps three summers, but as the man retired she sat up and beckoned Agistha forward.

"Come nearer," she said in a pleasant, decided sort of voice; "let me see your face."

The girl obeyed, dropping her apology of a veil, and stood meekly before the grand dame.

"You do not look very strong, yourself," said the latter presently.

"I am only weary, madam, I have walked so far. You will find me industrious, and stronger than I look."

"Well, perhaps so. Your face is honest, at least, and I have no time to be particular, as we must start inside of a half-hour. Take her, Chloe," turning to a dark-skinned slave woman who was plying a great fan above her mistress' head, "and give her clothing befitting my attendant. But remember, there is no time to lose."

The slave bowed low, and passed the fan to a small page not over eight years old, who had been crouched on the rug by the couch, and now scrambled to his feet. He was fair-haired and sturdy of build, and, Agistha learned later, a little Briton, recently bought from the new importation of captives sent from that unhappy country, whose king, Caractacus, was now languishing in chains at Rome. He had been sent to Ænone as a choice gift by a friend in that city.

After a brief delay the women returned, Agistha so greatly improved in appearance that her new mistress broke into a pleased laugh.

"Why, you are truly fair!" she cried, frankly. "I am glad, for I like bright and charming things about me."

As she ceased speaking Cleophas appeared to say that all was in readiness for his mistress to depart. At this Chloe made Agistha a sign and placed in her hand a long veil and mantle, the former of finest Indian lawn, the latter of silk from Persia, woven with gold thread till it glittered with every movement.

"Go wrap the mistress carefully in these, then follow her to her litter and see that she has everything she needs. I follow with the little master, Ian, for I am his nurse."

Agistha, trembling a little, obeyed, but as she began her unusual task it seemed as if some former knowledge came to her. She could remember some other lady standing thus to be wrapped in silken garments, and herself in some far-gone time looking on with a feeling of impatience at the delay. Only once or twice did Ænone correct her, and then by no means harshly, though with a decision which enforced obedience.

"There, that will do," she said presently, pulling the veil a trifle looser about the mouth and nostrils. "Follow me with the baby, Chloe. Where is Harold?"

She beckoned to the Briton boy, who as yet understood but few words of Greek, though he was learning rapidly, and the little train proceeded to the court-yard. Here several laden camels and asses were slowly filing out to the road, and others stood waiting. Forming a line on either side of the doorway were eight mounted guards in handsome liveries of blue with steel trappings, who remained like so many statues while the somewhat fussy Cleophas assisted his lady and her women to their places.

First Ænone entered a litter of dainty shape and lightness, mostly built of bamboo, the cushions and curtains displaying her special colors, blue and steel. In another lectica scarcely less handsome Chloe and her little charge was seated, while Agistha and the page, Harold, were placed upon the houdah, or covered saddle, of a kneeling camel just beyond.

Agistha watched the four Nubian bearers, white-turbaned and naked to the waist, lift the poles of their lady's lectica to their cushioned shoulders and step to position; the others, bearing the little Ian and nurse, followed; then her camel rose swaggeringly from his bended knees with a long-drawn yawn, and like clock-work the eight guards formed a hollow square about the precious family, one in front, one in the rear, and three on each side.

With a last look, to be sure all were comfortable, Cleophas mounted and rode up and down, getting the whole train in motion, for this was but its head, and the rest of the long, serpent-like body was waiting to fall into line outside. As they trailed out through the city gates in the twilight Agistha had just a glimpse of four men, foot-passengers with packs on their backs, walking in the same direction, and was pleased to see that they joined the pedestrians in the rear, having evidently put themselves under the protection of this caravan for the short night journey to the next caravansary.

But the following morning when she looked for them they were nowhere to be seen. They had doubtless risen at daybreak and gone their way. Would she meet them at Thessalonica?

CHAPTER XV.

THE POLITARCH'S FAMILY.

ÆNONE was the Greek wife of one of the politarchs who ruled the city of Thessalonica, Gaius by name, and was a woman of marked individuality and exceptional talents. She was musical, playing both the lyre and the viol, to which she sang enchantingly, and she was learned in the history and philosophy of her nation. She had studied thoughtfully the complicated and poetic mythology of both Greece and Rome, and, having considerable reasoning powers, she always felt they lacked the elements necessary to control her heart and life. She could not readily yield up her conscience to beings who were constantly liable to errors, and who were capable of the follies and petty foibles of humanity. She felt that the god she worshiped must have some greatness other than power, and must above all things be perfectly pure and true. She even went so far as to say that this being must be so above every human passion as to express a love that was universal and impartial, yet intense and personal as well, and a justice so absolute it could not err, either on the side of mercy or

severity. Gods who could love and hate, stoop to retaliation and bickerings, spy upon each other and show childish envy and malice, excited only her ridicule, though they might be the accepted deities of her country.

She could talk well on these subjects, and liked nothing better than to entertain her husband's friends at dinner, and enter into their deep discussions afterwards. She was looked upon as a skeptic, in consequence, and was in great disfavor with the pagan priests, who knew her influence was all against them. One or two Jewish rabbis who had been admitted to her home, claimed that she was greatly attracted towards their religion; though this she did not quite confirm. She explained that while its fundamental ideas were based on great truths, speaking to the inmost soul of man, yet these had become so overloaded with trivial forms and ceremonies as to have all spirituality smothered out of them by exactions as belittling as the superstitions of her own Greek religion. So, like most educated pagans of the day, she held herself aloof from all creeds, and gave only an outward respect to the rites of her priests.

Her suite made the journey to Thessalonica rapidly, reaching there the next morning but one, and Agistha watched with great interest their progress through the busy streets of the populous city overlooking the blue sea.

It being situated upon a jutting tongue of high, rocky foundation, the streets rose, terrace-fashion, directly from the shore, and the rolling land back of the city swept away into hills and peaks, whose green sides were divided into large and beautiful gardens, while the white houses of the lower city nestled amid the deep green foliage of palm and date trees, relieved occasionally by the cold gray-green of the olive.

To one of these suburban gardens our party took their way, but long before reaching it were met by another little company of half a dozen mounted men, whose rich costumes, half civic, half military, bespoke their rank. The foremost was Gaius himself, a tall, slender man of proud carriage, who rode like a centaur. He now dashed forwards, his face alight with joy, to greet wife and child, and was soon riding by the side of the first litter, his boy lifted to the saddle in front of him, while Ænone leaned eagerly out to watch the two with love-lighted eyes.

The other men, friends and relatives, having greeted her also, considerately held back their horses a little, leaving the two to their rapid interchange of question and comment.

"You are late; I expected you last night," said Gaius.

"Yes, and we should have been here but for Lucilla, who was taken ill on the road and delayed us some hours at Amphipolis. I found another maid, however, so I left her to be cared for by two of the pack slaves, who will bring her on as soon as she is able to travel. But tell me, dear, why must you go to Rome?"

"Oh, it is on account of these Jewish troubles, I believe."

"Jewish? I thought they had been very quiet ever since their outbreak under Caligula."

"So they have, but they are a seditious, uneasy set, and Caligula's persecutions only quelled, not subdued them. We always have to keep a close eye upon them, and there are rumors afloat that seem to need looking into."

"I see. But so many of them are good friends of ours! I do hope you will not be called upon to work them any mischief."

"'Mischief'! Really, my lady, that is an odd way to speak of your Emperor's rule."

She laughed with him. "Well, you know well enough what I mean. I have, somehow, a natural antipathy to the stirring up of such things. What is claimed against them now? That same matter of a new king?"

"Probably. I really do not know. And as likely as not this is only another of Claudius' annual scares—one never knows. If he had half the bravery of his wife, he would be quite a man."

"Have a care, Gaius! We are in the open street. You would not wish him to possess her wickedness, too?"

"No, but sometimes weakness is worse than wickedness—in a ruler. How Ian has grown—bless his little heart! And you are looking charming, my wife. The mountain air agrees with you."

"I am glad you think so, Gaius. With your presence, our little trip would have been perfect. It seems too bad we should have to be separated again so soon. When do you start?"

"To-morrow."

"So soon?"

"Yes, it must be. So you have had to be your own maid?"

"Oh, no; I found another at Amphipolis, and she has proved a real treasure. She was

brought me by some traders—such a pale, frightened little creature, and in rags—but she is really growing fair to see, with good food and treatment. You must—oh, Gaius! is that safe? How your horse plunges! Do give me the baby!"

"Entirely safe," laughed her husband. "Why, this is Selim, my new Arabian, priceless for fidelity, though full of his play at times. Is he not a beauty?"

"In truth he is! His coat is like satin. Ah, there is the dear old home! How beautiful it is! I never so realized it before. Do tell my bearers to stop at the gate. I want to walk up the terraces and see how the roses are doing—though it is late for them, I know."

"Yes, they are past their prime, but very fine yet. I will walk with you. Yes, yes, my boy; you shall ride still, if you like, and father will lead the pony for his little man. Now hold tight, my son."

Agistha, watching the trio, felt her heart contract with a sudden spasm of pain. It was not envy—she rejoiced in their joy—but more as if she had witnessed something of which she ought to be a part. It appeared for an instant to transport her into another existence, where she beheld like scenes of refined love and happiness, amid pleasant surroundings. There ought to be a fourth, though—a little girl, who seemed mingled with her own identity, clinging to the lady's gown, and with breathless interest watching the boy on the big horse.

These strange, dream-like suggestions came to her only at such moments, when all about her were grace, beauty, and affection, and she felt sadly that they could not be memories, unless of some former life in a sphere brighter and better than she had ever known here.

When the company had entered the wide villa-like mansion, surrounded by broad, pillared galleries, Agistha hastened forward to wait upon her mistress, a task she was learning through affection to perform deftly and well. For Ænone won the hearts of those who served her. She was even in temper, decided in her commands, and just in judgment. She did not expect impossibilities, but quietly insisted upon conscientious service, and while her slaves were never publicly, and seldom privately punished, her friends said they were more faithful than most slaves. Be that as it may, the mere threat of being sold brought the most unruly of them to terms, and their only idea of a promotion was to be given a service nearer the mistress. Agistha felt that she had been fortunate in securing such a place, and was most grateful to the Christian men for it. She kept a sharp lookout for them every time her duties called her upon the street, and longed inexpressibly for a chance to thank them in person.

She saw nothing of them, however, and had almost given up expecting to do so, having settled down to her pleasant life amid these new surroundings with little desire for change. Several weeks had passed when one Sabbath her mistress came in from a drive in the new chariot with the baby and his nurse, and said:

"Agistha, I wish you to accompany me out after the noon meal. Have on your street attire."

Agistha watched the sun-dial eagerly that afternoon, pleased at the prospect, and when it marked the ninth hour she and Ænone, closely veiled and plainly wrapped, started off on foot, an unusual proceeding for the somewhat luxuriously-inclined lady. They walked rapidly, Agistha keeping respectfully an arm's length behind, and after crossing several streets, made their way into a large structure built of marble from one of the quarries not far distant, and rich in gilding.

The pagan girl thought it could not be a temple, however, for it lacked the many statues and images she was used to seeing, so was puzzled when they had entered, to find herself in the latticed gallery of a place where people had evidently congregated for worship.

It was, in fact, a magnificent Jewish synagogue, very unlike the small structure at Philippi. Ænone made her way to a seat with the deftness of one familiar with the place, and they were soon comfortably settled close behind the gilded lattice-work, almost overlooking the raised seats of the rabbis just below the dais and desk of the Presbyter.

Agistha looked curiously at the symbols about the altar, none of which had any significance to her; admired a long, richly-embroidered curtain just behind a white-draped table, and wondered over a tiny door in the wall behind the desk. But as she glanced towards the rabbis' seats she caught her breath in astonishment. There, conspicuous among the bearded elders, were the two good men of Philippi!

Even while she gazed one rose—the very one who had commanded the evil spirit to come out of her—and stepped to the desk. An attendant brought him one of the Scripture rolls from the niche in the wall (thus relieving Agistha's curiosity about the little door), and, unrolling it, he began to read.

His voice was full, sonorous, and majestic. Agistha felt rather than saw her mistress press closer to the grating, and she too bent forward eagerly. He read but a short time from the psalms and prophecies, then began to talk in a conversational and winning tone, setting before his hearers in a confident manner the true understanding of the Messiah—"that He must suffer and die, and rise again from the dead," and after presenting this to his listeners most convincingly, he declared in a fearless tone:

"And Jesus whom I preach unto you is this Messiah!"

A murmur ran through the assembly as he wound up the roll and returned to his seat. At once another rabbi sprang to his feet, asking questions and raising doubts, while from that time till the closing benediction the first speaker was kept busy answering, denying, persuading and correcting, all with a calmness and decision that made every word forcible.

Through the whole Agistha listened almost as intently as her better-informed mistress, for though a great deal of it was beyond her comprehension, she could and did understand that this Jesus, the Messiah, was He whom her friends of the cave worshiped and loved. Knowing this, and believing fully that Paul was "a servant of the Most High," she accepted Jesus with the faith of a little child. Once she turned to look at Ænone, and saw that her gray eyes above the veil were intent and almost tearful.

At length the service was over, and as the two women lingeringly turned to go, Agistha felt sure she had just a glimpse of the youth Herklas, and another man—a small, bright-eyed person—pressing forward as if to speak to Paul and his companion; but the next instant they were lost in the crowd and she was obliged to hurry after her mistress, lest they be separated, for the synagogue was large, and to-day filled to its utmost capacity.

After they had reached home and Agistha had ordered some refreshment for her mistress, they wandered out to one of the wide galleries opening upon the inner garden, and the maid began playing with the little Ian, while his mother watched them thoughtfully. At length she said, suddenly:

"Agistha, where were you brought up? You really seem to have no religion. You pray neither to the gods nor the fates, you wear no amulets, you never consult the oracles, nor study the stars. What are you, I would like to ask?"

Agistha blushed and looked almost frightened. This seemed, even to her unawakened mind, a grave charge.

"I fear I am nothing, my lady," she said very humbly.

Ænone burst out laughing. "You need not look so frightened! Do you feel too humble to address yourself to any god? That is the way you act. It is not a common attitude, I assure you. No matter how low a man may fall, he always seems to think he has a special claim upon his gods!"

Agistha during this speech had been trying to collect herself. She was fond of her mistress, but somewhat afraid of her, too. At length she answered timidly:

"I mean I was never taught, madam. No one told me anything except how to chant the oracles, so—"

"The oracles? You chant the oracles! What do you mean, child?"

"I was possessed of the spirit of Python, my lady—so my masters said—and they made me do it. Sometimes I could not—then they beat and starved me; then my mind would get all confused and I would say whatever Flavius willed, and then they treated me better; but I was wretched all the time, and in my clear moments I knew it was a lie."

"You poor child! And did you run away from them?"

"Oh, no; they took me to the tombs, and—"

"What?"

"And left me there for dead. But for some reason they did not bury me."

"Horrible! Horrible!"

"When I woke from the long sleep I lay on the bier and I was frightened, for it had been raining, and now everything glistened under the moon, and all was so still and strange I thought I must be in some other world. Then some one told me not to be frightened, and came to my aid. It was the young man who helped me get my situation with you, madam—"

"Indeed!"

"And he took me to a cave where were three other good men who were very kind to me. They gave me food, and spread their abbas down for me to rest upon before the fire, then talked low and gently till I fell asleep; and when I woke next day they had gone, leaving me a nice meal to break my fast. I was following them here when I saw Herklas, as they called him, in the market-place, and begged his help. Then he and the stern elderly man brought me to you. I have found since that they are Christians, my lady, and if you please I would like to be a Christian too."

"How strange this all seems!" said Ænone musingly, with only a passing smile at the girl's simplicity. "What then did you think of the Christian Apostle who spoke to-day?"

"Oh! madam, that is strangest of all." And Agistha, warmed to a communicativeness unexampled in her previous experience, then told the tale of her first meeting with these Apostles in Philippi, throwing herself upon the protection of her mistress to keep her from those bad men, her former masters.

Ænone listened with many a sharp question and exclamation. The narrative intensely interested her. At once her speculative mind began to question and assert. Why had it been so clearly revealed to this childish person that the men were divinely appointed? She remembered something she had once heard in regard to the prophecies of Jesus, the crucified Nazarene, and tried to recall it now. What was it? That certain things should be hid from the wise and made clear to babes? Something like that, surely. Strange how constantly His utterances returned to her, when once she had heard them! He had certainly not succeeded in establishing a Jewish kingdom, but what if this Paul was right, and the only kingdom his Master wished to bring upon earth was that governing men's hearts and lives?

She looked up and broke into a gay laugh, as if shaking off some mental disquiet.

"How foolish you are, Agistha!" she cried. "You certainly must be better taught! One can not put on religion like a garment. And so it was a Christian youth who helped you in your extremity? Was he a Jew?"

"I think not, my lady. He spoke and looked like a Greek, though the others were Jews. He was like the statue of Apollo, tall and shapely, but with a more beautiful face, madam, for his whole look meant kindness and good-will."

"Well, well, bring me the baby now, and call Harold to take away this salver. Come, my boy—come to mother. I declare,

Agistha, you are nearly as much of a baby as he."

The girl stood meekly before her, the color coming and going in her cheeks.

"There! Mind me not!" cried her mistress relentingly. "But you shall have teachers. To-morrow bring your sewing and sit with me while Hipparchus reads to me. He is a learned eunuch who can teach you what religions there are, and then you may make a choice."

"I have made it, my lady."

"So be it! Perhaps you have done a wise thing, too—how can I tell? Only, those who embrace this belief seem so common." She had evidently forgotten the girl and was thinking aloud. "Even their Messiah Himself was low-born and died a criminal's death. Yet what sublime ideas He had! Supreme love expressed in supreme sacrifice—what could be more godlike, more unmanlike! Its force and beauty haunt me, and I never feel it so strongly as when my heart is filled with love for my dear ones. Perhaps—"

She looked up suddenly, catching herself in her monologue, and colored as she saw Agistha gazing at her, vaguely trying to follow her thoughts.

"Do not stare so, child!" she cried crossly, then smiled and gave the flushing cheek a friendly pat; and before Agistha had quite comprehended either mood, the mistress was engaged in a merry frolic with her baby, waking all the echoes of the garden with their laughter.

But the slave girl, slow of thought, crept away behind a rose tree and tried to recall all she had heard in the synagogue, like another humble woman, whose name even was as yet unknown to her, "pondering these things in her heart."

CHAPTER XVI.

TO THE HELP OF THE CHRISTIANS.

EVERY day when there was service at the synagogue the two women might have been seen in the gallery, listening eagerly to the words of the Apostles—Agistha with a simple faith that asked no questions, dared no doubts; Ænone with constant internal argument and resistance, yet with the persistent feeling that here might be the solution of all her difficulties; if only it were not such a wound to one's pride to acknowledge one's self pledged to a religion unpopular and ill-considered enough to have to keep itself in the background, that it might escape constant persecution! Yet she continued to go and listen, and sought opportunities, afterwards, to talk with her handmaiden about what they had heard, wondering meanwhile at the latter's simplicity and faith, yet half envying her, too.

While Paul and his fellow-workers were still in the city, Amasa and Herklas one day called at the politarch's house, with some exquisite linens from Egypt, and also some of exceeding fineness, enwoven with purple threads giving almost the effect of embroidery, brought from Tyre and Sidon.

Amasa was intent only upon the sale of his wares, but the youth, knowing this was the home of the Lady Ænone, was secretly hoping he might see once more the poor maiden whom he had twice rescued from suffering and privation—perhaps from death. The traders, being known to the slave people as honest, courteous men, were readily admitted by the porter, who only smiled at them from the doorway of his little room beside the vestibule, and kept his hand upon the good dog, Fides, who assisted him in his duty of guarding the door.

At the request of Ænone, who allowed herself many privileges not common among the Greek women—she having learned to follow Roman fashions somewhat—they were ushered into her apartments, where she sat with her maidens in what was called the "winter room." This delightful apartment, now made habitable by the cool mornings and evenings of late autumn, faced the south, so that through the gilded latticework of one whole length of wall the brilliant sunshine poured in, lying in broad checkered patterns upon the floor, only partially shaded by the inside vines that climbed around and over the diamond-shaped panes of mica, setting each in a frame of living green. Thick rugs, divans, cushions, and deep couch-like chairs, were scattered about, and at the end furthest from the sun stood a wide, oval-shaped charcoal brazier, its outer shell of steel carved into lace-like designs. This was supported upon griffins of bronze and gilt, whose tongues, in some way colored red, lolled out of their open mouths like those of dogs panting with the heat—a device which always suggested warmth whether there was any fire in the receptacle, or not.

Agistha, down on a rug in a nest of

cushions, frolicking with the baby, whose prime favorite she had become, looked up as the door curtain swung aside, and fairly turned white when she saw that the traders were Amasa and Herklas.

The young Greek's eyes sought hers at once and she knew she was not forgotten, while he felt, with something akin to

"And you are Christians!" she exclaimed. "But you," turning in her quick way to Herklas, "you are a Greek, are you not?"

"I am, my lady."

"I am not surprised that the Jews, who have always looked for a Messiah, should be taken with the tales of this Jesus, whose life seems so full of good and whose death

Agistha bounded to her feet with the cry, "Oh, dear mistress, they are my friends of the cave!"

triumphant joy, that her emotion was for him alone.

Ænone received the two men graciously, but when Agistha bounded to her feet with the cry, "Oh, dear mistress, they are my friends of the cave!" she became interested at once, and soon the four were busily talking, all forgetting for the moment that there was any difference in rank between them. Ænone eagerly asked questions, and the others respectfully answered them, satisfying her curiosity in regard to their present life and purposes, and thus naturally approaching the subject of their religion.

was so sublime, but it strikes me it is a long step for a worshiper of Apollo to take."

She was smiling at him, and the youth, flushing under her half-satirical gaze, answered modestly:

"It did not seem far to me, lady. I had been long discontented and doubtful. I felt that our gods were in many respects no better than I, and it seemed to me they must be far too busy with their loves, hates, and quarrels, to care for any one in humble life. So when I was told of the God who loves even the humblest, I was in a hurry to receive Him and give my love in return."

"It seems, indeed, a religion for the lowly and the burdened," said the lady. "And in these troublous times who knows when one may not be in sore straits himself, however fortunate now? But come, open your packs and let us see what the looms of Egypt and Phœnicia have to offer us."

The display proved tempting, and Ænone bought, though not largely, saying as she put aside one or two rolls of the finest linens:

"I will not take much to-day, but whenever you are in the city call again, as I may want more presently. My husband is now absent in Rome, and he likes to select the cloth for his own tunics."

The two men had been several times to the pleasant villa with their wares, when one day, as it was nearing sunset, and Agistha was attending her mistress in a stroll to and fro through the long, many-pillared peristyle which formed one of the enclosed courts of the great house, Herklas was announced, and presently stood making his salaam before them. He had no goods with him, and looked both hurried and agitated.

"Madam," he began quickly, scarce waiting for the lady's kindly greeting, "I have come to beg your help, if possible. But first, has your noble husband, Gaius, the politarch, returned?"

"No, and will not for a day or two. What would you with him?"

"Oh, madam, have you heard nothing of the tumult in the lower city?"

"Tumult? No! About what?"

"Concerning our friends, the Apostles, lady. I do not know what will come of it all, but the streets near their lodgings are filled with a crowd, shouting and threatening. It seems that some of the Jewish rabbis, angry and envious because they cannot answer Paul, and because notwithstanding them he keeps making converts among our best citizens, have stirred up the populace against the Apostles, and are urging it on to bloody deeds."

"Where do they lodge?" asked Ænone quickly, becoming at once the stern, self-controlled woman of authority, while Agistha sank back trembling with fright.

"With his kinsman, Jason the Jew, madam."

"I know him—a fine, honorable man! But surely he will not give those good men up to the rabble?"

"No, lady, they are well hidden and safe, thus far, but now we are trembling for Jason, who may suffer from the fury of the mob. He is one who would let himself be torn in pieces before he would betray a friend—and oh, if you could see the wolfish crowd! They are the lowest of the low, and ripe for any mischief."

"This must be looked after at once!" cried Ænone with decision. "You did well to come to me. Order my lectica, Harold; and Agistha, come with me."

"But, my lady," began Herklas remonstratingly, "the streets all around there are blocked with the mob, and—"

"Would they dare stop the wife of a politarch? You know his power is supreme here, Herklas. Even Rome does not interfere with it, unless to advise and caution. But call out my body-guard—the people will recognize and respect their livery, and—wait! You shall have a horse and be our leader. Can you ride?"

"I can, madam."

"Very good. We will go at once to the house of Jason."

The little cavalcade was soon under way, the two women in the litter, guarded by ten soldiers and led by Herklas, also mounted and hastily armed. But when they reached Jason's home, nearer the shore, only an excited group of neighbors and friends stood about, who hastened to inform the noble lady that Jason had been dragged to the justice hall before the politarchs, for trial.

"We will go there at once," said Ænone, and her stalwart litter-bearers broke into the swinging trot habitual to them, keeping well up with the horsemen.

As they turned into the forum gates they could see what a mob had arisen, for the whole space around the steps of the judgment hall was filled with their excited, clamoring faces, swinging arms, and bobbing turbans. At Ænone's word the guards, with Herklas as forerunner, began clearing a passage through the surging and compact mass; but though they spurred ruthlessly amid the people without a care where the horses' hoofs struck, yet their progress seemed terribly slow to the anxious women inside, consisting, as it did, of a series of jerky advances and long stops.

While they were in the thick of the crowd, Agistha gave a low cry and sank back, half fainting, against her mistress.

"Silly child, to be so frightened at this mob!" whispered Ænone through set teeth.

But she too started and looked anxiously around when Agistha murmured in return:

"Oh, it's my master—Flavius—the cruel one. See! He is urging those men at the left to cry 'Down with the Christians!' That man in a frayed yellow tunic, with the dark, scarred face. What, oh! what if he should look this way?"

"And suppose he does, girl? Would he ever think of finding his wretched slave in a litter bearing the colors of Gaius, the politarch? Be quiet, I say, and stop whimpering! He will never see you behind your veil, and if he did, you are so changed he could not recognize you. Ah, here we are at last! Herklas, come hither."

The youth rode close.

"No, stay! You will not do. It must be one of my own men whose livery is known to him. Here, Andrea!"

One of the guards spurred forwards.

"Dismount and go into yonder hall, and get speech with Hipparchus. Tell him I wish to see him at once."

After an interval of impatient waiting, during which Agistha leaned back, muffled to the eyes, and shiveringly watched the active Flavius as he kept the crowd keyed up to its work, Ænone watching also with keen intentness though in haughty quiet, Andrea appeared with the old lawyer, Hipparchus, a learned eunuch belonging to the family of Ænone.

Scarcely waiting to greet him, she broke out: "What is this, Hipparchus? I hear the worthy Jason is under condemnation. Is that true?"

"Yes, he is being examined now, my lady."

"And for what, pray?"

"For harboring some seditious men who are stirring up the people about a new king, and—"

"Bah! The same stupid old story that is made the cause of every unjust persecution of these Jews. Have you heard these Apostles speak, yourself? If you had, you would see the absurdity of such a charge, for they preach only peace, love, good-will, and self-sacrifice—never the seditions of public or private conspiracy. And Jason, too! You know his honesty, and what a good friend of ours he has been. Oh, if only Gaius were here! Is there no sense among the other politarchs, that they let themselves be ruled by a mob?"

"But you see, my lady, our loyalty has been questioned—especially that of our Jew-ish neighbors in the city. It was for that, as you know, that Gaius was called to Rome for counsel, and it will not do to let it be said that we harbor among us even the thought of a new king."

"No more! I am ashamed of you! Oh, were I a man! or were my husband, who is worth any two other men in Thessalonica, but here to speak for the right! Yet stay! Can they imprison Jason if security be offered for his person?"

"Not on this charge, lady."

"And the Apostles have not been found?"

"Not yet."

"Ah, ha! This simplifies things!" She laughed gayly. "Go offer security at once, Hipparchus. You understand that I will be responsible. Have our good Jason discharged, and we will argue the right of this thing later. Will you do this for me?"

He looked refusal for a minute; the lady Ænone was really too bold for a woman, though as fine a creature as ever lived! She was as dear to him as an own child, indeed, and when he looked up bravely to say "no," he met a winning smile that drew forth a reluctant "yes."

As Hipparchus slowly remounted the stately steps of the hall, Ænone gave the word Home!" and looked after him with a merry glance. She was as gay over her victory as she had been angry at the cause for it. Her moods were subtle and changeable as the stirrings of the wind, but pervading them all was the fine perfume of a generous, large-hearted nature. She now began to banter Agistha upon her pale cheeks and frightened eyes, dimly visible through her veil.

"Come, no longer fear!" she said with sunny imperiousness. "Let Flavius claim you if he dare! I only wish he would. I watched him narrowly, Agistha, and I have made a discovery. Let me whisper it—he has been a galley slave!"

"Oh, my lady! How can you tell?"

"I saw the brand upon his cheek. It has been cleverly concealed by a sabre stroke, leaving a cross scar above it, but it is there; I cannot be deceived. And furthermore, it is the brand given for a life sentence. The man is an escaped criminal—of that I am certain. How you look at me, child! Do you wonder how I know all this?"

"Ah, my lady knows everything; but this does seem a strange thing for you to understand."

"Yet the explanation is simple enough. I

have a sailor cousin who is in charge of one of the government galleys, and he has told me much. I used to go on board frequently when we were in Rome, and I learned each brand by heart. It was through curiosity, only—I always will be learning, and often, too, concerning matters that seem of little use to a woman of rank. But, Agistha, I have noticed already that curiosity is the key to wisdom, and wisdom, of whatever variety, is never wasted. It is like my coffer of odds-and-ends at home. Give a hasty glance beneath the lid and one would say the contents are useless. But wait! One day I need a silken tassel for my girdle, and I find it there; another day my sandal laces break—never mind; more are forthcoming. Or perhaps Chloe needs a bit of stuff to mend her tunic, or one of my crisping-pins is missing—a few minutes' search helps us both to what we need. So every bit of knowledge proves useful, no matter if it be but the brand upon the cheek of a galley slave—and here am I turning the coffer of my wits wrong side out for you!"

She ended with a laugh in which Agistha feebly joined, her fears vanishing in the warm atmosphere of protection and support which every one must feel when succored by this great-hearted, clear-headed Lady Ænone.

CHAPTER XVII.

THE BRIDE OF HERKLAS.

HERKLAS did not accompany the women home. A whisper from Ænone had sent him off, still mounted, upon some other business over which Agistha dared ask no questions. But after the delayed evening meal had been served and the mistress had spent an hour or more playing softly on her lyre, and occasionally breaking into sweet, low singing, there was a stir in the peristyle outside the women's apartments, and presently the page appeared to say that Herklas requested a short audience with the Lady Ænone, if she were pleased to see him that night.

She sprang up at once, flung her lyre upon the divan and started out; but catching a glimpse of her handmaiden's wistful face, she hesitated an instant, then said graciously, "You may attend me, Agistha," at which the latter rose to her feet and quickly followed.

They found Herklas somewhat dusty and disordered, as if from a long ride, and as he salaamed low he said apologetically:

"I waited for nothing, madam, but came to report to you, as you bade me."

"Yes, that is right. And what is the report?" she asked eagerly.

"The Apostles are safe on the road to Berea, lady. We went with them until sure they were not pursued, and then left them to other friends as trusty."

"That is well! And Jason?"

"The politarchs discharged him after security had been given, and he is in his own house, somewhat bruised and shaken, but not seriously injured."

"And—the other."

She shot a glance from under her lids at Agistha, but Herklas did not allow his gaze to wander.

"I have done your bidding, madam, and he is now in the inner prison, arrested on the charge of theft, and—"

"Theft?"

"Yes, lady. He was caught robbing a booth by the officers I sent to arrest him. After he is tried on that score, however, your testimony can be given against him."

"You have done well, Herklas! You have my sincere thanks, and more. But of that later."

She clapped her hands sharply, and Harold appeared from behind a curtain.

"Conduct this guest of mine to the small triclinium," she said briskly, "and tell my women of the culina to serve him with the best meal possible on such short notice. And you, Agistha," turning with a careless air to the girl, "may see that he is properly served."

She dismissed them with a wave of her hand, and returned to her private apartments, where, with a smile curling her lips, she once more resumed her lyre and her singing.

"One can see they are made for each other!" she murmured; then after freshly tuning the stringed instrument, she began a sighing little love song.

Herklas, scarcely believing in his good fortune, followed Harold, while Agistha, trembling, blushing, yet not reluctant, followed him. Neither spoke at first. He took his easy attitude upon one of the couches with a half-deprecating air, and she stood by, ready to minister to his slightest want, as was the attitude of most women to their lords in that day. Presently, however, the rich viands loosened the young man's tongue, and Agistha softly answered his remarks, her mood responding to his as clear crystal tingles to the touch of a golden bar.

He told her of his new life, with its beliefs, hopes, and work, to which she added the glad news that she, too, had taken the Christ into her heart. Finally, after much talk about themselves, which was not, therefore, selfish, since it also reached out to the help of others, he said:

"Agistha, to-night I have been told something which may change all my future plans. If events shape themselves, under God, as I believe they will, I shall remain permanently in Thessalonica, and it will be fitting that I should have a wife and a home."

Agistha dropped her eyes and trembled.

"I think your mistress favors me," he was continuing, but at the word "mistress" she broke into a cry of despair.

"Oh, yes, yes! But I had forgotten! It is my master I have to fear—my real master, Flavius! How dare I think of any future, when he is likely to claim me at a moment's notice?"

"Flavius?" cried Herklas, staring at her. "The suspected—but no, I must not betray the Lady Ænone's matters. But is he your master?"

"I know what you would say, Herklas—the suspected galley-slave. Alas! yes, that wicked man is the master I escaped from."

"Say rather who left you as dead without burial—the brute! He will never claim you, Agistha, never. Not only because he thinks you dead, but because—no, I have no right to tell you. Only, ask the kind Lady Ænone, and perhaps she will explain what I cannot. But one question more before I go."

He asked it so softly that even Harold could not hear, and her answer must have pleased him, for he left the house with a firm, quick tread, and a proud smile on his face.

As for Agistha, she soon appeared before her mistress so subdued in manner that the lady broke into merry laughter.

"What ails the girl?" she cried banteringly. "One would think she had been caught stealing sweetmeats!"

At which Agistha called up courage enough to ask: "My lady, is it true I need no longer fear my old master?—and why?"

"Ah, the young trader told you that, did he? And of course explained everything."

"No, madam. He said they were your affairs and he had no right to do so, but bade me ask you, who are so kind."

"What is it to him, Agistha, whether you are free or not? Ah, ha! your blushes answer. Well, well! it is all right, I am sure. He is true and good and beautiful. I will give you your wedding, my girl, and it shall be one suitable for the favorite of a politarch's wife."

"But Flavius? You forget that I am a slave yet, lady."

"I forget nothing, child! Your master, as you call that wretch, is now in prison, and will soon be returned to his proper service under government."

The girl smiled broadly. It was the first time she had really felt secure. Then her face clouded over.

"Ah!" she sighed, "the blessed Christ, whose follower I would be, forgave even his enemies, who were still more cruel than Flavius. I ought to do the same."

Ænone looked at her with astonishment. "Forgive him?" she cried. "He who beat and starved you, and, not content to ruin your present life, left you unburied, that even your soul should never have rest? Forgiveness for such a creature is an impossibility!"

But at that moment came to the speaker's mind the accounts not only of Christ and of Stephen, but of later martyrs also, who had sublimely forgiven under the tortures of a cruel death, and she grew thoughtful.

"Yes, even that does seem to be demanded of us," she murmured at last. "If Christ came to save sinners, surely this Flavius is one; and if the Christian's God can forgive such, should not the Christian as well?"

The lady shook her head as if it were a problem beyond her, then looked up with her merry glance.

"Yes, forgive him, Agistha, that is right. But let us be thankful that even your pardon cannot free him now!"

A few days later, Gaius having returned meanwhile, the once galley slave was called up for examination and fully identified as a murderer who had escaped years before during a frightful storm in the Tyrrhenean Sea, when the galley had capsized. He was supposed to have been drowned at that time, but by superhuman efforts managed to reach the shore. He was now "put to the question," and forced by torture to confess that he had not acquired Agistha by purchase or inheritance, but had stolen her from a palace in Rome, soon after his escape from the shipwreck, intending to negotiate with her wealthy parents for a ransom, but being afterwards in danger of recognition, had carried her with him to Nicopolis in Greece, still meaning in time to demand a ransom which would set him up independently for life. Meanwhile he left her, still a small child, in the care of a woman there. Later he took her with him to Macedonia, thinking that now he would sell her as a slave, for he believed it too late to try and restore her to her parents. But not readily getting his price for the puny, haggard, half-starved little creature, he kept possession of her, though leaving her for weeks at a time to pick up a living, as best she could, among his associates in poverty and crime.

At length the child fell seriously ill, and though she received only the precarious nursing of charity, was finally able to be about again, but with a disordered brain. Her singular powers of divination then first showed themselves, and gained her new interest, for the unscrupulous Flavius at once saw money in this acquisition. He had before this been connected with Alois, the Phœnician, in more than one questionable proceeding, and now the two resolved to go into partnership in exhibiting the girl, hoping to make a fortune out of her ambiguous utterances.

All this was literally forced from Flavius bit by bit, but nothing could make him reveal the name of Agistha's parents. Through severe suffering he persisted that he did not know, and when his tormentors turned the screws tighter he shrieked out names at random, evidently only to shorten the agony. Thus they became convinced that he really did not know, but his description of the house proved that it must be one of the palaces, for its vast peristyle was surrounded by marble columns and costly statuary, while a large fountain, beautifully shaded by flowering plants, played in its center. Other courts, smaller but as luxurious, he spoke of seeing in vista, and all showed enormous wealth in their plenishing.

He had gained entrance to this peristyle through the narrow fauces or passages leading from the garden to the peristyle, past the kitchens. The gate in the wall surrounding this garden had been inadvertently left ajar, and he had slunk in, hoping to steal something within the luxurious enclosure—a gay wrap carelessly flung across a seat perhaps, or a piece of silverware left from some banquet. But he found nothing portable,

so, seeing no one, he kept on until he reached the peristyle, where only a wee child was playing about the fountain. Obeying his first evil instinct of thievery, he quickly threw his girdle over her head to stifle her cries, and ran off with her wrapped close in his tunic, escaping without rousing a person, as it was the hour of the siesta, and all Rome lay asleep for the time being.

From this story he would not deviate, and was finally released from further torture, though only, subsequently, to be returned to the cruel galleys and his hopeless life of hard labor and degrading servitude.

While Gaius each night repeated to his interested wife these glimpses of crime wrung from the wretched man by rack and screw, she grew more and more engrossed in her little handmaiden, and a doubt began to assail her.

"Surely, Gaius, this points to the noblest parentage, and thus disarranges all my plans," she said once. "I had meant to marry her to young Herklas, but he is only a trader, and—"

"Ah! my wife, the trades are growing more honorable every day. Men must make money to keep up with the ruinously extravagant fashions. But how can you be certain that she is of noble birth? She might have been the child of some favorite slave, for aught we know."

"But you say Flavius confessed that she was beautifully clothed, so—"

"The most extravagantly dressed baby I saw in Rome was the Gallic slave boy, but four years old, of our brave young general, Otho. He looked like a little prince, and had his special nurse, as our own Ian."

"I know. It is the silly fashion of the times. But how can we know aught concerning Agistha? His description of the mansion would apply to so many."

"Truly. It throws little light upon the subject; and besides, the occupants are apt to change with the caprice of the emperor. The best way would be to make a list of all the patricians of twelve years ago and find if any sustained such a loss—but that would be a herculean task. You say she knows nothing of all this?"

"Not a word."

"Then what good can it do to tell her? It may make her discontented, and spoil a sweet disposition, to no purpose."

"But have we a right to keep it?"

Gaius thought they had, and they debated the question some time. At length Æxone sensibly broke up the discussion by asking abruptly:

"Which of the patricians did you see most of, Gaius?"

"Well, Aulus Clotius, I think. He is very civil to strangers, and I have met him before when he was in this city."

"Let me see—he is the officer who was conspicuous in the last triumphal procession, is he not?"

"Yes, the son of Aleutius, who died about thirteen years ago, some think by his own hand, because Caligula had a grudge against him. At any rate, for a time his widow and orphans, though not banished, lived in great seclusion and were not recognized in Court circles."

"There were other children, then?"

"Yes, one other; a daughter, I think?"

"And where is she now?"

"She must have died early. Pamphylia referred to her only indirectly, as if long since lost to her. Certainly she now has but the one son, Aulus."

A few weeks later Herklas and Agistha were married at the home of their kind protector. Before this event Herklas fully explained to both Gaius and his wife his future plans. These were, that he was to be installed at Thessalonica as deacon of the new church of Christ, and instead of traveling about the country, was to remain permanently in the city in charge of a shop of his own, the necessary funds having been lent him by wealthy friends in that body.

January was chosen as the time for the marriage, that being a favorite nuptial month with the Greeks, and before the day set, Gaius, in a talk with Herklas, revealed what he knew of Agistha's early history, leaving it to the young husband to repeat this singular story to her, or not, as he chose. Herklas was not ambitious in a worldly way, nor did he wish to awaken such ambitions in his wife, so after much thought he decided at present not to stir up the placid waters of her mind with such disconcerting ideas, fearing like Gaius its effect upon her peace. Thus, ignorant of all but the blessed fact that she "had been bond but now was free," both bodily and spiritually, Agistha entered into her new life.

It was a simple ceremony that changed the Greek girl into the matron, partaking still of many pagan rites and ablutions, but transfused and glorified by Christian sacredness and depth of feeling. Herklas secured

a modest house in the gardens back of the villa, and one evening, dressed in brave attire, with a new tunic of finest linen and a girdle of silk from India, he entered a chariot drawn by mules and gayly decorated with vines and flowers.

This was the nuptial car, and a low couch gorgeously trimmed in honor of the bride who was soon to be borne upon it, occupied its entire length. On one side sat Herklas: on the other Amasa, who acted as master of ceremonies. In great state, to low and winsome music, they were driven slowly through the streets, the people turning out in throngs to shout their greetings; and thus even before they were in sight, Agistha, tremblingly receiving the last touches to her rich attire, lavishly furnished by Ænone, heard the eager shout, "Behold, the bridegroom cometh!" and begged her maids of a day to hurry.

Soon she stood within the atrium, veiled from head to foot, her delicately-clad person emanating perfumes, her arms supported by proud mothers of boys (that thus might their happy fortune attend her new life), and awaited her groom. The car drew nearer, stopped. The music grew louder, more insistent. The groom entered with the violence of a love that would take everything by storm, and demanded the bride of her parents, making as if he would tear her away; all mere acting of course, for Gaius, who stood this night in the place of father to the blushing Agistha, readily seconded the groom and placed her hand in his, which simple ceremony of demanding and giving made them one.

The young husband then led his bride to the chariot, seating her on the couch-like throne, and placing himself at her side, while Amasa sat behind and diverted the crowd, who were full of the tricks and merriment common at a wedding.

All the younger people of the household formed a procession with torches, garlands, bells, and musical instruments of every description, and amid a merry din they left the old home for the new. The doorposts of the latter had been decorated with garlands and ivy leaves and laurel, and as the procession drew near it the custom was to sing a song to Hymen; but to-day Herklas had begged the singers to substitute a Christian hymn, and to its sweet notes of praise they entered their future home as man and wife.

Here in the hall, or ostium, stood Jason's wife, representing the groom's mother, and to her the bride's mother (represented by Ænone) handed over the young wife, to show that she no longer owed devotion to her own kinspeople, but to her husband's first of all. Then she was led to a private room to banquet with her female companions, while her husband received his special friends in the larger triclinium.

The feasting lasted several days, and sometimes grew wearisome to stomach and purse. The day following the marriage the bride and her maidens were kept busy opening the baskets of gifts, sent by loving friends, not only, but by sycophants, and all who had private ends to gain with her lord, if such there were. The most of Agistha's gifts were sent in real affection, however, for she had endeared herself to more than were found in the household of Gaius, while Herklas was a universal favorite.

So passed a few days, until no one could depart saying the master of the feast had been niggardly in the entertainment, and then came a still, home-like day which must have been very welcome to the loving couple. All the guests had departed, all the turmoil and confusion were at an end, and the two were left at last alone to prove each other, and to set up their own family altar, undisturbed by friend or foe.

CHAPTER XVIII.

HAPPENINGS IN PHILIPPI.

THE faithful at Philippi did not once lose sight of Paul in his wanderings, and with the liberality born of true love often sent him such sums as they could raise for his relief, which were carried over the road by devoted brethren, who gladly undertook the journey in order to see and converse once more with the beloved Apostles.

These donations were wholly voluntary, as Paul, no matter how weary with the day's toil, often worked far into the night at his trade of tent-making, in order not to be a burden upon his hearers.

Truly, in the best sense, Paul in his remarkable journeyings at this time proved that he was "all things to all men"—courteous among the refined, wise among the learned, tactful among the disputatious, busy where industry told, and with the greatest patience in inaction, when waiting was the will of the Lord.

In the house of Junius for a year or so there was little outward change. The two women wove industriously, and Salome added to this occupation that of carding and spinning wool and flax, which she had been kindly taught by Lydia. Junius, deprived of his office, had dropped easily into the despicable role of an idler—of whom there were far too many in every Grecian town—and sat about in the market-place all day, "hearing and seeing every new thing," discussing public affairs with others of like habits, and growing daily a little more intemperate, more ragged, and more unashamed, than the day before.

Elizabeth seemed much the same, calm, serene and sweet, but the contour of her face sharpened rapidly, and its pallor increased. She depended more and more upon Salome and Nadab. The latter was growing fast and promised to be her greatest solace and support in time. Thus working and loving together, they might have been almost comfortable but for the fact that everything in Philippi—its business, pleasure, home life, and public events—was based upon pagan ceremonies, and as Christians our little family found themselves debarred much that was otherwise desirable.

Even in the basket-weaving the question of expediency or brave right-doing often came up. Many wished the symbols of the gods woven into the baskets, or ordered such as had special uses in and about the temple services, and these orders Elizabeth felt she could not in conscience execute, while Salome was hindered from preparing the best and finest fabrics because they were for the use of priest, or Vestal, or to adorn those who joined in the processions to the gods. No Christian could in the slightest manner assist at such worship, and thus the calling of each often suffered, apparently, because of that higher calling which placed the kingdom of heaven first, and the acquisitions of this world last and least.

Then, too, it was almost impossible to apprentice Nadab to a good trade, for on the one side the heathen master preferred a boy of his own faith who would work, worship, and take his holidays exactly as he bade him, while on the other Elizabeth could not bear to place her son under the legal control of a master who "loved not Christ and his righteousness."

But God did not leave them desolate. In their own congregation they were loved and honored, and when help was absolutely needed it always came. If Junius had been one with them they would have considered themselves well off in their humble way, but he chose to attribute to the score of their "fanaticism" all the misfortunes resulting from his own conduct, shifting the blame from his own weak shoulders, where it belonged.

But even as things were, they did not repine. For a time, indeed, after the man's dismissal Elizabeth was very grave, and each morning her swollen lids betrayed the night's weeping; but one day she came forth from her chamber with bright eyes, a smiling mouth, and an air of such lightness and joy that each one noticed and said something in laughing approval. But when alone with her, Salome hastened to ask:

"What is it, dear? You look so glad, so happy! Has Junius promised better things?"

Elizabeth shook her head. "No, little sister, it is our Lord who has promised, and I have been shutting my ears—that is all. Last night, as I lay weeping, it all came to me with the sharpness of a rebuke. Why should I weep and repine? Why should I bear this trouble as if it were my trouble alone? Have I not been expressly commanded not to do so? I remember how Jesus once said that we 'would not come to Him that we might have life,' and I began to wonder, was it I who was holding aloof instead of Him, as I had felt? Then kept recurring many, many words: 'He that cometh to me shall never hunger,' 'It is the will of my Father that all who believe shall have everlasting life,' 'He that followeth me shall not walk in darkness,' and that beautiful request, 'Come unto me, all ye heavy laden,' and little by little everything grew clear. I had no right to agonize thus over my husband—it was distrusting Christ. It was as if I were bent double with some heavy load and a stronger offered to carry it, saying, 'It is really my load—give it to me!' yet I would still persist in clinging to the dreadful weight, staggering and groaning at every step, yet blaming that other even while refusing to yield the burden; and I said, 'Forgive me, Lord! Junius was yours before he was mine, and you love him. I give him to you to carry and to save. I will do my human best, and I will trust your heavenly wisdom and await your time. I have brought my burden—give me your comfort!' And oh! Salome, such rest, such peace as I felt! I turned over and slept like a little child. I rose like a glad maiden with

no care, for I know that my Lord is carrying my burden, that I may rest in His peace. Junius is His now, and He is 'mighty to save.'"

But Salome sometimes felt it would take a stronger faith than hers to be certain that Christ would save the surly, stupid man who seemed drifting further from them and from all good with every passing month. The young pagan captain was the only one of his old associates who seemed to have any notice or care for him, and he still continued to show a friendly interest in his affairs.

Cleotas, as the latter was called, could not readily forget Salome's spirited refusal to take part in the Lenæa, and, with his mind thus stirred to questioning, he watched that feast to the gods with new eyes, when it took place. The result was that its wantonness and license fairly confounded him, and he went home afterwards (with a clearer head than ever before) to ponder over this and the corresponding spring festival called the Bacchanalia, in which he had always thoughtlessly joined, sleeping off the fumes of strong wines and excitement later, without further thought than perhaps to boast of his ability to keep up the carousing longer than some men.

In his new perplexities he naturally sought counsel among his friends, and of these the converted jailer, now an officer of the church, came first to mind as he saw him almost daily in the way of business. Through him he was led to seek Luke, the beloved physician, who had personal care of the little flock in Philippi at this time, and ere long Cleotas became a true believer and helpful member of this body.

In the assemblies, held oftenest in private houses, he constantly met Elizabeth and Salome, and soon learned to look upon them as special friends. He was a brave, athletic fellow, with the strong man's instinct for protecting all helpless creatures, and the inside knowledge of their trials which had come to him made him anxious to help in every way. So, whenever possible, he gave Junius employment by the day, and secured public orders for the women, such as weaving mats for the justice halls and offices, or cloth for awnings and door curtains.

In this manner he won his way into their hearts, and no one thought it strange or unsuitable when, three years after Salome became a part of Elizabeth's household, she left it to go with Cleotas to a much finer home, as his honored wife. It was, even in the eyes of Lydia, who always took a motherly interest in the girl, a desirable marriage, for Cleotas was not only a sincere Christian, but an official in high standing, who had both means and influence.

Salome could now show her gratitude, and so generous was she that Elizabeth's cares were greatly lightened. More than this, Cleotas was able to help Nadab onwards in the difficult upward climb of a drunkard's son, and soon after the marriage made the youth his deputy, with fair pay, and every chance for promotion.

During all this time Junius seemed steadily declining, and Elizabeth still "waited upon the Lord" for his salvation. She was always gentle, and as loving as she could be with one of his disposition, while her treatment of him at his worst was courteous and considerate.

Once Salome, stung to anger by an exhibition of his brutality and Elizabeth's patience, cried out sharply, after he had stumbled from their presence:

"How can you treat him like that, Elizabeth? You really act as if you respected him!"

Elizabeth turned to the speaker, her face radiant with a great thought.

"I do," she said gently. "He belongs to God; he is one of the sinners bought with a great price, for all innocence, all virtue, all faith, suffer through his degradation. But Christ loves him, and it is His will to save him. I must respect him then, Salome; I dare not do otherwise!"

And Junius, through the slow deterioration of heart and brain, felt this, and secretly clung to it as a sailor submerged in deep and surging waters clings to the rope thrown from the stately, steady ship riding calmly above him.

"I am a man!" he would tell himself with a thickened tongue. "I am Elizabeth's husband, and she looks up to me. I will have to get the better of this sometime—yes, I certainly will."

But the days slid by and his resolves with them. The line seemed very slack now, and he hardly felt its pull in those thick, slimy waters. But ofttimes, on the ship, the captain can both feel and clearly see the rope which the half-drowned sailor scarcely knows has been thrown to him. Elizabeth knew it must be plain to the All-seeing Eye, and, groping by faith, she felt it too, and never ceased to pray and to believe.

CHAPTER XIX.

A GLIMPSE AT COURT LIFE IN ROME.

AS the intrigues, splendors, amusements and successes of his life at court filled Hector's time and thoughts, so did the holy influences, once powerfully felt, suffer neglect and decay. The virtues, especially those of truth and love, were not in demand among that inner circle of patricians who occupied the royal mansions. These perfectly understood that the Emperor Claudius was a drunkard; his wife Agrippina a shameless intriguer whose hands were not free from the stain of blood; her son Nero—while outwardly a brilliant and beautiful boy—in reality an ambitious tool without conscience or compassion; and even Burrhus and Seneca, statesman and philosopher, though the brightest stars in that night of sin, were often found stooping to hypocrisy and time-serving, hopeless to hasten the dawning.

How then could a young man entirely dependent upon courtly favor do otherwise than follow the lead of his betters and learn to close his eyes and ears, repress natural right feeling, and simply do as he was bidden, neither asking questions nor making comments?

So thought Hector; for looking about, he found no Daniels in Cæsar's household, and, failing either outward or inward moral support, he grew nearly as reckless and ready in crime as the rest.

He had not been two years in Rome when there was a complete change in the government. The weak Claudius was dead, having been poisoned by his wife, and Nero, her son, had been declared Cæsar by the Prætorian Guards before Brittanicus, own son of the murdered emperor, fully knew that his father's sudden illness was fatal. So perfectly and secretly did the subtle Agrippina lay her plots and mature her plans.

Aulus Clotius was naturally a strong adherent of Nero's, and the accession brought him new honors. He was made Tribunus Celerum, commander of the Royal Guards, and he and his household were invited to live under the imperial roof, which was large enough to house over a thousand people in roomy luxury. Hector advanced with him and won favor with the amusement-loving Nero because of his wrestling powers. Many a time, after a surfeiting banquet, the Greek was called in to amuse the company, and was pitted in private combat against some gladiator famed for his skill in the arena. Aulus sometimes told his client laughingly that Cæsar only sought a good opportunity to consign him to the same fate, and that if ever he lost the favor of the court he might know what his punishment would be—death in the amphitheatre.

At present, however, Hector stood well, and any disgrace seemed far away. He had been made a centurion in the Imperial Guards, and had a suite of apartments in one of the palace wings called the Prætorium. Here he lived in luxury with his family—his wife Céleste, once the pretty Gallic slave girl, now a freedwoman through the generosity of her mistress, and his two little children, a boy and a girl. During Nero's early reign Aulus had been out upon one long campaign in which Hector accompanied him, proving so brave and sturdy an adherent that the tie between them grew brotherly in its strength.

Pamphylia and Julia, hearing how, in close combat, Hector had twice interposed his body and shield between their lord and the spear of a fierce barbarian, felt they owed him much, and when the warriors returned gladly promoted the marriage between himself and the favorite Céleste, making her free that she might not dishonor him by a misalliance.

So everything went smoothly on the outside for Hector—but how was it within? A house left to perfect tranquillity through disuse should, it would seem, be better preserved than one kept in constant service, with childish feet pattering about, and a busy family giving it hard knocks. But this is not true. The disused house begins a slow, silent deterioration from the minute the family departs. Wind, sun, rain, and worm, take arms against it, to batter, scorch, rot, and burrow, from roof to foundation, and unless bright, active life comes into it again, the house is doomed.

So it is with a man's soul. When busy care, anxiety, temptation even, beset it without and within, while the love of Christ fills every part, it grows only stronger and better for the attrition; but let the love-light die out, let prosperity slowly smother it in outside beauty, and it surely tends to extinction. The soul of Hector was thus rapidly falling into ruin because too inactive and too empty, till deeds which had at first thrilled him with horror caused but a shrug of the shoulders, perhaps.

It was popular to join in the processions, so he and his family were sure to be prominent in these events, however immodest or grotesque they might be; for the same reason he was always at the cruel gladiatorial contests in the amphitheatre, watching them with an interest possible only to one who understood what strength and skill they involved, and too often he would not turn down his thumbs to save a poor overpowered wretch, because in his own proud strength he felt that the defeated gladiator had been too easy a prey.

Besides all these comparatively innocent employments, were many he never spoke of even in his own home, for was he not, with his one hundred men, always at the beck of Nero? What this secret service meant under his guidance, made Hector at first recoil and perchance try to withdraw from active participation. But to what purpose? He was in a net, and its meshes tightened with every crime committed.

Hector, however, salved over his conscience with the law made applicable to slaves, "A servant can do no crime when he fulfills only the will of his master," though he could not at all times stifle his self-disgust.

Thus passed the first five "good years," as they were called, of Nero's reign, because, with all their extravagance and crime, they were as nothing to what followed. During this era the young Nero found enough satisfaction in the license and power of his position to leave the governing of the Empire mostly to his wise counselors, Burrhus and Seneca, hence the outside world had little to complain of. But within the palace were all forms of wickedness. The young Brittanicus, whose only crime was that he belonged by right on the throne, was poisoned as his father had been; and his girl sister, who drew every breath in fear, was set aside for a slave woman, though her marriage with Nero gave her the empty title of Empress.

Of all these events Hector had a superficial knowledge, of some a conviction so deep that the stains rested heavily on his own soul, and yet each passing year greeted him as "a prosperous man."

It was nearly fifty-nine, over six years since the memorable night when Hector, a brave, unsullied youth, tore through the streets of Philippi calling aloud for his sister. He had just risen from his banqueting couch after the evening meal, and was playing with his youngest child, a sweet little girl, named in that sister's memory, Salome, when the door opened to admit a page, who announced Aulus Clotius, always a welcome guest.

Hector laughingly rose from his somewhat undignified posture on the rug, and put the baby by to greet his friend and patron.

"Ah, my lord tribune, you have caught me without my visor!" he cried merrily: to which Aulus quickly made reply:

"But thank the gods I am not an enemy!"

Their greeting was warm and brotherly, and they placed themselves side by side, ready for intimate discourse.

Age had not greatly changed either's appearance. Hector had broadened, and his bearing was distinctly military. Aulus was lined more with dissipation than with years, but his easy, carelessly good-natured air still clung to him. Both were handsome men, and, one in his official purple, the other in his military scarlet, attracted admiration everywhere. They flung a kiss after the grieving child, as she was ruthlessly borne away by her nurse, then Aulus turned and fixed his keen eyes directly upon Hector with the abrupt question:

"Have you heard the news?"

"No; what is it?"

"Nero Cæsar and his mother, the Augusta, have had another bitter quarrel this evening, and she has threatened to leave the palace this very night. She is now in her apartments talking excitedly with her maids, and I have been privately requested to bring you to the triclinium, where Nero still remains, that he may give you some orders."

"To what purpose?" asked Hector quickly, knitting his brows. "What would he with the mother who raised him to the throne of the Cæsars?"

"I know not," answered Aulus gloomily, "but he is purple with rage and drinking more heavily than usual. I am told it went so far that he even snatched off a precious amulet she gave him the night he was declared Emperor, and flung it in her face, saying he would have none of the good fortune it brought if she must be always taunting him with having received it through her."

"Bah! He was intoxicated."

"No, the meal had scarcely begun. He has been gracious all day, and sent for Agrippina and his poor little wife to banquet with him. I presume it is the same trouble. He wanted some favor for Poppœa,

and that always makes the Augusta furious. But come, the Emperor awaits you."

While thus conversing Hector had been swiftly exchanging his easy, ungirdled house-tunic for the military costume he must always wear on duty or in the presence of the Court, and soon, trimly girdled, helmeted, and buskined, he followed his noble friend across numerous courts and gardens of artistic beauty to the rose terrace, a magnificent enclosure near that part of the palace occupied by its head. Connecting with this was a small court, palm-shaded and fountain-cooled, and before entering this Aulus stopped and took from his bosom a large kerchief.

"I am ordered to blindfold you," he remarked quietly.

"What?" cried Hector, drawing back with the quick suspicion engendered by the trickery of the age. "Why say you that?"

Aulus smiled at the other's manner, and went on calmly folding the linen square.

"Do you not trust even me, Hector?" he asked with a hint of sadness in his tone. "But then, why should you?" he added quickly. "Who is to be trusted here? Well, friend, I must cover your eyes simply because I am to take you in by a secret passage which you are not to know—that is all."

"Secret passages lead to dungeons—and worse!" Hector muttered.

"Oh, come, my bold soldier, you have nothing to fear. You are not yet high enough to excite the jealousy of Cæsar, so be at peace, and thank Mars that you are only a centurion. Bend lower, please; I cannot reach you."

Hector obeyed, but still with dissatisfaction, and after being tightly bandaged, was led some distance and by many turns to a small door in the wall, guarded only by one sentinel, who stood inside, and admitted them after hearing a peculiar knock—four slow, distinct taps for the word Nero, and a loud and imperative one at the end for his title, Cæsar—whereupon the door flew open.

Traversing what was, could Hector have seen, a long and narrow corridor, with no light except from lamps kept ever burning, they turned into 'another at right angles to it, crossed this obliquely, and stopped at a door, where Aulus whispered the password into another sentinel's ear, then pressed his thumb upon one of the panels, at which the door flew open. The sentinel stepped respectfully aside, Aulus drew his companion through the narrow aperture, and it clicked to behind them. Hector drew in his breath a little at the sound. He had heard that ominous click many a time when he had been on the right side of the door, and some poor wretch upon the other, and it thrilled him now to the finger tips.

"Take off your bandage," said Aulus in his reassuringly calm voice; and the Greek obeyed.

He looked about upon a rather small apartment, surrounded by statuary, the panels between the full-length figures being cut into niches. These were fitted with doors of rich citron-wood carved into the fineness of lace-work, through which he could catch glimpses of rolls and mounted sheets of papyrus, the former slipped into cases of burnished gold, delicately-carved ivory, satin-wood, or embossed leather, the latter, called tablets, stacked up and held in place by weights of carnelian, agate, or malachite. It was, indeed, the tablinum, or room for the preservation of the family archives, and was approached by this secret passage from one side, while from the other it opened into the larger bibliotheca, or library, a handsome apartment, more for show than use in this palace. At right angles was a curtained archway which gave a long vista of rich apartments for family use, and opposite that was the door leading into Cæsar's private triclinium, or dining-room.

The secret door through which the men had entered was now invisible. Hector's roving gaze could neither place it nor conjecture where it might be, for before removing the bandage he had been given a whirl or two, and knew not which way he was faced upon entering. The door, in fact, was what appeared to be one of the niches for the books, and was known to only a very few in the palace. Even the guards in the passage were led thence blindfolded, by a trusty officer, and had little idea of its situation.

Our friends stepped along the tablinum to the door of the banqueting room, from which issued sounds of an angry voice, and occasional laughter. Aulus swept aside its heavy curtain, motioned to the page, and the two were at once ushered into the presence of that Emperor whom a fawning populace was taught to worship as a god. He looked little enough like it now. He lay sprawling on a couch gorgeous with gilding and Persian stuffs, evidently satiated with food and helpless with wine. Upon other couches scarcely less splendid were stretched

two of his favorites, their garments and jewels vying with his own in richness, and their countenances bloated with overfeeding and drinking. The room was softly lighted with gilded lamps, and a shower of perfumed waters fell in a soft spray from a small fountain just within the half-circle made by the crescent-shaped table. This table was heaped with every delicacy, served on gold and silver plate, and velvet-shod slaves passed to and fro, handing about the viands and instantly removing the stains of wine carelessly spilled by the intoxicated men. Nero was talking fast and furiously, while the others sometimes laughed, sometimes applauded, with drunken gravity.

The couches on which the women had rested for the short time their presence was allowed, were pushed back out of the way, and just as our friends entered, Nero was amusing himself and ending a sentence by flinging at the Augusta's a full wine-glass, which shattered against its woodwork, and ruined its gold-embroidered cushions.

This ought to have relieved him, but evidently did not, for, seeing the two new-comers bowing low before him, he jerked himself to a sitting posture and began swearing at them, while each—inwardly fuming though he was—could only bow the deeper, and meekly submit to the indignity.

When Nero's fury had expended itself somewhat, he cried abruptly:

"Well, speak, can you not? What have you come for, Aulus?"

"To bring the centurion Hector, as Cæsar commanded," returned the patrician as shortly as he dared.

"I commanded? Who says so?"

Evidently the fumes of wine had beclouded his memory for the moment. Tigellinus, boldest of his favorites, laughed and said ironically:

"How convenient is a short memory! Has Cæsar forgotten his grievance, also?"

"No!" bellowed the royal son, as he thought of his mother's defiance of his wishes, and stern admonitions of his folly. "No, and now I remember all. I sent for Hector because he belongs to my guards."

"Assuredly, Cæsar."

"But I do not need you, Aulus. Get out, will you?"

The coarse command made the haughty young patrician turn white, but he must needs swallow his chagrin, bow low, and back out, almost prostrating himself at every step. He accomplished the feat with outward equanimity, but Aulus Clotius never forgot that thickly-uttered order, nor the sneering laugh from the two favorites that followed his withdrawal. It was perhaps his first real rebuff, but by no means his last, for Nero was already growing jealous of his musical talent, which threatened to surpass his own. He had been vaguely made to feel the royal displeasure in various ways, but this was the

sionless, under the imperial scrutiny. Long practice as a guard had made it possible for him to seem more like a statue than a man.

"Well, you will do, methinks," said Nero at last, with a laugh. "My beloved mother, the Augusta," (the words were a sneer) "wishes to leave the palace to-night, and I, Cæsar, desire that she should do so. She must of course be properly attended. See that she is. Do you understand?"

"Then act! A good servant does not need specific directions; he allows circumstances to aid him."—See page 74.

first actual rebuff, and even Nero would not have gone so far but for his inflamed condition, which made him scarcely accountable for what he said.

"Come forward!" he commanded as Aulus disappeared; and Hector, fired with indignation for his friend, slowly approached the royal couch.

"I want to look at you," said the Emperor with a hiccough. "I want to see what stuff you are made of."

Hector stood motionless, almost expres-

Hector bowed low, his hand at his visor. Given permission to speak, he asked deferentially:

"Does Cæsar desire that the Augusta shall have a guard in addition to those in her own employ?"

"Yes, Cæsar does!" mimicked the emperor in the tone of a hectoring child, for Nero could not be kingly when he was intoxicated. "If her guards should grow quarrelsome on the road and the Augusta be in danger, overpower them with your stronger guard and make her safe and quiet. Do you follow me?"

Hector repressed a shiver of loathing, and bowed assentingly.

"Then act! A good servant does not need specific directions; he allows circumstances to aid him. Given a lonely night road, one or two women in litters, and a lot of drunken guards ready for a fight, and what chance will there be for those women, eh?"

The leer which accompanied these words filled Hector, hardened as he was, with horror. For an instant his fingers fairly tingled with the desire to throttle the ruffian who could so coolly plan for the death of a mother who had been the sole instigator of his present elevation.

The Greek swallowed his wrath, glad that he had no cause to speak and thus betray himself, and bowed to the ground. Nero beckoned him nearer, spoke a few rapid sentences in a lower tone, then with a careless wave of his jeweled hand dismissed him, after which he lifted the richly-colored glass of Falernian wine to his lips with as much unction as if he had not just ordered the murder of the mother who bore him!

Hector bowed himself from the room, the obsequious, well-trained servant outwardly—the disgusted, rebellious officer within. But luckily for him Nero never looked below the surface, and at that date had not dreamed that any would dare defy him.

———◆———

CHAPTER XX.

CLEOTAS.

AULUS was waiting in the tablinum, still white and cold from his rebuff. Silently he again bandaged Hector's eyes before leading him outside, and not a word was spoken until in the outer court once more, when, snatching off the kerchief, he asked with a grim smile:

"Well, is she to be murdered?"

Hector started. It was an ugly word to use in reference to a royal commission. But he answered as bluntly:

"That is the substance of it—yes. I am to attend her with my guards, and when they get into a tumult—"

"Who get into a tumult?"

"Her soldiers and mine."

"Oh, I see!" laughing shortly. "Well, when they do?"

"Then she and her women are to be—dispatched," was the gloomy answer.

"It is a nice commission!" observed Aulus sarcastically. "I do not envy you. How will you do it? The knife or the battle-axe?"

"The latter. It will look more as if the men did the deed in desperation, simply to stop their screams. Her guards are then to be overpowered, bound, and brought back to be charged with the crime, while my men receive a sestertium apiece for their brave defense of her."

Aulus laughed outright. "How ingenious! Nero never thought that out—it came from the fertile brain of Tigellinus. And the centurion of this brave band, my friend Hector, how much does he receive?"

"Ten sestercia," was the prompt reply; but in the tone was all the self-loathing Hector felt over the horrid deed.

Aulus turned and looked at him. "It is not the work for soldiers, friend."

"No, I can meet the lances of the Bedouins with coolness, but this work gives me a horror," assented the Greek with fervor.

"Do you know," said the tribune in a different tone, "I believe there is only one man in this palace who cannot be bought by Nero's gold."

"And who is that?"

"He is an officer lately sent here with dispatches from Philippi, and his name is Cleotas—a tall, brave, honest-eyed fellow. Nero, as you know, enjoys brow-beating these ministers from the provincial towns, so he began asking him about the Christians there, and said in that hateful, tantalizing manner of his, 'I hear you have a large and flourishing church of that sect—how is this?' Cleotas answered him respectfully that they were indeed flourishing, and it was doubtless owing to the fact that some good men had labored there, converting many. Then Cæsar began telling him that such a report put the city in a bad light with the government, and added, 'We shall expect you and your Duumvirs to see that this religion does not spread further, for we have no sympathy with it; and as for these " good men " you speak of, if they are like that Paulus of whom we are constantly advised as stirring up the people all through that region, the less we hear and see of them the better. Put all such seditions down with a firm hand.' And then what does that bold Macedonian do but answer, 'Then let Cæsar appoint a new officer to serve in my place, for

I, Cleotas, am a Christian also.' The words fairly took us off our feet! Even Nero started on his throne. Everybody looked to see the foolhardy ambassador ordered to a dungeon at once, and the guards grasped their short swords involuntarily, when, to the astonishment of the whole assembly, Nero burst out into a good-natured laugh. 'You evidently are not used to courts, my rustic friend,' he said leniently, 'and Cæsar will appoint when and whom he chooses. For the present Cleotas of Macedonia holds the office, and must exercise it in all justice to our advantage.' The man bowed low, but before he could speak again, I, who had attended him to the audience room, began my retreat, making him an imperative sign to follow, for I had no notion to stay there till I saw the bold, true-hearted fellow consigned to the torture. When I had him safely outside I muttered, 'For Jupiter's sake, Cleotas, how dared you? Men have been flung to the beasts for less!'"

"And what did he say?" asked Hector, deeply interested.

"He coolly told me he knew that perfectly well, but he had no fear; his Master was a greater than Cæsar, and 'Him only should he serve.'"

"But the strange thing is that the Emperor should take it in that way," mused Hector. "He is not wont to be so easy with men."

"True enough! I heard, however, that he said afterwards to Burrhus that he was so sick of fawning and flattery that the fellow's boldness seemed quite refreshing; and he certainly is letting him go without further instructions against the Christians."

"Is the man still here, then?" asked Hector quickly. "I would like to see a countryman once more, and such a brave one! Where can he be found, my lord?"

"He is lodged in one of the towers—I can show you the place. But have you the time? When does the Augusta start?"

"Of that I cannot be certain. One is appointed to watch and let me know. Meanwhile I have but to order my guards to be in readiness, and wait in my rooms for the word. If only he would come to see me there!"

"And why not? I will apprize him of your wish, and, if he is not too hurried, bring him with me."

"Ah, my lord, you are always more than kind to me."

"And take it out of you in return when-ever possible!" laughed Aulus, as with a wave of his hand he hurried away.

Hector had not been long in his own atrium when, with a flourish, the little page announced the two guests. With his heart beating unaccountably our centurion arose and stepped forward to greet his fellow-townsman. He saw a tall, frank, keen-eyed man of something over thirty, with an expression denoting good-humor and firmness in about equal proportions. The two greeted each other with warmth and soon were deep in talk, Hector eagerly asking, and Clotas fully answering, questions about Philippi in general and some of its inhabitants in particular.

When they had talked some time Hector observed slowly, with a long sigh:

"I was very happy there! I should never have left, but for the loss of my sister."

"She died, then?" asked Cleotas sympathetically.

"I could almost say I hope so, though I do not know," returned Hector in a tone of deep sadness. Then, as if impelled by some impulse stronger than his usual reticence about private matters, he repeated in detail the story of that eventful night.

The two men listened in perfect silence—Aulus with the peculiar air of deprecating sympathy he always wore when the matter was referred to; Cleotas with his keen eyes fixed upon Hector, wonder and conviction growing in their depths. The latter had barely finished when the Philippian broke out excitedly:

"You say this happened over six years ago? Her name—what was your sister called?"

"Salome," was the answer.

"And you—why, of course, you are Hector!"

He sprang to his feet, and, his host having also risen in a vague astonishment, clasped him in a close embrace, after the warm oriental fashion.

"My brother!" he cried. "Know that Salome lives, is well and happy, and is my own loved and honored wife!"

Hector could not believe his senses, and for a minute the demonstrations of joy and relief from Aulus Clotius quite overpowered his own.

"Do you not understand, Hector? I have always told you she was not abducted—that she must have escaped to safety. Where is your tongue, friend—can you not speak?"

No, for a time Hector, strong man that he

was, had all he could do to battle with his emotions, and it was Aulus, full of excitement and interest, who asked the questions trembling on his lips.

When Hector learned all, and fully realized that Salome owed rescue, care, protection, maintenance, and a marriage far beyond his expectations for her, to the despised Christians alone, he was deeply touched, and the softening influences of that almost forgotten night in prison, when the earthquake proved a friend, returned to him. Their talk was long, rapid, and absorbing. For a time Hector even forgot the hideous commission which soon must claim him. A messenger from his company, who came to ask special instructions regarding the armor to be worn, brought it all back once more, and he was obliged to turn with an awful sense of wretchedness and loathing from the life of purity, love, simplicity, and faith, which Cleotas had been depicting, to the depths of deceit and crime in which he himself had so long been submerged.

In that moment of tenderness, of revived affection, of intense longing, his life stood out clear in all its wickedness, and his inmost soul recoiled. Yet to-night he must compass a crime more horrible, more unnatural, more revolting, than any yet required of him. He must murder a woman, a mother, at the behest of a son who owed to her alone the imperial power he was now wielding against her.   While still tingling with the delight of finding his own sister safe and well, he must steel himself to make way, by brutal means, with another man's mother! The thought grew unbearable, and cold drops stood out upon his brow as he realized the hideousness of his position.

Of course, to Cleotas this emotion was accountable only as the result of his own surprising news; but Aulus, knowing all the facts, felt it must be more than that, and was not astonished when the sudden appearance of the little page, to announce another messenger in waiting, made Hector leap from his place, and exclaim in broken accents:

"Oh, I cannot, cannot do it!"

Aulus looked after him with concern, Cleotas with mild surprise, as he hurried from the chamber to the anteroom, to confer alone with the man.

Shortly he re-entered, his face now radiant, his manner filled with joyful relief. Aulus stood up quickly, a question in his eyes—what could have happened?

Hector threw him a look. "Something I have been dreading is averted," he said aloud in partial explanation, for Cleotas also seemed curious; then as he passed close by Aulus he managed to whisper: "She is not going—the auguries were not propitious!"

Aulus understood, and his face broke into smiles of amused relief.

"Another case of a woman's changing her mind!" he thought in his satirical fashion. "For once it has worked well, I must own." Then aloud, and in a careless tone: "No one can tell how many disagreeable duties occur in the life of a centurion—and not the least of these are his long night services. I am glad for you, Hector, if you can rest to-night."

Hector bowed his head comprehendingly, and turned to Cleotas.

"I shall see you on shipboard to-morrow, but you must come in the morning and with us break the fast. I want you to see my wife and children, and take to Salome our love, and whatever gifts we can secure in the short time allowed us. And to-night, brother, when you pray to your God in the name of the Christ, remember me, for I am beset with temptations, and life is hard for a soldier who is at the beck of royal masters!"

Cleotas nodded brightly. "I know all that, and I used sometimes to feel I was as much a slave as any bondman of them all. But now it is different, for Christ has made me free. I do what I know is right, and no man, be he Cæsar himself, can make me do otherwise."

"But how dare you? Here the least word of rebellion will doom us to scourgings or torture."

"I take the risk," said Cleotas calmly. "For I do all through Christ who gives me strength. Ah! if you could talk with our beloved Luke, or with our brave and glorious Paul, or indeed with sweet Elizabeth, sister and friend of our Salome, you would quickly understand. For, you see, it is God working in us, and we have only to let him influence us, and leave all results in his hands. I am but a bluff official, not given to eloquence, and so can best honor Christ by sturdy deeds; but these I have mentioned not only act the Christian part, but win others with loving and appropriate words. However, brother, I can pray for you, as Jesus taught us how to do that; and when I ask each day that you be 'led not into temptation, but delivered from evil,' my prayer will be heard and answered. Only hold yourself in readiness to be blessed and helped."

———◆———

CHAPTER XXI.

TREACHERY IN THE HOME.

TIME did not improve matters in the palace. Nero's peace with his mother, after the disgraceful scene of the banquet, was not long-lived, and less than four months later, in the spring of the same year, the poor woman fell a victim to his hatred and her own ambitions.

Nero had managed, by alternately coaxing and harassing, to induce her to depart to her country seat at Antium, where, after plotting her death by drowning—which plan proved a failure through her quickness and knowledge of swimming—she was put to the sword by Cæsar's minions; a murder in which Seneca was unwillingly involved, to his lasting discredit, but from which Hector escaped as participator, he being just then needed in Rome to help quell a riot among the people.

A little matter of that kind was soon crushed out, however, and Nero, relieved of his most daring admonisher, his mother, prepared to assert his will and give rein to his passions without a thought of consequences. His divorce of Octavia, his pure and fair young wife, and the attempt to cover her with public dishonor, which even he could not carry through against the outraged sense of the people, was the next event in the reign of this tyrant, and was almost immediately followed by his mock marriage to Poppœa, the beautiful but unscrupulous woman who proved the bane of all who loved her.

Poppœa did not favor Aulus Clotius. She had an old grudge against him, and was quick to perceive Nero's jealousy of the man. This she used every subtle art to inflame into hatred. Nero was ready enough to respond to all ungenerous impulses, but the young patrician stood too high to be lightly thrust aside just now, when the temper of the multitude had been greatly tried, so the Emperor contented himself with dealing him one or two blows that greatly hurt his pride and crippled his ambition. Aulus, who had been for some time commander of a cohort, fully expected to be made general of a legion as soon as circumstances rendered

the promotion possible, and great was his chagrin to see a far less able man given the command, while he was appointed prætor instead, an office civil rather than military, which confined him in Rome, and was to him an almost empty honor; for, being the youngest of the prætors, he would have little voice even in judicial matters.

Though the pill was coated with fair words and the assurance that it was given only to keep him a fixture at court, Aulus thoroughly understood it, and felt all its bitterness, as he put aside his helmet and donned his robe of office, for he knew that from this hour his fortunes would begin a sure decline. Besides, he loved his soldier's life and loathed the squabbles and defeats which made up the judiciary councils of the day, and his soul grew sick at thought of the degradation there must be in pretending to rule under a tyrant who was also devoid of common sense. But his wife and mother secretly rejoiced that he was thus spared to them in safe citizenship, not appreciating the inner circumstances which made the civil life galling to a man like himself.

The next rebuff was a curt order to vacate his apartments in the palace, as they were required for a friend of the new empress; and the family made haste to repair to the old home near by.

Hector loyally requested permission to go with them, and even as Aulus admonished him for thus jeopardizing his own fortunes by clinging to an unpopular master, his eyes glittered with moisture while he wrung his henchman's hand, touched to the heart by his devotion. To repay him, Aulus fitted up some of the best apartments in one of the quadrangles about the inner peristyle, where the fountain was always playing, the rooms occupied by Pamphylia and her women being opposite, while the family and state apartments were nearer the street and opened upon a larger court.

After the visit of Cleotas Hector could not rest until he had managed to bring him, with Salome and the three little ones, to Rome, and Aulus now kindly furthered the plan by offering to appoint Cleotas his lictor primus, or head attendant and man of affairs, who would give orders to the rest of the household, assist in judicial proceedings, and always ride at the shoulder of the prætor, in distinction from the two common lictors who ran in advance, to clear the street and command the respectful homage of the crowd for their master.

It was a great day for the little household at Philippi when Cleotas received, by special courier, letters from Aulus Clotius and Hector, detailing this plan, and furthering it by sending a special guard to conduct them hither, and Salome could scarcely await the necessary delays of preparation when she remembered that she was really to see her beloved Hector once more. She hurried to tell Elizabeth the news, and was astonished to have it received with a burst of tears.

"Why, Elizabeth—sister—what is it?" cried Salome, in real distress. "Surely you must be glad to think I shall be re-united to one of my dear brothers at last."

"Oh, indeed—indeed I am!" cried Elizabeth, struggling with her tears. "Only, I shall miss you so, Salome! You cannot realize how dear you have become to me."

"Dearest friend," whispered Salome, kneeling beside the older woman, and drawing the weary, weeping face to her breast, "I can, because I know how much you are to me. Would that you might go with us! If—" She checked herself, then went on quickly: "We will leave Nadab in a position to assist you in every way, and we shall not forget you, even if so far off, Elizabeth—you know that?"

"Yes, I know. You were going to say, 'If Junius were different'?" looking up with a glance that she tried to make composed. "Salome, God is long in answering me, but I feel sure He will—sure! But just now I am greatly cast down, for my husband has been away two days and nights, and though I sent Nadab, he could not find him in the usual haunts. I fear—I scarcely know what."

"Elizabeth," said the younger woman, after a thoughtful silence, "you remember what I told you of Nero Cæsar's words respecting the Christians here, when the illness of Tuema caused Cleotas to be sent to Rome with the dispatches?"

"Yes, I remember. Cæsar has never liked our worship, and persecutions have been frequent; but so far here in Philippi we have been unmolested."

"Yes, so far. But see what the good Paul has been made to suffer. Then, too, there are rumors that many have been put to the question in Rome. Cleotas, who knows all that is taking place here, says there are people acting as paid spies to discover something against us ever since the last edict forbidding our assembling together, or practicing our ceremonies. He does not know just who they all are, but—"

Elizabeth started and turned a pallid face upon her. The eyes of the two met—in one an agonized question, in the other a sad and reluctant affirmation. Elizabeth clutched her friend's arm and shook it in a passion of denial.

"No, no, Salome! He could not—he would not! He has had money lately, but he declares he earned it tending the wine shop for Hæram. Do not tell me—" She sank back, half fainting.

Salome's eyes had not withdrawn their assertion; they had only drooped with regret and sorrow, and Elizabeth knew from her manner that the unspoken charge was but too well founded, or it would never have been brought up. But the wife could not talk of it, and quickly changed the subject by asking some question regarding Salome's departure.

This took place a few weeks later, and when Elizabeth—who, with Nadab, had accompanied them as far as Neapolis—watched the dingy lateen-sail spread to the breeze and slowly clear the harbor, she turned away forlorn and lonely, feeling that life would be but the more difficult in future. But the sensation could not secure a firm hold upon her even then. Before she and her son were half way back to Philippi she was again resting on the promises of Christ, and behind the impenetrable armor of her faith was serenely facing all that life might have in store for them.

"'I will never leave thee nor forsake thee,'" she whispered in her loneliness; and feeling for the hand of Christ, was comforted.

Lydia was now about the only friend to whom she could turn in trouble, and she was denied frequent communication with her because Junius so disliked her. He had never pardoned the severe reproof the strong woman had given him about the time his insignia of office was taken from him, and he sullenly resented every favor she bestowed upon his needy household, secretly cursing her because of her good fortune, independence, and honesty, and well knowing how poor a thing he must seem in her energetic eyes. So Lydia seldom came to the little home, except for the religious services often held in its upper room, while Elizabeth rarely ventured to arouse the wrath of her husband by going to her friend.

The new fear that now tortured the poor woman day and night lurked in the question: "Is Junius really spying upon us?"

She wished, now it was too late, that she had asked questions, had insisted on knowing why Cleotas suspected him, had indignantly denied it all to the end. She looked at Junius often as he came and went, taciturn, gloomy, and forbidding in expression, and wished she dared broach the subject and have all these tantalizing doubts set at rest. But she was always dumb before him, afraid to evoke the surly temper which never lost its power to wound her.

So passed some little time, during which Junius was away often for days together, while his wife, sick with doubts and torn with conflicting duties, could live only by creeping closer to the heart of Jesus and resting her burden upon Him. If there was danger, she felt she ought to warn the little congregation; but how could she tell them she suspected her own husband of being a spy? In her anguish, one day, she forgot her gospel of trust, and, growing terrified in her human weakness, sought out Lydia and, on some flimsy pretext, begged her to have the meetings held in her home for a time.

She hoped in this way to avert the vague danger, but she simply hastened what she meant to hinder. The man had means of learning what he wished to know, and when he found that the Christians assembled at the house of the woman whom he hated, he felt that he now had everything in his own hands. He could ask no better revenge than causing the arrest in Lydia's house.

But as time went on and nothing happened, Elizabeth began to feel more secure. She told herself that Salome had mistaken her news, or Cleotas had suspected without cause. It was always easier for her loving heart to exonerate than to blame her husband, and now in her remorse at doubting him, she grew kinder and more forbearing than ever. She had not given up attending the meetings when possible, though she would never go when Junius was at home, lest he should follow and do mischief. One night, after he had gone out as usual, she rose to wrap herself in her chlamys, then stopped, hesitating and nervous, scarcely knowing whether to go or stay. On one hand was the command of the Master, "Cease not the assembling of yourselves together;" on the other, an intangible reluctance which had seized upon her so strongly as for the moment to smother her serenity and trust.

While in this state of indecision Junius suddenly stood before her. She had not heard a sound until she looked up to meet his gaze, that seemed to burn her with its intensity. She felt a glad relief at the sight of him, then quickly noted two things—he was not intoxicated, he was excited. His eyes were bright, sharp, restless, his manner alert and watchful.

"Were you going out?' he asked abruptly, glancing at the long scarf which she had thrown across the couch in her moment of indecision.

She thought that he suspected her—meant to follow her, perhaps—and she answered truthfully:

"No. I had thought of it, but was about giving it up. I am a little tired and nervous."

He nodded. "I shall not be back to-night," he said in a crisp voice, utterly unlike his usual slow, thick utterance. "Do not sit up for me. Bar the door carefully, and put your lights out early. Some of the garrison are making holiday over news from Rome."

He left as abruptly as he had entered, and she thought sadly:

"Ah, I see! He has been asked to sup with the officers and is pleased with the honor. He means to be out with them all night. What will he be to-morrow?"

She sighed, and threw herself down on the couch. She was lonely, sad, heart-broken. Tears welled up into her eyes and overflowed; sighs rose to her lips and broke in sobs. She needed consolation, companionship. She longed for the little service where, if even two or three were gathered in His name, they were assured of His presence in their midst. "Why should I not go?" she thought desperately. "I am not so afraid of the streets as of those in my own home. Junius will never know nor care where I am while he is feasting and drinking."

She rose, dashed aside the tears, and quickly wound herself in the long chlamys, covering head and face except the eyes, then, locking the door behind her, slipped like a shadow through the quiet streets, until Lydia's house was reached.

But Junius was not at a banquet. Through a treacherous slave in Lydia's employ he knew all that was necessary to his purpose. The Christians were to have a forbidden meeting there, that night, and the leader of the service was to be the keeper of the jail, whom Junius hated as he did Lydia, and for much the same reason. He would have an opportunity to strike a blow at them both by betraying them to certain Roman officers who had orders against this "seditious sect," and by betraying them he could fully avenge his wounded self-esteem —the one really strong characteristic left to him after years of besotting indulgence. Only, he must be certain Elizabeth was not there. Low as he had fallen, morose and cruel as he often was, the nobler part of him still loved and honored his wife, fully appreciating that she was his best earthly friend. Elizabeth must be spared.

So, before communicating with the officers, he had hastened home to assure himself of his wife's safe presence there, and upon leaving her had gone at once to the Romans.

The immunity which Nero had previously granted the Christians had been rather through indolence than tolerance. He was too busy with his spectacles and personal competition in the musical festivals to care for so obscure a sect. But Poppœa, whose influence was now supreme, had her reasons for favoring the Jews, and the influential of these were constantly stirring up the government to sterner measures against the followers of the Christ they had repudiated. They told the most shocking stories of the Christians' rites and practices. The breaking of bread and drinking of wine "in remembrance" were construed into an actual feeding upon human flesh and blood, and infants were said to be stolen for this revolting ceremony. Other dark practices were imputed to them, and the constant charge of conspiracy against the throne was waved in Nero's face whenever he needed special rousing. A late edict had forbidden the Christians every privilege of worship, and the decree had been lately brought to Philippi by Roman couriers, while Roman officers were instructed to enforce it to the uttermost. Hence what Junius looked upon as his opportunity.

When, after leaving Elizabeth, as he thought, safely housed for the night, he hurried back to the Castle, it was but to meet with unexpected delays. The decurion who led the men detailed for this work was not at first to be found, and an hour slipped by before the detachment was ready for service. But at length, guided by this new Judas, they started on a brisk march down into the city, choosing little-frequented streets to avoid stirring up a crowd.

When they were near the pleasant home of Lydia they broke ranks, and after a short consultation with the treacherous slave who had been won by bribes, they were one by one secretly admitted into the enclosed garden, where they could surround the house.

Here, as they stood in the deep shadow awaiting further orders, the men could plainly hear the sound of soft, sweet singing from some upper room, at which they wondered, for it scarcely seemed a suitable accompaniment to the hideous ceremonies imputed to the obscure sect.

Elizabeth had found only few at the meeting, but the moment she had received their gentle greeting, "Peace be with you," her sore spirit felt lightened of its griefs, and she was thankful she had come.

The jailer did not, for some reason, appear to take lead, and his chair was occupied by a young brother from Thessalonica, who had come to visit the church in Philippi and bring news of the brethren further west. He was a fine-looking man, ready of speech, easy of manner, and with such a genuine love of the Christ that it transfigured all he said and did. As he told them what Paul had suffered through misrepresentation, envy and malice, Elizabeth felt that her troubles were not worthy to be mentioned in comparison, and meekly asked forgiveness for her depression when she knelt in prayer, after the humble and devotional method growing more in favor daily.

The little group rose from their knees consoled and strengthened, and were in the midst of a low and tender hymn when the doorkeeper suddenly sprang into their midst, wild-eyed and white as death, with the terrifying words:

"Fly! Fly! The soldiers are upon us."

In an instant some quick-witted brother had extinguished the lights as the hasty tramp of armed men and the clashing of their spears sounded in the room, but in that one instant some had escaped. As the guards poured into the place, the torches of the link-bearers lighting the scene smokily, it was seen to be nearly deserted. A few were cowering behind benches, or fleeing madly into corners, but two or three knelt in the center, motionless and unresisting. Among these were Elizabeth and the stranger.

The would-be fugitives were quickly secured, the worshipers dragged to their feet, and a scene of horror followed as the guards went from room to room, striking down those who resisted, and dragging others from their hiding-places. But Lydia was not among these. She, with a very few who followed her, escaped by a secret way of which she only had knowledge, and were over-looked by the soldiery, who supposed all had been secured.

Elizabeth from the instant of warning had made no sound, offered no resistance. She simply dropped to her knees, recom-mending herself to Christ, and calmly awaited what might happen. Presently she felt herself being dragged across the floor, and looked up to say:

" I can walk, sir; do not exert yourself. I am not faint."

The rough prætorian, used to scenes of blood, but not expecting calm courage in a woman, looked at her in astonishment and relaxed his grasp.

" Can you?" he asked almost gently, and simply held her arm without gripping it.

She walked beside him firmly, but scarcely in the full possession of her senses. It seemed like a dream, and she could not realize it all. But she felt no fear, she had no wish to cry out. Something sustained her so that what might have been a horror, mak-ing every nerve to quiver with fright, be-came but a weird, shadow-like proceeding in which nerves were dumb and spirit steeped in calm. She always afterward remembered the night as one might recall a trance-like dream, and she called the " something " which so stayed her soul the presence of her Lord.

She knew there had been a hurried march, in which chains clanked and arms gleamed in the moonlight, then an assembling of the trembling little company on a wharf, where they sat huddled together in the night chill until they could be consigned to some galley not yet at the landing.

This appeared towards dawning and they were hustled aboard, driven like sheep into a corner of the hold, and left there to groan out their fright and despair through the rest of that night of agony. But Elizabeth slept and dreamed of heaven. She thought Junius came to her there and begged her forgive-ness, telling with penitent tears that he had God's gracious pardon. So the hard resting-place, the guards, the dangers of the ocean, were forgotten while she wandered with her restored lover and husband in fair places.

Once the guard who had chosen her as an especial charge came and looked down upon the women prisoners—there were but two—to find one in the attitude of prayer, and the other sleeping like a child in its mother's arms.

CHAPTER XXII.

A DESOLATE HEARTH.

JUNIUS did not appear with the sol-diers. Having led them to the house of Lydia, his errand was accomplished and he lingered only through curiosity, well hid-den in the shadow of the street wall, to wit-ness the result. He heard the noise of the quickly-ended struggle above, and soon, with a chuckle of inner satisfaction, saw the sol-diers reappear with at least a half-dozen prisoners huddled in their midst. Two of these were women, but in the uncertain light it was difficult to get a clear idea of their veiled figures. One, however, who walked erect and with firmness beside the half-fainting figure of the other, he felt sure was the proud Lydia, and a pang that was mingled satisfaction and regret flashed through him. In that moment of her down-fall insistent memory recalled a thousand kindly deeds from her to his household and shamed him for this dastardly requital.

A groan from one of the prisoners smote his ears as the company passed by his re-treat, and surprised him into a shiver of dis-may for the awful consequences of this night's work. Junius was quite himself for the first time in months, and though he had kept sober for a distinct purpose, and that an evil one, the divine soul within him, freed for the moment, showed it still had power to make itself heard. Just now its noiseless reproaches made him miserably uncomfort-able, and he was glad to slink away in the darkness and hasten to his home. As he passed swiftly through the deserted streets, singularly quiet after the brief commotion which had driven the guilty and the timid— a large share of Philippi's population, in fact—to shelter, he felt glad he had Eliza-beth to go to.

" She always calms and comforts me," he thought. " She is a woman of rare sweet-ness, I must own, and I have often made life a burden to her, doubtless. If she were not such a fanatic she would be almost perfect."

Yet truth compelled him to own that her faith in the teachings of Jesus had but deep-ened and strengthened all her better quali-ties, only—here was his grievance—it gave her some secret sustaining power to endure his own cruelties against her. A wife had no business with help outside her own hus-band! He told himself it made her less sub-missive.

Yet inwardly he resolved to be kinder to her than he had been. He would take some of this ill-gotten money and buy her a new tunic—she needed it sadly, poor thing!—and the next time her large, soft eyes reproached him he would turn away and say nothing, rather than lift hand or voice against her.

He soon reached his humble dwelling, and was not surprised to find it dark and securely locked. Elizabeth had evidently obeyed his instructions to the letter. He had means of admitting himself, and soon had lighted a lamp and proceeded to the little chamber, which to his astonishment he found empty. He looked around dazedly. Elizabeth gone? Oh, no! She had simply carried her sleeping-mat to the roof this mild night. He would just take a look to make sure.

Shading the lamp with his hand, he passed up the outer stairway and peered across the flat space before him. Yes, there she lay. He could see the dark figure's outline against the white parapet. How relieved he felt! He thought he would satisfy himself, however, by a closer look at her. It would steady his nerves, which were somewhat shaken by the evening's occurrences. So he crept softly over the flooring of baked clay, and bent above—not Elizabeth, but Nadab! He woke the youth quickly, with a curse, and before the latter's sleep-laden eyes were fairly open, shrieked into his ear, "Where is your mother?" for an awful terror was beginning to grip his heart-strings.

"Mother?" asked Nadab confusedly. "Has she not returned from the meeting?"

"Meeting?" hissed the terrified man in return. "Did she go? Are you certain? How do you know?"

Nadab, fully aroused now, looked sharply at his father to satisfy himself that this was not the frenzy of a drunken man, then answered calmly:

"Well, and if she did? She will soon be back now—or shall I go and fetch her? I presume, however, there will be women coming this way: there always are."

"Peace!" shrieked the tortured man. "Tell me if you are sure she went to that meeting."

"No," said Nadab slowly, gazing with astonishment at the excited man. "No, I am not sure, because I did not see her go. But she never goes anywhere except to the meetings or to Lydia's."

The last words but added intensity to the husband's forebodings. To Lydia's! To the house where he had led the soldiers, making merry in stifled whispers over the unconsciousness of their prey! To Lydia's! He remembered the two female figures in the grasp of the rude soldiery—one half-fainting, one proudly erect—and was seized with such an agony as only a strong man can feel when for the first time he sees himself guilty of some horrible crime.

Once, the other day, when he had asked the decurion from Rome the question, "And why are Christians wanted at the capital just now?" the officer had answered with a laugh: "There is a fresh load of wild beasts from the jungles, and we must find food for them."

The laughing words came back now to burn themselves into his consciousness. As in a flash of light he saw his Elizabeth, fairest and purest of women, standing for one uncertain minute in the broad arena of the amphitheatre, surrounded by fierce, starving beasts let loose from their dens upon her, and it seemed as if all the neglect and unkindness of a lifetime had become animate to torture him through her sufferings.

"Hurry, Nadab!" he called hoarsely. "Run to Lydia's—I cannot go. Rouse the slaves—find Eumene! Make sure—make sure whether she was there, or not. Do you hear, boy?"

"Was there? You mean is there, of course. If she had left, she would be here by now. And I would not be anxious, father. Lydia always sees that she has company home, even if she has to send one of the slaves with her."

"Go! go!—hurry!" was all the wretched man could say; and Nadab felt that for some reason this frenzy of his meant more than any drunken ravings he had ever known.

While the youth was away Junius paced to and fro before the house, watching every shadow, hearing every flutter of a leaf, in the desperate hope that Elizabeth might appear. Oh! to see her come around that corner, her graceful figure stepping lightly, her modest face veiled in white! His Elizabeth!—fairer than the day he married her. His wife! who was to him the embodiment of all good, all hope, all faith in a better life to come!

He called distractedly upon the gods he knew; he invoked the Lares and Penates of his desolated hearth; he cried to the stars shining coldly in the midnight darkness, and then—because He was the God Elizabeth loved and worshiped—he called upon the Christ to help, to forgive, to bring her back to the husband who, all too late, was learning her true worth.

He grew a trifle calmer at length, and when Nadab reappeared with a well-wrapped female figure beside him, the greatness of his relief made him almost faint.

"Elizabeth!" he sobbed, holding out his arms. "My wife!"

It was Lydia who answered. Sweeping aside her veil, she turned her blazing eyes upon him.

"Vile, unhappy man!" she cried in an outraged voice. "You sought to betray us, and have bereft yourself! Elizabeth was near the outer door and one of the first, doubtless, to be seized. I escaped at the earliest word of alarm, calling upon her to follow, but she either did not hear, or had no time to obey. They took her with them."

Junius staggered back against his desolate house-wall, and a deep groan burst from his lips. Lydia was safe! Elizabeth was taken! And he, the traitor, the spy, was left to bear his success as best he could! They passed indoors. Poor Nadab, hardly yet comprehending, followed them, weeping silently.

A few words convinced Junius that his wife was indeed on her way to Rome to confront all sorts of unknown horrors, and the man in him woke from sloth and selfishness to deep repentance and earnest action.

"Lydia," he said brokenly, "your reproaches are just. I, and I alone, am to blame! I believed my wife was safe, and in betraying others to ruin I have been overwhelmed myself."

Lydia, seeing his misery, was softened. "You have not the power to ruin any of us, Junius. That rests with God, and He will not let your treachery cause us harm that is not in His perfect plan for our future betterment. Your sin is just as great, for it was willful and malicious; but, thank God, Elizabeth is in the care of One more tender and trustworthy than yourself. But she is doubtless lost to you forever."

"No, no!" The cry was sharp with anguish. "I shall follow her to Rome. I shall save her, if possible; and if not, I will at least die with her. Nadab, will you come with your father, or stay behind?"

"I will go to my mother," said the lad; and Lydia, bursting into tears, besought Heaven's blessing on their enterprise.

Their preparations took but a few hours. They had little money and must make the long journey by land, mostly on foot. It was a terrible undertaking, but they did not stop to think of difficulties now—only of results.

Lydia, convulsed with weeping over the sad fate of her friend, drew Nadab to one side and pressed her purse into his hand.

"Take it," she whispered, "and make it shorten the way whenever possible. But husband it well, lest it be spent unworthily."

Nadab bowed his head, and thought, "But how shall I ever keep father from spending it for strong wines during all that long journey?" For neither yet understood that Elizabeth's prayer was answered and her burden rolled away. From that night on, Junius never touched the red liquor again.

Meanwhile, in Thessalonica, Agistha sat awaiting the return of Herklas from his journey to Philippi and wondered that he did not come, for he was one of those honest and comfortable people who never promise what they cannot in all human probability perform, and he had said he would be back three days ago.

Feeling restless and uneasy, she thought she would take her baby boy, Gaius, and go to the "great house," as they called the villa of Ænone, for a little visit with its mistress.

She found the latter in her private room surrounded by her women, to whom she was giving rapid orders, but she stopped to welcome Agistha, fondle the baby, and exclaim excitedly:

"What do you think, child? Gaius is called to Rome for an indefinite time, and he is to take Ian and myself with him. We are to start in a day or two, and I am very busy giving orders for the conduct of my household while I am gone, and making preparations for the journey. But sit down, Agistha, and I will dismiss the slaves for a while.— Go! You have your orders for the present and can come for more later.—There! Now we can have a good rest and visit. But how forlorn you look, my dear! Have you been crying? What is troubling you?"

Agistha broke down at this, and sobbed out:

"Herklas has not come back."

"Is that all? Foolish child! What is there to worry over? He has simply been detained."

"But he is three days behind time. And he promised, Lady Ænone. You know Herklas always keeps his word."

"Yes, he is careful about it; but even the best of men fail sometimes. He has found old friends who are making merry over him, be assured. Indeed, I never expect Gaius till I see him—ah, here he is now!"

The master entered, starting a little as he noticed Agistha; then, seeing the traces of tears, he said quickly: "You have heard, then?"

"Heard—what?" she asked, looking up at him with anxious eyes.

Gaius turned to his wife perplexedly. "I was about to ask you to go to her. There is news from Philippi—I just heard it from some traders on their way west. Does Agistha know?"

"No, no! What is it? She is worried because Herklas does not return."

Both the women had risen, and Agistha stood holding her baby closely, quite pallid with alarm.

"I hope the report is exaggerated," he said kindly, "but they say that while he was addressing a secret meeting they were raided by soldiers, and a part of them carried off to Rome."

"And Herklas—did he escape?" shrieked Agistha.

Gaius sadly shook his head. "They say he was certainly taken. But do not feel that all is lost, Agistha. I am going to start for Rome in a day or two, and I have some influence there. Be assured I shall use all I have to procure his release."

Agistha dropped to her knees and held up her arms—the baby still in them—crying:

"Oh, master! dear, kind Gaius, take us with you! Take your little namesake and his mother. Oh, beg for us, dear mistress! Take me as your slave—anything—only let me go to my husband!"

"There! there! Of course you shall go. Say that she can, Gaius. I will make her my first lady-in-waiting, and Chloe can look after little Gaius and Ian together. Say yes, husband!" pleaded Ænone, her kind heart wrung with grief for her favorite.

"Well, it shall be as you wish. I did not intend—however, it is no more than Herklas would do for me. Yes, yes, she and the babe shall go."

"My blessed master!"

"Run, Agistha, and put everything in order at your home. Ah, Gaius, you never fail me! There, weep no more, little one; we will surely save your husband."

"Be ready by Thursday, for I cannot delay another hour. But what if this news should prove to be a mistake?" said Gaius.

"Then he will certainly be here by that time to speak for himself. If he is not, I will be ready for the first boat."

Agistha was as good as her word. When morning was still in her first blush, next market-day, the Lady Ænone's train was awaiting embarkation upon a special galley finely fitted up, and flying the imperial colors. Above it a gay awning was spread, and cushions were placed beneath for the greater comfort of the ladies.

But Agistha scarcely noticed these details. It would have been all the same had this been a dingy merchantman from Alexandria, the floors swimming in bilge-water, and the sails torn and soiled with hard usage. Pale and still, she crossed the gangplank with her baby, but one idea in her mind—she was going to her husband.

CHAPTER XXIII.

IN PROUD ROME.

IT was a long sail from Neapolis to Rome, and one embarking late in the season was never sure of not being forced to winter somewhere on the way. But Cleotas and Salome with their little family had sailed in early springtime and been favored with fair winds throughout the voyage, thus they made a quick and pleasant passage. Hector and his wife Céleste, with their little Aulus and Salome, were waiting impatiently to greet the travelers, who landed at one of the lower wharves on the Tiber, and were thence transported by a barge to the city landing.

Upon this barge, gay with streamers and music, were the Roman family, and Hector had spared no expense or trouble to make this welcome to his long-lost sister and her family a truly royal one.

It was a glad hour. The meeting between Hector and Salome was full of deep emotion for both. Looking upon her noble, matronly countenance, he felt that she had grown older in wisdom and self-control, as well as in years, and thought that even as a maiden she had never been more attractive. He liked her gentle firmness with her children, and was pleased at the deference and respect her manly husband paid her.

Hector had found a dwelling for them in the north-eastern suburb, near the gardens of Sallust; the encampment of the Prætorian guards, whence his duties took him daily, being not far beyond. Before he would let them occupy it, however, he insisted they should all visit him in his own home, that the families might make acquaintance at last.

The two ladies soon became warmly attached, and Hector daily grew more appreciative of the sturdy virtues which kept his brother-in-law so evenly balanced, and so unafraid. As he went from station to station, enforcing that discipline which made the armies of Rome invincible, Hector felt that there was a better kind of discipline, not enforced, but voluntary, and full of joy inexpressible—the discipline of a soul brought into harmony with the Higher Will; and as he studied this Christian brother, brave as he had never been, he first marveled, then loved, then longed to imitate. But alas! Self-interest and iron law, under the most lawless of sovereigns, seemed to bind him in chains too strong for breaking. Like Agrippa, he was " almost persuaded "; but also like him, the glitter of worldly rank outshone the Heavenly beams.

In a few weeks the new-comers were quite at home in the Imperial City, and Salome never tired of going about in her litter to admire the high and massive buildings with their wilderness of columns, the narrow paved streets teeming with their motley crowds, the shops beneath the great houses divided into living apartments above, which were gay with every salable luxury, the temples beautiful as artists could fashion—though to her thought degraded to base uses—and the blooming gardens of the patricians, both public and private.

Everywhere she observed statues dedicated to different deities, for if pagan worship was strong in Philippi, it was all-in-all here. These statues, placed in the intersections of the streets, outlining forums, baths, theatres, and halls of justice, decorating every shop and booth, standing guard over every private doorway, were of all substances, from the precious metals and the finest Italian marbles down to hideous little carved effigies, rudely fashioned from a block of wood. Every shop was dedicated to some deity, every trade made oblations to some patron of the skies; even the children's toys were consecrated to Bacchus, the god of fun and revelry. Nothing, however trivial, took place without consultation with the Augurs, who calculated their prophecies from the flight of birds, or the direction of the lightnings in a storm; or appealing to Horespices, who gravely inspected the entrails of fowl and beast for their decisions, and gave them with a solemn voice, although, as Cato has told us, " they could not help laughing when they met in the streets " over the credulity of the masses who heaped their coffers with silver.

Salome noted, too, in her thoughtful manner, the intense contrasts in life here displayed. On one hand was a poverty that bereft life of all freedom, beauty, almost of hope; on the other, a luxury that seemed steeped in wildest extravagance. At the least movement the higher patrician glittered with splendor. His clothing was a mass of gems. His lectica, or chariot, shone with gold and silver-work, and was upholstered in the richest stuffs from Damascus. Lictors ran before him with their fasces (a bundle of rods with an axe in the center), clearing a passage through the crowded streets, which were only the width of a village lane; and, not content with this, the most showy fashionables trailed about with a retinue of slaves, until the nuisance was getting almost unbearable, for the confined roadways were often blocked by this foolish display.

The short winter was blossoming into spring when, one day, Cleotas came in hastily and sought his wife in her distaff-room. His face was quite pale with some unusual emotion, and he looked at her keenly an instant, where she sat calmly at her embroidery, before he said in a controlled voice:

" Salome, I have strange news for you."

She half rose, startled at his manner. " What is it, Cleotas? Has anything happened to Hector—to his family?"

" No, it is about Junius. Junius is in Rome."

" In Rome—here? And without Elizabeth? Surely he has not forsaken her!"

" No, she—sit down, dear. It is a long story—she is somewhere here, or on the way."

" Here—or at sea? How strange you are, my husband! Tell me all about it."

" I will, Salome, but it is a sad story. Elizabeth was arrested with some other Christians, and the soldiers started with them for Rome—at least they are known to have sailed from Neapolis not three months after we left there, but—"

" And have not reached here yet? Oh, they are lost at sea!"

" No, Junius and Nadab think they are

not, or we would have had news of it in some way. But they may have been wintering somewhere, driven by storms to seek shelter in a foreign port."

"So Nadab is here also? Poor boy! He must be heart-broken. But Junius—has Junius done all this for her?"

"Yes, and evidently is a changed man, Salome. He refuses to touch wine, though greatly worn with his long journey, is thoughtful and kind for Nadab, and—"

"But where are they? Why did you not bring them here at once, Cleotas?" springing to her feet with hospitable solicitude. "Surely you would not let them lodge elsewhere?"

"No; they are here, my dear. I left them to make their ablutions and replace their soiled garments before seeing you—for there is something more, my wife. You say Nadab must be broken-hearted. True, he is very sorrowful, but youth and hope brace him to bear this blow. It is Junius who is broken in spirit."

"Junius? That surly, neglectful, cruel man! It does not seem possible."

"Yes, it is, because remorse is what tears the heart-strings beyond repair, my Salome, and Junius is remorseful to self-abasement because—he is to blame."

"To blame? For Elizabeth's arrest? Oh, the wretch! the unnatural monster! the—"

"Peace, peace, child! Not so fast! Let me tell you all;" and amid Salome's sobs and broken exclamations, Cleotas made her understand just how the sad event had happened.

At first she felt as if she could never forgive Junius, never even see him, but Cleotas reminded her gravely:

"Salome, we pray to be forgiven as we forgive. If God should not even overlook our mistakes, in what evil case we would be!"

Weeping and torn with conflicting emotions, she threw herself into his arms.

"Oh, my husband! You are so kind, so good, so strong! Show me the right, that I may pursue it."

"There is only one way, and that is the Christ's, my child. We must help and comfort Junius and Nadab, and with them watch and wait for Elizabeth, to give her such succor as will be possible. There is, of course, the faint chance that she may be even now languishing in some dungeon here in Rome, though so far diligent inquiry has failed to locate her. But when you see Junius and comprehend the entire change in him, you will feel differently."

Cleotas had spoken truly. One glance into the haggard face and deeply sorrowful eyes of the bereft husband filled Salome's warm heart with sudden pity. Its expression was so pathetically humble, despairing, patient, that it would have touched a stone, and Salome was far enough from such hardness.

He and the Thracian girl had never liked each other, but now the desolate man turned to her as the one who had been nearest and dearest to his wife, while Salome, stirred to deepest sympathy, soon grew tender to him in their common sorrow, and felt a daughterly affection developing for this Roman whom she had once despised.

For a few days Nadab's young grief was almost forgotten in the novelty and bewilderment of his surroundings. He roamed the streets all day, looking, looking, till his eyes ached, and felt each night that he had only just begun to realize the extent, grandeur, and singularities of this capital city of the whole world.

But Junius, if he noticed, did not heed. Each morning he took his long walk across the city to the wharves, and there spent his day between the Emporium, or grain pier, and the Marmorata, a special dock for landing stone and marble, not knowing just where or when he might see some storm-tossed barque come sailing in, bringing the most precious freight this world could give him—his Elizabeth.

Sometimes, seated upon a post, he looked out upon the waters of the Tiber, here broadened into a harbor-like roadway from the ocean, and watched with his longing eyes the strange craft from every port along the Mediterranean's shores. He saw the government galleys equipped for warfare, the fishermen's junks starting out for their season's work, the patrician pleasure-barges, gay with streamers and silken awnings, and the low, black, square-hulled convict ships.

But the ship he sought—the one which would bring news of the wife he had betrayed—did not come, and sometimes, looking into the soft blue of the dancing waves, he wondered if it would not be better if both were sleeping far beneath them together? For oh! what might not await her in Rome? Again he would be seized with the conviction that she was already there, lodged in some forgotten dungeon, and he would wander distraught from forum to castle, asking wild questions, and growing momentarily more unmanageable. At these times it needed all the persuasions and assurances of both Cleotas and Hector (the latter having been enlisted in his cause) to quiet him. But these days were few. Generally he was patient to dumbness, and only his gaunt, hungry eyes betokened the agony gnawing at his heart.

One morning as he entered the shipping office where he made his daily inquiries, he saw a man he had often noticed there before, a patrician of high rank, undoubtedly, whose frank face and agreeable manner attracted him. This day they advanced at the same moment, and he courteously made way for Junius, giving him a sympathizing glance as he did so. But Junius had scarcely finished his queries when the man stepped forth quickly, to say:

"Just what I was about to ask! Are you interested in these people, too, my friend?"

Junius bowed his head. "My wife is on board, sire," he answered, with the respect befitting the other's rank.

"Indeed?" The patrician seemed interested. "I see you wear the dress of Macedonia, my native country; may I ask what city you are from?"

"From Philippi, sire."

"Ah! And I am of Thessalonica. The ship about which we are anxious had several Christians on board, I understand."

His look was inquiring, and Junius answered it. "It had. My wife is one of that sect, sire. They arrested her at a meeting, and I have come by land to see what can be done for her relief."

The other listened intently. "At a meeting? It must have been the same. See here, my good man, the wind is sharp this morning. Come with me to my home for a little. I too have on board this missing galley a friend who was also arrested at a meeting in Philippi, and I would gladly learn something more definite of that event if possible. My chariot is waiting outside. I pray you come."

Junius consented, but with reluctance. It was torture for him to recall that night even in thought, and how could he acknowledge to another his part in the sad result? But his repentance was sincere, and he felt it a well-merited punishment that he must always be pointed out as the betrayer of those whom he now gladly claimed as brothers and sisters in Christ. Then, too, he might glean some new facts or gain some new friends helpful to Elizabeth, and for her

sake he could not refuse this man's courtesy. So he followed him into his finely-wrought chariot, with scarce a thought of its magnificence, though once Junius would have swelled with pride over such an honor, and was borne swiftly to the palatial home of Gaius—for this was he—upon Palatine Hill.

Here he followed the latter through vestibule and ostium into the atrium, or parlor, where even the absorption of Junius was not so great as to quite blind him to its beauty. A noble vista opened before him, of which this lofty apartment was but the beginning. From the paneled walls, painted in rare designs, beautiful statuary was set out on pedestals of onyx and malachite in rich relief, while the floor, inlaid with marble in charming patterns, was a work of art in itself. Directly in the center was the impluvium, or square of water, from the center of which rose a feathery spray, and above this cooling basin, protected by a brass railing, the roof curved inwards from all sides to an opening corresponding in shape and size, through which the light poured in, transforming the vapors into broken rainbows, wavering and graceful as ribbons blown in the breeze. A striped awning, now rolled to one side, could if necessary be drawn across this skylight, shutting out the too ardent sun of noonday.

Gaius seated his guest upon an ottoman, drew another close beside him, and the two were soon in earnest converse. Junius told the whole story plainly and without reserve, even to his own baseness and low estate. Gaius listened without comment, but as he glanced now and then into that countenance upon which its story was graven in lines cut by regret and despair, he could not feel other than intense pity for this misguided, suffering man.

"I aimed," said Junius slowly, "to strike at two people who had incurred my displeasure, and God drove the blow home to my own heart."

"Then both those people escaped?" asked Gaius.

"They did."

"Strange how little we control events after all!" mused the politarch. "Even Christ pleased not Himself, yet no act of His ever went astray." Then turning brusquely to Junius he asked, "What think you of your wife's faith? Was Jesus of Nazareth the Christ?"

Junius bent his head. "I believe He was and is," was the earnest answer; and Gaius felt this was a conviction of slow growth, perhaps, but laid in foundations deep and strong.

As they conversed further the host told how, upon his own journey to Rome, undertaken so near the same time, the ship had been obliged to keep to a southerly course, in order to avoid a long and terrible storm which raged for days along the Adriatic shores and doubtless occasioned much delay to shipping in that region. He had long ago decided that the convict ship must have gone into winter quarters, if not lost at sea, and was now daily expecting word of it, since navigation was opened once more. He said, moreover, that he had positively assured himself these special prisoners were not in Rome, as he had instituted the strictest search for them through every prison and castle.

When Junius finally departed, it was to feel greatly encouraged and strengthened, and the parting was most friendly, each promising to acquaint the other with any news he might receive.

February had passed, March was coming in shod with sandals of green, and it was early morning. The air was soft with odors and crisp with recent rains, and the streets were lively with slaves hurrying to the houses of their masters for their daily rations of food. Not till later would the heavy teams for traffic be allowed, and now there was plenty of bustle without noise, for the bare feet trod lightly, and the servants knew better than to disturb their indolent sleeping patrons by too loud talk and laughter. One of them, however, ventured to approach the house of Cleotas, arouse the porter, and inquire for Junius. He was summoned, and the fair-haired youth of a foreign cast of countenance (whom we would have recognized as Harold) stepped forward with his message.

"Sir, my master, Gaius, the politarch, has news of a certain ship lately landed at Puteoli. There are said to be Christians on board, notably one of celebrity well known both at Philippi and Thessalonica—the Apostle Paul, who is being brought to Rome for trial. My master intends to go by land to meet these people, and would be pleased to have you and your friends accompany the party, of which there are not a few."

Junius thanked the messenger and promised to join the party immediately. Then dismissing him, he hastened to send the word to the private rooms of Cleotas and Nadab. It quickly brought the household, excited, inquisitive, and eager to join the expedition. Cleotas and Nadab prepared to accompany Junius, and Salome was almost rebellious at being left behind, for once bewailing her sex, that it should prevent her.

But she did not cease to aid her women in making ready the early meal and helping the men in their preparations, though tears kept rising to her eyes as she thought that her dear Elizabeth might be of the convict group, and if so would be longing for one loving face of womankind to greet her after this long and wearisome journey. She mentally resolved that she would at least be carried in her litter as far as the Porta Latina, an arched gate of the inner wall, or possibly even to the place of tombs beyond, and after the departure of the others, went about her own preparations, comforted by this thought.

She was sitting at her embroidery, awaiting the time to go, when Nadab came rushing in again in great excitement.

"Come, hurry!" he cried with boyish roughness. "There are ladies going, too—some from the politarch's household, and others—and I have come back for you. We are to join them in the suburbs. I will run and order your litter while you make ready, and then will conduct you the shortest way to the arch under the aqueduct—what do you call it?"

"The Porta Capena? So far as that? Oh, Nadab, how good you are! I will not keep you waiting a minute."

Salome hurried to call her maids, and was at once in the center of a bustle of preparation, while Nadab ran out to summon her litter-bearers and promise them liberal recompense for their swiftest work. Then he mounted his mule and impatiently awaited her outside, though in fact it was not five minutes later when Salome entered her litter, and the little group started briskly down the hilly street.

CHAPTER XXIV.

THE MEETING AT THE THREE TAVERNS.

IT was always a slow task making one's way through the crowded Suburra, but having left behind that somewhat unsavory locality, with its many shops and questionable resorts, they rapidly skirted the Palatine, its roomy palaces and gardens in sharp contrast to the squalor behind them, and struck off at a goodly pace past the villas lining the way. Presently they reached the Porta Capena, its arch always dripping from the aqueduct above it, and clattered on quite into the suburbs, where fine mausoleums lined the white-paved road for miles.

It was a spring morning, and the whole atmosphere was rich with those first faint earthy scents which each year thrill us anew with their promise of future verdure and beauty. While Salome was delightedly sniffing the perfume of the newly upturned farm-lands on either hand, she heard Nadab give an exclamation, and saw him make a dash forward. Leaning out between her curtains, she quickly discovered the cause. The party they were to accompany stood awaiting them, gathered in a knot beneath a clump of mulberry trees, and a horseman spurred forwards instantly at sight of Nadab, to cry out approvingly: "In excellent time, my boy! We have but just arrived."

Then the speaker came close to the litter to whisper merrily, as he bent to the beloved face between the curtains:

"Ah, my Salome, you always conquer in the end! I was happy to be able to send for you. Here they all are, the Lady Ænone and her friends, and waiting to greet you."

He gave a quick command, and the litter-bearers brought their burden abreast of the more beautiful lectica in blue and steel, from which a bright, intelligent face, its veil pushed aside for the moment, looked forth as the owner said:

"And this, then, is the wife of Cleotas? I am glad to know her, and have her company this fair morning. Let me present my friend, Agistha."

A pale, sad, young countenance, with darkly shadowed eyes, peered out, and Agistha and Salome greeted each other in friendly fashion. Others of both sexes were in the party, but Gaius with a laughing word took command, urging haste, and the little procession, headed by two lictors, proceeded on its way, the horsemen in front, then the litters—the Lady Ænone's taking precedence—and lastly Nadab on his mule.

In this way they traversed a distance of seventeen miles to a place of resort known as the Three Taverns, where, in consideration of the tired litter-bearers, the party was to rest, enjoy the noon meal, and await

the coming of Paul and such other Christians as might be with him.

None of the company had reason to expect to meet any nearer friend than he, yet, in spite of themselves, in the hearts of both Agistha and Junius was a trembling hope that the dear partner each longed for might be found with Paul.

As the women gathered in the room set apart for them in the inn, they soon made acquaintance and talked eagerly, for they had been brought together by a common interest. All reverenced the great Paul and longed to prove their friendship, even though he came to them in chains, and Salome was full of excitement at thought of seeing once more the man who had first thoroughly convinced her of the truth as it is in Jesus. But as she watched Agistha's tremulous absorption and lack of appetite, she pushed aside her own hot wheaten cakes and honey to ask eagerly:

"Is it possible you really expect to see your husband in this company? You see I know of your loss from Junius, who has told me of you. If so, then doubtless Elizabeth will be with them, too; but I dare not hope it."

"I am not sure that I 'hope' it," replied Agistha, "but I do feel it. Ever since I awoke to hear this news, I have felt that I should see him—but oh! what then? What then?"

She turned away, choking with emotion, and Salome's pitying eyes met Ænone's.

"True enough," she murmured, "but I had not thought of that. I have been all absorbed in the idea of seeing these good people, of hearing, perhaps, some news of my friends, and I forgot they come as captives, to be consigned to the dungeons beneath the forum before we can do more than exchange a word with them."

Yet, in spite of future forebodings, present hope could not but buoy them up. Only to see those from whom they had been so long separated, if this was to be, only to be sure they were alive, was a great boon, and insensibly their spirits rose as each felt all the others in perfect accord with herself. Gaius presently came in to say that some of the men had decided to ride on, hoping to meet Paul's party soon, and would leave the lictors behind to attend upon the ladies. These now gathered close behind the lattices to watch them ride away, then settled themselves for a longer, or shorter, waiting.

The afternoon dragged slowly on, and

nothing happened. It was nearing the ninth hour. Two or three, including Ænone, had fallen asleep, and Salome was dozing, when Agistha, who had been sitting in severe quiet within the embrasure of the window overhanging the court below, made a quick movement and bent forward attentively, her hand behind her ear. In the distance, far and faint, she thought she could discern voices and the tread of many feet, mingled with a clicking noise that suggested the impact of steel on steel. From where she sat only a portion of the paved court was visible, but that portion included the wide-arched opening connecting it with the street. It was thence she now turned her eyes in a piercing gaze. The sounds she had heard grew more distinct, and she knew them, now, for the tread of feet shackled by fetters.

Yes! Here through the arch comes a mounted guard—another—their shirts of mail gleaming like fish-scales in the sun; two more, then—oh! how her heart beat as her glance ran like lightning over the first four of the prisoners, all chained together! Not one was known to her. But here come two more between soldiers, with wrist-fetters only, and these she recognizes as Paul and his companion, Aristarchus of Thessalonica, a well-known brother there. Are there no more? Ah! what is this? Two women on a pillion. She looked quickly around and called, "Salome, madam, come at once!" then turned back to her eager watch, while Salome, thus suddenly aroused from her light doze, sprang up and came forward with a shower of questions.

But Agistha did not answer. Instead, she raised a hand, and gave a cry that awoke all the sleepers, "My husband! My husband!" for behind the women, again in fours, are other men, and among them—though bearded, haggard, and browned like an Arab—Herklas!

Her cry was caught up by Salome, who had recognized Elizabeth in one of the women, and the two simultaneously made a dash for the corridor outside, followed closely by Ænone and the other women. So far, Salome had no idea of the name of Agistha's husband. It had not been mentioned before her. When Gaius or Ænone had spoken of him they gave him his title in the church; the few times Agistha had referred to him she named him as her husband; and in the brown-bearded man just marched into the court of the inn, there was

but little trace, to a casual glance, of the boy who had left home nine years before. Then, too, her whole thought now centered in Elizabeth, except such as all gave to the Apostle, whose fate they watched with deep interest.

When the women reached the court they found it filled with an excited company—not only their own group, but quite a party who had gone further on, even to Appii-Forum, the first mule-station on the twenty-mile canal built by Augustus to drain the Pontine Marshes, and an important point for travelers approaching from the coast. So it was a large cavalcade of horses, donkeys, and foot-passengers who now thronged the paved square to its utmost capacity.

But our hurrying women had only a dim impression of the scene as they poured out of the house door. Agistha, who had outrun the rest, slipped in and out amid the throng, supple as a serpent, and Ænone followed at her heels, scarcely less excited. But Salome turned from them and ran close by the wall with her eyes fixed upon a pillion, half concealed between two mounted men who hovered close about it, and whom she saw to be Junius and Nadab.

"Elizabeth!" she called, "Elizabeth!"

At the cry Herklas, in the center of the mass, turned surprisedly—turned only to see a slender figure, which did not at all belong to the strangely familiar voice, reaching for him despite the guard's angry protest—and forgot the odd impression in the rapture of beholding his wife at his very side, and behind her his tried friend and patron.

Salome was answered by Elizabeth's sweet voice, placid as ever:

"Here we are, all safe, dear sister. My husband, my son, and you. How gracious is the Lord! Ah, Salome, this pays for all."

She clasped her friend close, then turned again to Junius, whose eyes scarcely left her face. The joy, the surprise, of finding her own where she had looked only for new strangeness and fresh terrors, made Elizabeth radiant. One glance, one word, his very presence, had been enough to convince her of her husband's repentance, and it seemed to her for the time being that she was indeed repaid for months of peril and hardship by sea and land, in this unexpected joy vouchsafed to her.

But Elizabeth, even in this supreme moment, could not be selfish. She said eagerly:

"Dear Salome, let me bespeak your kindest attention for my friend here with me.

Her name is Eunice, and you have met her at home. We were taken together, and I can never tell all she has been to me on this terrible journey!"

Salome hastened to greet the delicate young creature who had outlived so many perils, but had time for only a word, as the soldiers ordered back the crowd, and formed quickly about the prisoners, commanding that they seat themselves on the pavement, as food would be given them before they resumed the march. One of the guards thrust Junius aside and bade the women dismount, but Gaius now appeared, ready to greet the friends of his new friends.

He saw the look upon the husband's face at being thus treated, and said cheerily:

" Ah, friend, I see you have been made happy as well as Agistha. And this is the dear wife you have looked for so long? Peace be with you, lady. And now, courage, all! I know the centurion in command, and as soon as I can get speech with him I shall ask that we be allowed to serve all these Christian friends, also the guards, who must not be overlooked,"—he bowed courteously to the helmet beside him, and received a ready military salute in return,—" with a good and abundant meal; then with bodies and spirits both refreshed, we can accompany them on the last stage of their march."

The guard's visage expressed satisfaction, and he considerately stepped back, leaving the reunited to themselves. Thus Gaius, winning all with courteous words and well-bestowed gifts, was allowed to carry out his hospitable plan, and soon as excellent a supper as the inn could furnish was smoking on a hastily-improvised table in the court.

Once more these dear ones met in perfect accord, putting aside, for the time, all fears and forebodings, to enjoy to the full a meeting fraught with hope and comfort for each. Paul conversed with those who had come so far to greet him, hearing their good report of the churches he had founded, and giving in return such counsel and spiritual advice as would linger in their memories for life.

For Elizabeth it was an hour set out in whitest light. With hands clasped in those of husband and son she turned her shining eyes upward in thanksgiving for the mercies of God. When Junius brokenly tried to explain the terrible mistake which had brought her here, she checked him.

" It was the will of the Christ, my husband. He has honored me by allowing me also to come to testify in Rome, even as Paul will do. And in spite of shipwreck and the many perils we have gone through, these months have been blessed to us all, for Paul has directed us, and Christ has been with us, to save and comfort. Do not reproach yourself, or pity me—and never, Junius, speak of forgiveness between us two! I have always pleaded for you as you never could for yourself; it is enough that God has answered me, and you are His— and mine."

The brief rest over, the little company took up its line of march again, and even the chains seemed to have grown lighter because of this companionship and cheer. The guard in charge of the women, through some mysterious influence, even allowed Elizabeth to ride in Salome's litter, saying it would lighten the mule's load, and fell a pace or two behind, allowing Junius and Nadab to ride on either hand. Evidently Gaius and Cleotas had busied themselves to some purpose! Thus they marched, sometimes talking low and intimately, again listening to the wise discourse of Paul, anon breaking into singing, sweet and holy.

But a change was made in the cavalcade as they neared the city. Elizabeth was requested to resume her seat on the pillion, the prisoners were bunched together, and the guard formed a hollow square about them. In this orderly manner they were conducted to the forum, and there formally delivered over to Burrhus, who consigned them to the captain of the guard to be led to the dungeons.

With wet eyes the party from Rome called out their farewells, watched them till they disappeared, then slowly turned away to their homes, unable to do more for those they loved. Yet that night Junius slept like a child, and Agistha, clasping her baby to her heart, thanked God for this sweet day, whatever the future might have in store.

CHAPTER XXV.

A TEST OF LOYALTY.

A WEEK or so before the coming of the prisoners to Rome, Hector and Aulus Clotius were closeted with a man who gave evidences of a long journey, and whose air of furtive anxiety bespoke him either a fugitive from justice, or a messenger bearing secret tidings which would imperil his life, if discovered. He, in fact, announced himself as an ambassador from Marcus Salvius Otho, the former husband of Poppœa, now in Lusitania, and owned to bearing dispatches of a treasonable character. He claimed it could scarcely be wondered at that this outraged and banished husband should hate his usurper and long to be avenged, saying further that his spies at court had kept him constantly informed of events there. When he thus learned of the covert rebuffs aimed at Aulus Clotius, he shrewdly singled him out as one who would be ready to further the interests of any opponent to the throne. In a word, Otho was longing to supplant Nero, and felt that Aulus would prove a powerful ally, could he win his allegiance. His influence with the army was great, and his bravery proverbial.

This was well known to the messenger himself, who had long been acquainted with Aulus in the army, and could judge of his abilities, he being also a military officer, though in another branch of the service. Hector, as one more directly in touch with the Prætorian Guards, had been also admitted to the interview, and sat in grave silence as the messenger unfolded his plan.

This was cunningly devised and complete in detail, but as Aulus examined the papyri, and listened to the concise explanations, he shook his head dubiously.

"Rome is not yet ripe for the change," he protested. "We all know what Nero is, but the populace does not. He gives it plenty of festivals, games, and spectacles—why, he has just had fifty lions, thirty leopards, and twenty-seven magnificent tigers added to the dens in the amphitheatre! Then coin is plenty here, if the provincials do complain, and favors are given largely. No, Plutus, it will not do! We must wait."

The messenger turned his dark, disappointed face upon Hector. "And do you, too, counsel delay, my brave centurion?"

Hector was sitting with his chin upon his hand and his eyes bent on the floor. "I am thinking," he answered slowly, "whether it is worth while to exchange the leopard for the panther. If one's bones are to be crunched, it matters little about the teeth, save that the sharper they are the quicker the end."

Plutus laughed with some amusement. "You think Otho but a new Nero with another name?" he asked.

"I fancy either would hold Rome in his palm and squeeze it for his own indulgence.

If there were a man, now, who could be careful of his subjects, watchful of their interests, self-forgetful even unto death, and—"

"Bah! Would you expect a Christus?" laughed the messenger. "You see how little He was fitted to keep His Jewish kingdom. Why, He died like a thief upon the cross! No, no! what we want is a man, indeed, but not such a man! Rome would not know what to do with a ruler who did not ride over her in his chariot. She adores a tyrant!"

Hector sighed. He felt this was too near the truth to be denied. Nero had reached a summit whose glory set him apart, and the populace gazed, and hailed him a god. But Hector, knowing the stains upon his record, the pettinesses of his character, the cowardice beneath his bravado, felt a deep disgust which it was difficult, always, to conceal. He had begun to long for purity, and this hypocrite in a high place revolted him to the depths.

The interview was long, but conclusive. Both Aulus and Hector refused to act in the matter, and after mutual pledges of profound secrecy, Plutus withdrew. When he had left their presence Aulus turned to his client.

"Hector," he said impulsively, "I am glad you stood by me in this. You said rightly when you inferred that such a change of masters would be but a change of evils. And yet the day is coming—yes, we will live to see it—when this people will turn and rend their Cæsar, even as now they deify him. Do you not believe me?"

Hector nodded thoughtfully. "It is only a question of time, Sir Prætor." Then in a lower tone: "But, meanwhile, if he is determined to crush you? I have heard of this latest slight, my Aulus; you were entirely ignored in the last festival. Where every singer appeared, the voice of Aulus Clotius was silent; where the viol-players numbered fourscore, the instrument of the brave general and prætor was absent."

A quick flush dyed the other's bronzed cheek. "Such an insult is in reality an ovation, my Hector. Nero will not see himself surpassed, so he bars me out. If his malice ends there, I am fortunate. The son of Aleutius can exist without a stage success—he will leave that to the Emperor!"

The tone was bitterly sarcastic, but his laugh rang out as carelessly as ever. "Come, come! what matters? Cæsar cannot rob me of my recollections, nor dare he hinder the Prætorian Guards from flashing their swords in military salute whenever I appear; no more can he take from me the love of my mother, wife, and children—nor of such as thee, my brave, true Hector! Let him enjoy his triumphs; the earth is wide."

A few days later a sudden order summoned the prætor to the palace, and at the hour when the party of Gaius was on the Appian Way, nearing the Three Taverns, Aulus was waiting in the anteroom of Nero's judgment hall, trying to subdue his forebodings and steel his countenance into utter indifference towards whatever new blow the tyrant might have in store for him. He was not kept waiting long, and when he entered the wide apartment beyond, he was almost dazed by his reception. Instead of the supercilious smile or the frowning brow to which he was used, Nero turned upon him a look of frank pleasure, seemingly, and cried with heartiness:

"Come hither, Sir Prætor! I have a question to ask of you."

Bowing low, and wondering what this might betoken, Aulus advanced to the foot of the throne, and bent his knee before the curled and perfumed Emperor. But when he rose he could not restrain a start, while his face paled perceptibly—at his right hand stood Plutus, the messenger, an inscrutable look upon his face and his eyes discreetly lowered.

"I am lost!" thought Aulus, and drew himself up proudly, resolved that Nero, who had once been his familiar friend, should not be gratified by signs of weakness.

But Cæsar was speaking. "Aulus Clotius, general and prætor, do you know this man?" He pointed to Plutus.

Aulus gazed at the messenger scrutinizingly. "Unless I am mistaken, Cæsar, he is Plutus Aurelius, a commander of cavalry, and a brave soldier."

"Indeed! And this is all you know of him?"

"It comprises most of my knowledge, sire. In detail, I know him also to be a good talker, and a man of rare ability as a disciplinarian."

Nero laughed. "Then you have talked with him?"

"Often, Cæsar."

"With what purport?"

Aulus seemed groping for definite recollections. "It is difficult to remember all, O Cæsar, but generally upon matters of warfare, as I bethink me."

"And have you never talked of Cæsar?"

"Undoubtedly."

"With what conclusion? Come, let me hear all."

The Emperor, with a smile of cunning, leaned easily back and tapped the golden lion-heads of his throne-arms with his long finger-nails.

Aulus noted the manner, and a feeling of desperation came over him. So far he had told the truth, if not the whole truth; every answer had been in consonance with facts, if not with the fact which Nero was striving to obtain from him. He felt that in reality concealment was of little use, for undoubtedly Nero knew all; still, honor would not permit him to betray a comrade-in-arms, even to save himself. In his desperation he suddenly resolved to make a bold stroke, let the consequences be what they might, and with the quick resolve came something of that grim daring which made this man a hero in real stress and danger.

Bending a little forward and letting a twinkle creep into his eye, he answered easily:

"At last Cæsar has awakened my memory. I did talk with Plutus and express myself too freely, doubtless. I said the noble Cæsar had failed woefully in judgment once, for he had spoiled a good general to make a poor prætor when he called me to that office. And Plutus agreed with me."

Nothing so pleased Nero as dauntlessness, and the mingled humor and audacity of this answer fairly took him off his feet. He broke into laughter, which proved contagious. His favorites joined in, Aulus felt his own face twitching, and Plutus suddenly put his hand over his mouth as if to conceal his risibles. For the minute Nero's better self was in the ascendency, and he showed clemency, which so well, but alas so seldom, became him!

"It is bravely said, my Aulus," he cried, when he could speak for laughing, "and I cannot misdoubt your judgment, however you may that of Cæsar, for a poorer prætor never wore the toga! Go, rascal! I am done with you. And if you are presently ordered to take command of the legion about to be sent into Gaul, blame yourself. Such bluntness is best fitted for the field. Go!"

Dazed and delighted, Aulus made haste to retire, fearing that another word, or look even, might alter this benignant mood.

When safely outside, however, he thought regretfully: " But poor Plutus is in sad case. I have not betrayed him, thank heaven! yet it is plain enough Cæsar knows all. I shall never see Plutus again. Some dungeon will swallow him up, unless for his former bravery he is permitted to fall upon his own sword, or open his veins. Peace to his ashes!"

Imagine, then, his astonishment, the next morning, to meet the cavalry commander in the forum, not only alive and well, but looking smiling and assured. Aulus was almost too surprised to speak, but his expressive face, as he held out his hand in greeting, made the other break into laughter.

"You had evidently consigned me to oblivion, my brave Aulus!" he cried merrily. "Is it not so?"

"What else could I do? I saw Cæsar must know all—or enough at least "—he lowered his voice and looked cautiously around,— "but I was determined not to be your betrayer."

"So I perceived, my noble friend, and thank you for it! But is it possible you do not understand, even yet?"

"Understand? What?" Aulus gazed at him perplexedly.

"Truly, general, you are a poor prætor, as you say, if you cannot unravel such a simple knot of duplicity as this."

A wave of color flushed the open face of Aulus, then faded slowly. "Do you mean— was that message—were those papyri you would have had me sign, really from— Cæsar?"

"Whom else?"

"And I—great Olympus! If I had signed them! It was a plot then to prove my loyalty?"

"Something of that nature, doubtless," smiled the other.

Aulus looked actually blank with astonishment, then came a quick recollection. "But I said—Jove! What did I say, Plutus?"

The other laughed outright. "Never mind what you said, comrade. Would I be base enough to betray one who shared his waterskin with me that blazing day on the plain of Astivari? You did not and would not sign—that was my report, and Cæsar once more loves his old friend Aulus, though he does sing far too well to please him. Learn wisdom, friend! Be dumb henceforth; have a rheum that shall ruin your voice, dash your viol against a tree, and be content to

worship Mars rather than the Muses, delightful though they be."

"It is good advice and I will follow it. Plutus, you have warmed my heart! Rome has at least two men who can be trusted to stand by a friend—pardon the egotism that makes me glad I am one of them. And see here, comrade—if fortune favors me once more, ask what you will of your brother-in-arms, for we stand or fall together."

Hector shared with his patron the sudden and astonishing accession to favor which followed upon this farcical performance of Nero's. Our centurion felt it even before he knew the cause. He saw it in the salute of the guards on duty as he went to the Prætorium for his morning inspection; he read it in the kindly nod of Burrhus as they passed each other in the gardens later; and he knew it when a kindly message summoned him to the presence of the emperor, and he was bidden, as of old, to strip off his shirt of mail and engage in a wrestling match with a burly ambassador from one of the provinces, who had been boasting of his muscle.

It was a short encounter. Restored courage and anticipation made Hector invincible that morning, and he soon had the astonished Bithynian upon his back, with one knee pinning him to the floor, while the banqueting chamber rang with applause.

"Well done, Hector!" cried Nero heartily. "I told you he would win, Tigellinus! There is a trick he has that only an Olympionic knows, and it is a sure throw every time."

"I would like well to see him try it on Anisarchus," remarked the favorite gloomily, for he had lost a heavy wager. "He is simply unapproachable."

"Oh, you mean the gladiator?" asked another. "He is certainly a remarkable wrestler. Has he ever been vanquished?"

"No, and he has been matched against a score, at least, of trained men from every country. Such muscles! Such long, powerful arms! They say his grip is like that of a steel vise."

Thus they talked on, but Hector, being dismissed with a gift, heard no more, and thought little of the matter, for what likelihood was there that he would ever meet this famed wrestler, who was a condemned criminal, only saved alive, so far, by the downturned thumbs of the populace who delighted in his prowess!

As our centurion passed outside the palace

gates into the street he heard his name called, and looked around to see one of his guards hastening towards him, who, after saluting, placed in his hand an order. It was signed by Burrhus, and bade him take personal superintendence of a Jewish prisoner lately arrived in Rome, who, being free-born and notable, had been permitted to remain in his own hired house, well guarded. Hector was further ordered to detail a certain number of soldiers to relieve each other in being chained to the prisoner, and, in fine, to keep him with discretion and care, after the usual manner.

He hastened immediately to the designated street, and was soon in the presence of Paul, whom he at once recognized as his own fellow-prisoner in the past, for whom an earthquake shock had wrought a miracle.

Hector treated the illustrious prisoner with marked respect, exchanging courteous remarks upon the strange and varied events which had brought them together once more, then the centurion asked if there was anything he could do to further the Apostle's comfort during his enforced confinement. But Paul had no complaints nor requests to make concerning food, warmth, or personal comfort of any description; only two favors he begged — papyrus, stylus, and ink, that he might write to his beloved brethren in the church; and the permission to call together the Jews of the city, that he might personally address them upon the subject of the Christ. These requests Hector at once granted, and, giving strict orders that the Apostle should be indulged in every reasonable desire, he left a detail to guard him, and, bidding him a courteous good-morning, took his way to the house of Salome, to tell her of his renewed favor at court and (what he supposed would be news) all about the arrival of Paul the Apostle, as a prisoner who had appealed unto Cæsar for trial.

CHAPTER XXVI.

AN IMPERIAL COMPACT.

THE new prisoners, with the exception of Paul and his special companion, Aristarchus, were consigned to the dungeons of the forum, two of the largest cells being given them, with an unlocked door of communication between. Here all the men were confined, while the two women, Eunice and Elizabeth, were placed in a smaller cell not far away.

This prison was in charge of an official well known to Hector, Euphrastus by name, and as the former came from his interview with Salome, who had told him all about the Christian prisoners, he was pleased to see the man lounging on the steps of the judgment hall.

"Peace to you!" cried Hector, showing his pleasure frankly. "You are the very one I desired to see. I have in mind a favor to ask of you."

"The gods keep you!" returned Euphrastus. "But what is the favor, pray? You know it will be granted, if in my power."

"Thanks, friend! It is not one that will greatly strain your generosity. You have a new batch of prisoners, I learn, and they are Christians."

"Right as usual, Hector!"

"Well, then, I simply have a curiosity to see them. Cannot you let me accompany you upon your rounds this morning?"

"Noon, you might say, for the sun is high. However, I have been slow about the inspection this morning on account of some fresh orders I was awaiting. As to your accompanying me—well, it is not strictly allowable, but—what is your interest in these people, forsooth?"

"Curiosity," was the prompt reply.

"I see. You have heard of their obnoxious practices. Queer, too, for I find them as docile as could be desired. They do nothing worse—that I can discover—than to sing and pray together. I have seen no bloodthirstiness in them, and they give me no trouble whatever. Yes, come with me; I am going down now to number them out."

"For what?" asked Hector quickly.

"Have you not heard? They are to be sacrificed in the games at the amphitheatre, at the celebration of Poppœa's birthday. So many to the beasts, so many for the naval combat, and the rest to fight with gladiators."

"But the women?" cried Hector in horror.

"Who told you there were women?" asked Euphrastus, turning upon him suspiciously.

"My sister, the wife of Cleotas. She has been permitted by Burrhus to visit them."

The answer seemed satisfactory. "They will doubtless be portioned to the wild beasts," was the careless reply. "I have no orders for them so far, but as they cannot fight, what other disposal could be made of them?"

Hector did not answer, and the official went on relating incidents peculiar to his profession. In this friendly fashion they entered the wide corridor beside the judgment hall, and at its end descended the stairs which led downwards by successive flights far underground. Once there they pursued a somewhat rambling course through the network of passages undermining the great building. At intervals Euphrastus stopped to fit a key into a lock, open a heavy door, and thrust his head within a cell in which Hector, glancing over his shoulder, caught dim glimpses of some haggard being crouching in the quiet of despair. At length at his word, "Here are the Christians!" Hector awoke to animation, and looked eagerly as the door swung wide, for while the two approached a murmur of tuneful melody reached their ears and he knew that, after their happy custom, these men were singing hymns of comfort and good cheer.

The music ceased as the door creaked rustily on its hinges, and every eye was directed towards it from within, for no one confined there knew at what moment the summons might come—the summons to trial, perhaps; more likely to death without a hearing. By the light of the lamp in his guide's hand Hector let his eye run over the group before him. He saw grave, self-controlled, intelligent faces, worn with the long journey and privations, but neither wretched nor desperate. On many, indeed, was a smile of absolute brightness, and on all an expression of security and peace marvelous to behold in such a place.

As he gazed, noting all this with an eye trained to observation of human nature, another man came in from the adjoining cell, his chains clanking as he made his difficult way along. He was younger than the rest, with a face and form such as sculptors choose when they would embody their choicest creations. Now browned, bearded, and somewhat bent with the heavy fetters as he was, he still showed the manly beauty which had always made him notable.

As Hector devoured this youth with inquiring glances, his own face quite concealed beneath his helmet's visor, the latter looked straight at him with large, honest eyes, in which was the old boyish expression, unmistakable to one who had loved him so well. Hector was almost betrayed into a cry of recognition, for he knew the prisoner to be his longed-for brother, Herk-

las! It was all the soldier, trained to absolute self-control, could do to stand there like a statue, when his whole soul was crying out in fond welcome, when his arms twitched to enfold the boy he had cherished from babyhood, when his eyes ached with the tears welling into them, and his throat with the sobs he must suppress. He had no eyes, no thought, for any one else, and he waited with a passionate desire to hear this prisoner's voice, knowing that evidence would be conclusive.

Euphrastus, meanwhile, had drawn forth his tablets and stylus, and was calling each by number—for a Roman prisoner dropped his name with his liberty—and marshalling them side by side along the opposite wall. Hector, standing motionless and absorbed just within the locked door, was to them but a Prætorian guard on duty. They attributed to him a heart, as well as garments, of steel, and thought that with cold, unmoved eyes he was gazing through the holes of his visor, alert only to quell any disturbance. How could one of them have imagined that behind that shirt of mail the heart was beating to suffocation, behind the closed visor the face was working with tenderness, and that the shaded eyes were swimming in tears!

"Number Seven!" called Euphrastus; and the youngest prisoner answered clearly, "Here!" as he took his place in line.

It was enough—Hector knew! The boy of his own raising, the lad for whom he had labored like a father, the brother who had been cherished in his inmost heart, was here—a Christian, and doomed to a horrible death!

A groan welled up from his tortured soul, but died upon his lips. He dared not give it sound. The dim and crowded cell swam before him, but he moved not. Roman discipline quelled his weakness, and kept him the grim, silent sentinel, though faint with feeling.

The numbering continued till all were crowded about the three walls of the narrow room, and Hector, gradually conquering his first agony of recognition, grew intensely interested in the scene, noticing that while all looked expectant and some curious, not one but was serenely courageous in bearing. Euphrastus, holding his lantern high, looked them all over carefully, then once more consulted his tablets. After an interval he slowly called the even numbers, and bade them stand forth from the rest. They did so, and the keeper noted them down with accuracy.

"These," he whispered to the silent Hector at his side, "are for the naval battle."

Next he called the odd numbers. There being eleven prisoners in all, there was one more of these than of the even. He noted them as before, with the whisper:

"These are for the beasts."

"Let me select the men, my Euphrastus! I was once skilled in the training of the arena, and we would fain make these combats interesting."

"True!" answered the keeper, well pleased. "Then give us your judgment, friend. I doubt not it will be far better than my own."

Hector, thus permitted, ran his eyes

"Number Seven!" called Euphrastus; and the youngest prisoner answered clearly, "Here!"
as he took his place in line.—See page 96.

Hector repressed a shudder. Herklas was Number Seven! There would have been a chance for him in the naval combat, for he could swim—there was none here! But Euphrastus went on:

"I am to select two out of this greater number as gladiators; one for the net, and one to be done to death by Anisarchus, the champion wrestler."

A sudden inspiration came to Hector, hardly defined as yet, but bringing a ray of hope. He whispered back eagerly:

quickly over the group. One of the men—Number Three—was thin, long-legged, and wiry.

"Take him for the net-throwing," he murmured; and Euphrastus, with a laugh and admiring oath, at once approved.

Hector's second choice seemed to take him longer. He scrutinized each more than once, but at length appeared satisfied.

"Let the opponent of Anisarchus be Number Seven," he said in a voice hoarse almost to extinction.

"Jove! That slender, beautiful youth? He will be crushed like a mouse in the jaws of a cat."

"Be not so sure, friend. He is quick and muscular. It will be at least a livelier battle than if any of these older men, with stiffened sinews and slow movements, were chosen. Indeed, I feel more and more satisfied with my choice."

Hector's hoarseness and agitation had disappeared. He seemed almost gay. Whatever his sudden resolution, it gave him courage and hope, and after they left the cell, while ascending to the upper air, he was so talkative and merry as to keep the other in a roar of laughter.

They separated the best of friends, Euphrastus vowing his self-elected helper a good fellow; and when the latter said carelessly, at parting, "I may want to take another look at my gladiators sometime," the keeper answered heartily, "Whenever you wish, comrade!"

But the instant he was alone Hector gave way. Seeking a secluded bench in the public gardens near by—a rustic seat embowered in a jasmine vine, making a shrine to Minerva—he threw himself down upon it, and clasping his arms over the back, bent his head upon them and groaned aloud.

"My brother! My little Herklas!" he murmured in a voice thrilled with tenderness, while wave after wave of recollection rolled over him, until his heart grew weak with the strain.

Long he sat thus, great sobs racking his frame as he wavered betwixt the joy of once more seeing his brother and the torture of such a meeting.

"Do I find you only to lose you again?" he groaned. "Oh, God of the Christians, hear and help me in this extremity! Thou hast shown me my brother—help me to save him! Give me Cæsar's ear, O gracious Lord, that he may grant my request; and fill me with Thine own invincible strength in this encounter, that Herklas may be saved a cruel death. For Christ's sake!"

He rose, calm and strong, and returned to his duties, uplifted by a purpose that dominated all lesser thoughts, and a consecration to Christ that, in spite of grief and fear, brought him a certain bliss and comfort which no earthly woes could take away. It needed but little reflection to convince him that it was best not to tell Salome what he knew. Why rack her with his own torture? Already she was sufficiently grieved over

her friend Elizabeth; why add to this a still more bitter trouble? No, she had long since given up Herklas as lost. Let her remain in calm unconsciousness of his presence and give all her energies to her dear friend. She could not save Herklas; he might. If he did, there would be a glad reunion, indeed; if he did not—then let her never know the awful truth.

Hector at once began laying his train of operations. By a little diplomacy, easy now that he was in favor, he managed to be detailed, with some of his men, for special guard-duty in the palace. Once there, he was careful to take up his own station, every evening, in the corridor leading to Nero's private apartments, and, as he expected, found it often devolved upon him to assist the royal inebriate to bed after the late suppers. Once or twice, when the Emperor was not too stupid with wine, he recognized the wrestler and had him in for a friendly bout with the gloves, as he felt his muscles needed hardening, and at these times Hector managed adroitly to introduce the name of Anisarchus, and, if possible, excite both Nero and his favorites into talking and laying wagers over the wrestler's powers.

It was evident that Nero, for some reason, chose to depreciate the champion's fame, and he frankly said more than once that he would like to see the swaggerer beaten, for he was growing altogether too pompous over his repeated successes. Evidently Nero did not enjoy pomposity in any one but himself!

At length an evening came when Hector was summoned, as usual, and this sort of talk ran high. Presently Burrhus, who was present, remarked absently:

"Well, whether or not the man is all he claims to be, he will have an easy victory, at least, at our Cæsar's games next month."

"Why, how is that?" asked Lucan the poet.

"Because one of the condemned Christians is to be pitted against him, a young, slender, handsome fellow of Macedonia. He will be like a kid in the grasp of a mountain bear!"

Hector did not look up, nor start even. He held himself with iron steadiness and listened.

"Too bad it could not be a more even combat!" yawned Tigellinus from his couch. "I would like to see a real wrestler stand up against him."

"Yes, one like our good Hector, for instance," added the Emperor graciously. "If only he were in training, now, he might give the boaster something to do—eh, my centurion?"

Hector bowed low. "The noble Cæsar is too flattering, but"—he hesitated one instant, then plunged on, his heart beating wildly, but with determination on his face and a prayer in his soul—"but if our Emperor would wish to see his servant meet the champion wrestler, it is in his power to command it."

Nero was pleased. Anything that reminded him of his high estate was incense in his nostrils. He turned upon the inwardly-shaken Hector with a smile.

"Cæsar has too much regard for his loyal soldiers"—he emphasized the word "loyal" significantly—"to condemn them to the mutilation and disgrace of the arena. He leaves that to captives, criminals, and slaves, who are condemned, or who willingly risk all for money. You know such a trial of strength is to the death."

"I know, O Cæsar!" Hector drew in his breath hard. "Yet to please my lord I would gladly risk all. In fact, though he may think me a fool for my temerity, I will willingly meet this Anisarchus in the place of the Christian prisoner, and it shall be a combat to the death. But if I conquer I ask one reward—that Cæsar give me for mine own the handsome young captive whose place I take in the arena."

It was said. Hector, bowing to the ground, felt the room whirl around him amid a confused clamor of laughter and hand-clapping. Then Cæsar spoke, and all stopped to listen.

"So you long for a slave of your own, Hector? And more, for a good-looking one. How the lowly do love to ape their masters! But what would you with this slave, when the soldiers under you are at your lightest beck?"

Hector smiled. "I cannot beat them, Cæsar."

"True enough! And that is a satisfaction, I own. Well, so be it. But I fear I will lose a good soldier by the exchange. You are not in training, Hector."

"There are three weeks yet, O Cæsar, and I have been daily attending the gymnasium, for some time. Pray let me try, under the conditions."

"That you get the slave? Oh, yes, take him by all means—if you live through it—and beat this Christian nonsense out of him.

That will be good practice for your muscles!"

"I have Cæsar's word?" asked Hector once more, knowing so well the tyrant's changeable moods that he dreaded trusting to them in so important a matter.

"Assuredly; here are my witnesses and—but wait! You have a stylus and papyrus, Lucan—I see them thrust into your girdle. Come now, draw us up a compact in verse, can you not? Let us see what you can do as poet and lawyer combined."

Lucan, flushing uncomfortably, could not refuse, though he felt the task beyond him; and while Hector stood by, outwardly the impassive soldier, inwardly the fearful, supplicating brother, Lucan wrote busily, the rest looking on with faces full of merry curiosity.

To these it was but a break in the monotony of their splendid feasting; to the other it was an hour upon the rack. At length the poet looked up with a sigh of relief. "It is written, noble Cæsar, but I fear it is neither poetic, nor clerkly."

"If only it will hold!" murmured Hector almost involuntarily.

"Never mind!" laughed Nero, unheeding the low-spoken words. "I suppose it will be just as binding if I put my seal to it. Read, Lucan!"

And Hector breathed again.

The embarrassed poet was doubtless right in his opinion of the document. It might not, perhaps, have stood in any court, but Nero was his own court, and respected nothing save his own seal and signature. Freely translated, it read as follows:

"This compact holds 'twixt parties two:
Primus, the great Imperator,
Nero Claudius Drusus, who
Rules all the earth in peace and war;
Secundus, Hector, known to men
As of the guards Prætorian,
And honored with the rank and claim
Of Celeres, centurion.
Hector, secundus, here agrees
To meet in combat to the death
The far-famed Anisarchus, who
Is champion wrestler—so he saith.
And should said Hector, in fair fight,
Twice throw this man and still endure,
Great Cæsar, primus, promiseth
Above his seal and signature
This guerdon, namely: That the man
To Anisarchus doomed before
Be given Hector as his own,
To have and hold for evermore."

The reading was greeted with shouts of

laughter and merry jests, Nero's sounding above all the rest, as he cried:

"You are right, Lucan! It would stand in neither law nor literature, but it may in Cæsar's will. Come, I will sign it."

Instantly a slave stepped forward and bent over to form a table of his broad back, while another brought ink, wax, and stylus. Hector watched breathlessly as the royal name was affixed, the melted wax dropped upon the papyrus, and the royal ring pressed into its molten substance for a seal.

"Here, it is yours to keep," said Nero, flinging it carelessly in Hector's direction. "Cæsar needs no reminders to carry out his promises. Take it, and do your part, or it will be the worse for you. I wish to see a really decent match. Go!"

Hector, bowing low, withdrew, the parchment grasped in his palm, but when he was alone in the outer corridor he raised it to heaven in his right hand, and looked up reverently, as he murmured:

"Now the God of the Christians strengthen this good right arm, and you shall be mine, my brother!"

CHAPTER XXVII.

A VAGABOND BEFORE THE MAGISTRATE.

IT was fifteen days later and nearing noon. A small group in earnest discourse was gathered in the peristyle of the palace of Aulus Clotius. One was the prætor himself, and the others were Pamphylia his mother, and his fair wife, Julia. They were talking over his recent promotion (as he esteemed it) to the generalship of a legion of the Celeres, or royal troops, and what it doubtless portended—his soon being ordered to Gaul to quell a mutinous uprising there, which threatened to be serious.

"If only we could go too!" said Pamphylia, sadly. "It is so trying waiting for news by the slow couriers, and I am sure something has happened to you if the despatches are at all delayed. Oh, the hardest part of war is the women's part!"

"Yes," said Julia, coming to her husband's side, and throwing an arm about his neck, "and mother's fears make mine all the greater. But you will not go till after the birthday celebrations?"

"No, I shall stay for those. I must see Hector through this mad freak of his. I cannot think what has come over him to insist upon trying his strength with that burly Anisarchus, and for so paltry a consideration—one slave! Surely he has the means to buy himself a servant; and if not, I would gladly have given him a man out of my first consignment of captives. But he will not listen to my arguments or promises, nor will he fully explain his motives. There must be something more than this silly desire to acquire human property. Sometimes I think the old wrestling fever has possessed him—as my war fever now and then dominates me in times of peace, until all my veins are in a turmoil of hot blood—and that he can no longer control it. He is ready to risk death, even, to prove once more his own powers."

"That is what Céleste thinks," returned Julia. "Even her pleadings do not move him—fight he will and must!"

"Mayhap his sister's interest in the prisoners has awakened his," said Pamphylia thoughtfully; "and from what I hear of these Christians, now, the sect must have been greatly maligned before. I understand that you, Aulus, have been exerting yourself to clear this woman—Elizabeth, is her name?"

"Yes, to please my old friend Gaius, as well as Hector and his sister. Not only Elizabeth, but her companion, Eunice, though I hardly think the latter will live until next week. She is failing rapidly. Yes, I have done my best for them, but in vain. There must be plenty of victims for the spectacles, and these cannot be spared."

"But women!" cried Julia. "That seems too hard! Men can make a show of defense, at least, but with women it is only slaughter."

"Nero loves slaughter," said Aulus calmly. "He fattens on it. What a master to serve!" His tone expressed deep disgust. "I have been thinking often, lately, of the sentence that seems to come naturally to the lips of these Christians: 'One is my Master, even Christ.' It would be a happiness to serve such a Leader, who called Himself 'friend' and 'elder brother' to His disciples. I sometimes revolt at the service I give to Nero; I cannot help it!"

There was a moment's silence, then Julia remarked:

"I hear that this man whose place Hector takes has a wife in the city who is under the protection of a friend of yours; is that so?"

"Yes, this same Gaius of Macedonia—a fine fellow, too! He is working with me in this matter, and seems deeply interested. When we were together, the other day, I noticed that he turned and frequently examined my countenance in a critical manner. Finally he said apologetically, 'Pardon me, but there is something about you occasionally that reminds me of this very person we have been speaking of—Agistha, wife of Number Seven in the prison. I cannot say whether it is your expression, manner, or voice—hardly your general complexion, I think, for she is darker than you—but it is there, and unmistakable.' Naturally this interested me. Now, why do you not both go to call upon the Lady Ænone and her friend? Perchance you, mother, can tell whether it is all imagination with Gaius, or not."

"We have intended to go for some time," said Julia. "Suppose we say we will to-morrow, mother—does that suit you?"

"Perfectly, my child. To-morrow let it be."

The next afternoon was very warm, and Agistha, worn out with grief, left her baby sleeping and strolled into the peristyle, where the fountain was playing to freshen the air. She had heard of the man who had, strangely enough, bargained for her husband's life by the risk of his own. But she knew nothing of him, except that he was a centurion, and she spent hours in vain imaginings as to the outcome of the matter. If the soldier won, Herklas would be a slave—and she?

"I shall beg to follow him," she told herself with loyal determination. "I must be with my husband, even in slavery!" But she dared not let herself hope too freely, for what if the man should fail?

She was dreaming thus to-day as she sat in her loose robe, leaning gracefully against the stone rim which encircled the basin of the fountain. One slender, sandaled foot was bracing the inclined body, and one bare, round arm was thrown against the marble rampart for her cheek to rest against.

She wore no jewels in her grief. Her loose curls of dark hair were confined only by a triplicate bandeau of silver cord gleaming amid its soft duskiness. The loose tunic, of an amethyst shade, was bound to her slim body by crossed ribbons of the deeper hue of purple verging upon crimson, replacing the ordinary girdle, its fringed ends falling low over the long gown. With her dark lashes lying upon her waxen cheek, and her arm softly pink against the marble's cold whiteness, she was a vision of pensive loveliness.

The entrance of Pamphylia and Julia, following Harold the page, was so quiet that Agistha was not at first aroused from her deep reverie, and the older lady had time to think, "How charming!" while the younger, after one glance, turned with a hasty whisper:

"Why, mother, she is your very image, only younger!"

The little rustle they made aroused Agistha, and she sprang to her feet with a courteous welcome, as Harold spoke their names. But while she greeted the elder lady the eyes of both lingered in meeting, and each felt so drawn to the other that it was difficult to keep the salutation within the bounds of conventionality. When Ænone appeared the three were conversing without a break, and almost before she had greeted the guests, her eyes flashed from the Roman matron of noble blood to her own loved but humble companion; but, though she checked the exclamation that sprang to her lips, Julia had noticed the glance and broke out in her lively fashion: "You see it, too, do you not? They are enough alike to be mother and daughter!"

Pamphylia looked at Agistha with a sweet wistfulness, which made the other's cheeks flush with pleasure. She longed to throw herself at the dear old lady's feet, even as the latter could scarcely keep from crying out, "Come and kiss me, my child!" and while Ænone and Julia exclaimed, the others drew closer in soul.

The call was prolonged to an unusual length, and the four separated, at last, with mutual promises of future meetings, though amid the courtesies Agistha's face grew somber—what future was there for her?

"It is really wonderful, mother!" cried Julia, as they entered their waiting cisium, or light cabriolet, drawn by two perfectly matched mules and driven by a tiny Nubian. "She has your voice, even, not to speak of that flower-like droop of the neck, and that sudden upward honest gaze into one's eyes whenever directly addressed. It put me in a sort of daze to watch you both, and see the similarity. Are you sure she does not belong to some branch of your house, and has thus inherited a few of the family traits?"

Pamphylia smiled. "Would it were so! I confess I was strongly drawn to her, but I have the impression that she is a Macedonian, and none of our family are found there, you know. It is, I suppose, only one of those freaks of nature which sometimes make two people, even of different nationalities, so marvelously alike as to deceive their nearest friends. Really, the wonder is that there are not more such resemblances. Think of the limited number of features we all possess—a nose, a mouth, two eyes—and the millions of creatures who bear them, and yet we are astonished when any two closely resemble each other!"

Julia laughed. "What a philosopher you are, mother! But it is marvelous, now you remind me of it—this diversity in similarity. Surely the gods must give deep thought to their work, and have great unity in plan. I wonder at it, too, for there are so many, and they are so full of their own affairs, it would scarcely seem as if they could have any time left for us."

"Doubtless they divide the cares, as the honors," returned Pamphylia, then lapsed into thoughtful silence, as she often did when their beliefs were discussed, for there were many things which puzzled—some which revolted—her in the worship of the day. Though by nature loyal to both "king and creed," her better sense told her that many practices were far from being worthy the purity of her regard, and this often faltered into questionings which tore her heart and burdened her conscience.

The lively Julia was soon telling her husband all about the call, and speculating upon the resemblance.

"It is a little odd, notwithstanding mother's philosophizing," he remarked, as she finished her detailed account. "I would like to see the lady. Well, let us hope that poor Hector will win for her sake, as well as for his own. He is practicing in the gymnasium every day, and seems confident and happy enough."

"But the captive women!" cried Julia. "They are doomed."

"I fear so," returned her husband sadly. "Poor things! It is a terrible fate."

Yet, in spite of this sympathy for individual cases, both were soon gayly discussing the choice of seats in the amphitheatre, for even the best of the Romans took these degrading, blood-thirsty spec-

tacles as a matter of course, and would have felt defrauded could they not have witnessed them.

They were in the midst of lively conversation when a servant entered, bearing a silver salver whereon lay a small tablet of papyrus, which he presented on one knee to his master. Aulus caught it up and read it, then turned to his wife.

"I am summoned to the judgment hall," he said briskly. "Some criminal who comes under my jurisdiction has been apprehended;" and kissing her, he hurried out, for he was still acting as prætor, not yet having received his official discharge.

He soon reached the hall, and took his seat, ready for his magistratic part in the proceedings. In the prisoner's enclosure stood a man who wore the peculiar headgear of a Phœnician. He was lined and marred with dissipation and misery, more than with age, and he looked both hungry and wretched. He had been discovered within the garden of Gaius, probably bent on plunder, and the latter sat in one of the witness seats at the left, ready to testify against him. The prætor began his investigation with the usual question:

"What is your name?"

"Alois," was the answer.

"From Phœnicia?"

"Yes, sire."

"How old?"

"Forty-two."

"Free-born, or slave?"

"Manumitted slave."

Thus the examination proceeded, the prisoner testifying with an air of desperate carelessness, as if it made little difference to him what the outcome might be. He seemed to have grown indifferent to his own fate. When asked what was his object in concealing himself in the garden of Gaius, he smiled in a peculiar manner and answered calmly: "I wanted to see my slave."

The cool reply produced a sensation.

"Your slave?" cried Aulus Clotius. "A creature like you have a slave! Now tell the truth, or we shall be obliged to resort to the screws."

The prisoner shrugged his shoulders. "Nevertheless it is true. I owned a half-share in a slave, and this man, Gaius, took her from me. She had been gone many years, but I discovered her retreat at last, and had the curiosity to see her again, for I had supposed her dead. I was fond of her."

Gaius looked flushed and embarrassed under the glances cast upon him by the lookers-on, as he began to see the significance of this man's answers, and feared it might involve himself in much unpleasantness and Agistha in trouble; for the laws governing runaway slaves were severe, and here undoubtedly was one of the wretched so-called masters of that unhappy woman. How had he found them out after so long an interval? and how was he, Gaius, to explain the intricate affair? He felt that the whole truth was the best policy, and, rising, turned courteously to the magistrate.

"Sir Prætor, may I address the prisoner?"

"Assuredly," returned Aulus; "but pray keep to the point at issue."

"I will, sire. What was the name of this slave you claim?" he asked in a clear voice.

"Agistha," said the man.

Aulus started, and looked from one to the other. He recognized the name at once.

"Where and when did you obtain her?"

"Seventeen years ago, in Amphipolis of Macedonia."

"Of whom?"

"I bought a half-interest in her of Flavius, a Roman."

"And a galley slave," added Gaius quickly.

The man gave another shrug, and answered with a sneer:

"Very likely. He was none too good!"

Gaius turned to the magistrate. "Sir Prætor, this man, I believe, speaks the truth, but in order to show why I retain and protect this woman, Agistha, as I believe in right and justice, I must tell you her story as I had it from the lips of Flavius himself, which I can verify from writings on record at the judgment hall in Thessalonica, where he was tried under torture, found guilty, and relegated to the galleys."

Then in well-chosen words he related the singular narrative of the stolen child. As Aulus listened, his interest grew more and more intense. He grasped the arm of his prætor's chair and gazed at the speaker, his face paling and flushing with emotion. At length, impatient of details, he called out sharply:

"And this child—how old was she when stolen?"

"About three, methinks," answered Alois, wondering at the patrician's manner.

"She could talk, could she not? Did she never give any other name than Agistha?"

"I know not," returned Alois slowly. "I did not see her until later, but I fancy Agistha was the name Flavius gave her. However—"

"Well, why do you hesitate?"

"Because it may be nothing. Once when we were severely pressed for money he handed me a little gold chain and charm, which he said had been hers, and bade me erase the name engraved on the pendant, so that we might sell it. I remember because it took me all day—"

"The name! The name!" shouted Aulus impatiently.

"Cleone," said the man deliberately.

Aulus fell back in his chair, pale to the lips, while Gaius, astonished, strode forward to his assistance.

"No," he said, faintly raising his hand, "I am not ill—only—this child was my sister!"

The announcement was met by a stunned silence, which Gaius broke.

"Are you certain, Sir Prætor?"

"It must be so. Her singular resemblance to our family, the time, the circumstances, the name, the place—all convince me that this lost Agistha is my lost sister, Cleone, who was stolen from the peristyle of our palace when an infant nearing four years."

He turned abruptly to the guards attending the prisoner. "Loose this man!" he commanded.

The order was at once executed.

"Alois," he added, "you are to accompany the honorable Gaius and myself to his house, that together we may converse with the lady and see if all your assertions are true."

"But, Sir Prætor," put in Gaius, "she knows nothing of the things concerning her infancy. We have kept them from her—her husband, my wife, and I—lest they trouble her mind, and she has no memory of them."

"Her husband!" At the words Aulus turned with an odd expression. "Her husband is the condemned Christian?" he asked in low tones, stepping to the side of Gaius.

"Yes."

"And my Hector is to match the wrestler for him! How strange! If he wins it will be a new tie between us, indeed! But come, let us to the lady."

"You will give me time to prepare her?" asked Gaius. "She is weak with trouble."

Aulus laid a hand upon his arm. "My friend, do you feel it necessary to protect my own sister from my rude haste?" The tone was full of sad reproach. But before the other could explain his caution, Aulus added quickly, while the tears flashed in his eyes: "But the gods bless you for your care of her! I have no words to thank you."

They entered the handsome domus, and the master hastened to summon his wife and acquaint her with the wondrous news, that she might, in turn, prepare Agistha. But she laughed at him.

"We need no preparation for joy!" she cried amid her rapturous exclamations over the good news. "Agistha has borne sorrow with a staunch heart. A bit of prosperity and happiness will not harm her."

However, she sent to summon Agistha to the atrium, saying she had strange news for her, but in no wise concerning Herklas—with whom his wife's every thought was woven, these trying days.

Meanwhile Aulus Clotius and his prisoner remained alone, and the former studied the latter with eyes made critical by new interest.

"He looks forlorn and hungry, poor wretch! but not vicious," was his unspoken comment. "He said he was fond of her, and seems, from the story, to have interfered when she was cruelly used. We will see."

With the thought Gaius entered, accompanied by his wife, flushed, excited, and beautiful in her joy.

"Your sister?" she cried, scarcely waiting to greet her guest. "I knew she was of gentle blood; that has proved itself in every way! And you"—flashing about upon the prisoner—"are the master she did not fear—Alois?"

He bowed humbly.

"She has told me he tried to be kind to her,"—addressing Aulus again—"but was overruled too often by his more cruel partner. Do you know what has become of him, Alois?"

"He is dead, madam. The galleys soon kill a man. He will trouble us no more."

The curtains parted again and a hesitating figure stood just within them. The slender white form in its classic garments was sharply outlined against their dark richness, and Aulus drew in his breath with delight as he gazed.

Agistha turned to the mistress. "Harold said you desired my presence here, Lady Ænone."

"Yes, I—we—Agistha, do you see who is here?"

She looked and paled. "Alois?" she whispered. "He has come for me!"

"No, no, child! Be not frightened. Here is another who claims your notice—the noble Aulus Clotius, general and prætor."

Agistha turned to him with a sweet smile. Peace to you, sir! I have met your mother, and was greatly drawn to her, and to the noble Julia."

"And both to you, fair lady. I note a strong resemblance between you and my mother."

There was a slight tremble in the prætor's voice, but he commanded himself well.

"Yes, it has been observed upon before. It flatters me."

"Agistha," asked Ænone, who could wait no longer, "did you ever hear the name of Cleone?"

"Cleone?" The younger woman spoke the word lingeringly as if in a dream. "Cleone! It suggests a noble court with marble columns, and a fountain spraying in the sunshine. I seem to see a boy at play, and a little—little girl. There is a lady too—fair and sweet. Oh! it is like a beautiful dream long since vanished!"

Aulus had risen. He could no longer control himself—he must tell her! Then he sank back with the thought, "No, it will startle her. We must come at it gradually," and had reseated himself even before he perceived Ænone's imperious gesture to that effect. For the matron had taken this affair into her own hands.

"Agistha," she said quickly, "Alois has told all your story. You were stolen, when a mere babe, by Flavius from a house—a palatial domus—in this very city. Your name was Cleone. Now can you recall—"

"Oh, it comes! it comes!" With the cry Agistha shut her eyes tightly, and clapped her hands over her ears. "Wait! I remember. The boy—he took care of me—I loved him. But his name was difficult—I called him Ollie—Ollie!"

Aulus gave a cry of rapture. "My sister! My Cleone! It is true, and I am Ollie! Oh, my baby darling, dost not remember me?"

She opened her eyes and gazed at him. The veil of the past seemed rent in twain.

"Ollie—brother!" she cried, and the two sprang to each other's embrace, all barriers between them forever removed.

Even Alois wiped his eyes. Ænone sobbed outright.

"Send for my mother!" cried Aulus in a

transport of happiness, "or no, let me—let us all go to her. Alois, you are free because you had one tender thought for my beloved sister; and I will take you into my household and give you comfort and protection."

The man let his eyes rest upon Agistha. "I mourned her as dead," he muttered, "and when I heard differently my heart yearned over her. I regretted those years of oppression and wanted to do her good in some way to atone for all. I have learned kinder thoughts and manners from some people I have been with—they call them Christians. I wished to tell her this very story and help her to recover her home. Let me serve her, for I am fond of her."

"Then come with us," said Aulus kindly; and Agistha added:

"Yes, Alois, come with us."

Gaius and Ænone would not be left behind. The palace was not far distant and they chose to walk. Pamphylia and Julia sat at their embroidery, just a bit dull and sleepy, the latter telling herself she was glad that a few days more would usher in the Games.

Aulus hastened into their room with a quick tread, and a face alive with varying expressions.

"What! Sitting here alone?" he cried merrily. "There are guests in the atrium."

"And nobody announced them?" cried Julia, rising.

"I announce them, for I brought them. Mother," his voice shook in spite of himself, "the Lady Ænone and that fair Agistha, who resembles you and me, are awaiting you."

"How kind of them to thus return our visit without delay!"

Pamphylia rose and gently shook into even folds her soft, dove-colored tunic, rich with steel embroidery. "Come, Julia, we must not keep them waiting."

"Mother,"—Aulus drew her arm within his own,—"have you never thought we might, sometime, come upon some trace of our Cleone? Does not even this resemblance touch you to wonder?"

She stopped to peer into his face, which he tried to keep impassive.

"Ah, Aulus, I dare not wonder—nor hope. I have been so often allured and then deceived. Leave me in peace."

"Yes, mother, but"—they were nearing the atrium—"I have heard a strange tale about this fair lady."

Julia pressed closer to listen, as she followed.

"She is of Roman birth—a patrician—and she was stolen when three years old from—"

"My son, why do you torture me?"

At the cry, he swept aside a curtain, and she stood in the large reception chamber. Back at its far end, beyond the impluvium, was a small group; here, close at hand, was one slender figure.

"Mother!" it cried in a small, pathetic voice, "mother, know you not your little Cleone?"

Pamphylia looked and believed. The rest, waiting breathlessly to see her faint or fall, had no need for fears. Ænone was right when she said joy did not harm.

"It is my child!" she said in a strong tone of deep conviction, and reaching out her longing, empty arms, she drew her baby to her breast.

CHAPTER XXVIII.

ELIZABETH IN DUNGEON AND ARENA.

EUNICE was indeed dying. The outdoor hardships through which she had passed, though they had weakened her frame, might have been withstood, but the dampness and gloom of the dungeon added thereto were more than she could endure. Her end was near. Elizabeth, before whom a hideous death loomed on the morrow, was now indifferent to all but her companion, who lay against her breast gasping for breath. Through the efforts of Cleotas and Hector a mattress had been provided her, and a small lamp burned feebly in the close cell, while the prison leech had just departed, the medicine he left behind sending out a strange, pungent odor that filled the air.

Junius, Nadab, and Salome had been there also, but were permitted only a short interview on account of the sufferer. Elizabeth's good-night had been calm and tearless—indeed, all had tried to subdue their feelings in respect to the near presence of death, and had simply whispered lingeringly:

"We will see you again in the morning."

Elizabeth, bending over the close comrade and friend of months, almost envied her the natural death so rapidly approaching, but put out of her mind her own horrible expectations of the morrow, the better to nurse and comfort the sick one. The latter was breathing heavily, now, quite unconscious, and it was with difficulty that her faithful friend could rouse her to receive a portion of the medicine to be given at stated intervals, marked by the hour-glass the physician had left on the stone floor at her side.

As Elizabeth prepared the mixture—this strange-smelling powder stirred into thin wine—her hand trembled with weakness, and was almost transparent against the lamplight, while her sweet face with its large, clear eyes and delicate features seemed cut from marble. In spite of her care, she spilled a considerable portion of the powder, which lodged amid the folds of her tunic and yellowed it slightly wherever it clung. But there was enough left, she was glad to see, and gently raising the sufferer's head, she held the shallow measure to her lips.

Too late! For an instant the drooped eyes lifted surprisedly as if at some remarkable vision, then dropped back in her head. There was an unmistakable noise in the wasted throat, and Elizabeth felt the form straighten and stiffen in her arms. The poor prisoner—the blessed Christian—had passed to her reward!

Elizabeth laid her gently back and looked down upon her for a long time, with something like a smile on her lips. "To-morrow I will be with thee in Paradise!" she murmured, then pressed the tired lids softly down, and gathered the worn robe decently about her limbs. "Rest, sweet soul, and be forever with our Lord!" was her inner benediction, as she at length stepped to the cell door and gave the signal agreed upon to the guard without.

He soon entered. "Is she gone?" he asked.

Elizabeth bowed her head, but as he stooped with rude haste to lift the wasted figure, she added quickly:

"Gently, friend! She is a woman."

The appeal, so softly spoken, seemed to touch even his calloused soul. With an apologetic mutter he controlled his hurry to something like decorum, and calling another guard, the two bore the body out slowly and with perfect decency, the one left behind gazing after the gloomy little funeral train through a mist of tears. But Elizabeth was faint from weariness and lack of rest, and soon that deep exhaustion of mind and body, which seems so near to utter extinc-

tion, gained possession of all her senses. Sinking back upon the lately-vacated mattress, she dropped into a state partly sleep, partly insensibility, and knew no more till the day was come again.

It is evidently a special day in Rome. From earliest dawn the streets have been teeming with the plebeian classes hastening to and fro on busy errands, all tending to one spot—the great amphitheatre of Taurus in the Campus Martius. Here a group of carpenters, their girdles bristling with tools, go chattering by to finish some delayed work on the safety rampart surrounding the arena, for it is said these new beasts are large and powerful; next two tent-makers hurry along, with rolls of sail-cloth, great needles, and waxed threads, to repair a rent in the velarium, or roof-awning, caused by a sharp and sudden gust of wind last evening; then a party of country people in curious garb, speaking as curious a dialect, go pounding by on bare feet of horn-like hardness, intent on what they are soon to witness; and in rapid procession follows a company of burly, beetle-browed men, almost naked, and loud in talk and arrogance, for whom the crowd separates in admiring curiosity—they are gladiators. Some merchants' slaves come next, with goods for the booths which their masters have had constructed just outside the amphitheatre, and behind them are three jockeys in gay attire, leading a group of prancing horses, whose tufted heads show them to be participants in the chariot races to-day; while, crowding their high-stepping heels and exchanging jokes and laughter with the street-loungers, is a company of mountebanks leading a tame and funny bear—in fact, it is easy to see it is circus-day in Rome! Circus-day for the populace—doomsday for the condemned.

As the hours advance, the crowds thicken and change. Amid the slaves and plebeians can now be seen, often, the gay car of a party in rich attire, all carrying small banners of one color; or the lectica of some senator, sporting the ribbons of his favorite contestant in the Games, most of them denoting certain chariot-drivers, this sport having grown rapidly in public favor lately.

There is a flourish of trumpets, the gleam of a golden eagle held high, the flash of steel in the sunlight, and a cohort of the royal guards sweeps by, ready to take its place in the Campus and preserve order over the two or threescore thousands likely to assemble for the day. Following these is a rabble of common people, mostly small boys and slaves, and they make directly for the Campus, intent on watching some of the military evolutions to follow, for this plain has always been used as a parade-ground and sporting-field. Now, however, it is largely occupied by buildings of great splendor, their marble columns stretching along the streets in all directions—baths, temples, theatres, and mausoleums—nearly all memorials to some great man long since laid low in death. Facing some of these is the succession of terraces called the Janiculum, all beautiful with gardens and stately homes, and considered the healthiest spot in Rome.

Past all this the people pour, and finally reach the immense oval-shaped structure where the Games are to be held. As they near its vicinity the crowds grow denser and more lively, for the sound of martial music is heard, and they know that before a great while a fine flourish of trumpets will announce the opening of the Games. They no longer linger among the columns of the wide porticoes, but pour into the stone building through the many wide entrances, and hasten to secure a ticket at the small loggia where the jam is thickening, and there is a constant noise of cries, imprecations, and laughter. Once inside, the breathless ticket-holder may stop to glance around him, for the foyer is wide and comfortable. Standing in one of the openings between the segments of seats he can see the great ellipsis of the arena walled in to the height of perhaps fifteen feet, the broad rampart topped by a bronze railing ending in sharp spikes, as a further protection against any sudden dash of some powerful beast, goaded to desperation.

On a line with this wall is the podium, or gallery, reserved for the favored aristocratic class. Midway of its oval, and close to the terminal markings of the course, is a canopied enclosure displaying the purple and gold of royalty, with chairs on either side for the tribunes, prætors, ædiles, curules, and censors, who assist in the government. Opposite is a segment separated from adjoining seats in which is a pleasing flutter of white, and he knows this vicinity is claimed by the Vestals, the only women allowed outside the latticed gallery set apart for them, three tiers further up, save such as may be found in the exclusive space reserved for the Emperor.

The flow of the people along the præcinctiones has been incessant for the last hour, and the nimble locarii, or ushers, have been busy verifying the numbers on their tickets with those on the benches of the higher galleries where the populace is seated; the poor slaves being relegated to a sky gallery close up under the awning. Here the velarium is now rolled back, and tugs at its guy-ropes like a confined sail, while away below there is a bustle of sand-strewing over the arena, the sound of a hammer driving some loose bolt home in the iron gates confining the beasts, and beneath all, like the low thunder of the surf before a storm, rises the uneasy growl and grumble of these savage creatures in their dens that underlie the great structure.

The vast audience is nearly seated at last. The locarii are leaning back against the curving walls to catch their breath; the students of the schools, accompanied by their instructors, have demurely taken places under their severe eyes, only to break into mirthful chatter later; the velarium has been finally adjusted at the proper angle to exclude the sun and admit the air, and the people are telling each other it must be nearly time, for the editor has just taken his raised seat ready to conduct the programme, when there is one clear, long-drawn trumpet note, then a great clarion blare that may be heard far over Rome—the Games are begun!

One last quick rush of the inevitably late, and the doors are closed. The editor rises and salutes the Emperor—who politely responds—then turns with a gesture towards the end of the ellipse, and through the suddenly-opened gates pours a great procession made up of all the participants of the day—poets, musicians, wrestlers, net-throwers, leapers, runners, tumblers, athletes, armed fighters, riders, chariot racers, a train of tame elephants and other beasts, and lastly a long, pathetic, slow-moving line of doomed captives, many from far countries, who, not understanding a word that is spoken, only realize in their trembling isolation that something terrible is about to happen, from which there is no possible way of escape.

Through the kindness of Gaius and Aulus, both of whom are in the podium, Junius and Nadab are well seated in the first row of the second mæniana, and now with eyes dulled by weeping, and faces drawn with grief, they watch for a last glimpse of their loved one amid this glittering show of man and beast. The women have all remained at home—Salome, face downwards on her couch, in bitter weeping; Agistha (now Cleone) with her new-found mother and sister, sometimes walking wildly to and fro, sometimes dropping to her knees in earnest prayer; while Pamphylia fondles the laughing baby, Gaius, and feels that he is more nearly like the child she long ago lost than is this distracted wife, who can find no solace outside her religion.

The procession has but half circled the arena when Nadab touches his father's arm.

"Is not that Hector, the centurion? See—amid that group of gladiators with the bronze headgear!"

Junius nods half obliviously, for his eyes strain onward to the less showy ending of the motley, serpent-like string, and presently he utters a stifled sound, between a sob and a groan—there is Elizabeth! She is pacing slowly in her flowing white robe, her hands clasped lightly before her, and her eyes down-dropped. She seems almost to float, so light is her movement, and there is such an absence of all emotion—even expression—in the still figure that one might think each step involuntary; that she was walking in her sleep.

At length the long train has made the entire circuit, and passes out of sight, to be replaced by a band of discus throwers, who have a lively, innocent game, preliminary to the more blood-curdling scenes to follow.

It was nearing noon, and the people were growing weary with the heat and long sitting, when, to whet their somewhat jaded appetites, it was announced that the beasts would now appear. Junius at once stiffened into an immovable quiet. Nadab moaned and hid his eyes. But Cleotas whispered presently:

"Not yet, friends. These are men, and each has a short, two-edged sword to fight the monsters with. There are our Christian friends and many more—but no women."

It was a short but bloody spectacle, and Nadab, sickened and faint, leaned heavily against Cleotas, whose face was gray with sympathy. When the dead had been removed with long grappling-hooks, and fresh sand sprinkled over the stains, there was an instant's pause. Then from one of the doors entered a single figure in simple white, the dark hair banded neatly in place, the hands softly clasped, the eyes upraised as if in prayer. Junius and Nadab saw her as through a haze of blood, yet presently their eyes cleared, and their tortured nerves grew still. Something in her gracious presence seemed to rebuke their horror.

She advanced slowly, but with perfect dignity, and apparently without fear, though four fierce leopards, just released from their barriers, were slipping and snarling around the wide space in which she stood. Junius, thinking he could not endure the sight which must follow, yet felt his eyes glued to that strangely solemn figure, and Nadab, moaning, crouched and looked, and murmured:

"God will save her yet!"

Elizabeth appeared to see and hear nothing. All her thoughts followed her eyes' uplifted gaze—her soul was with her Lord. For the moment an ecstasy of faith, of love, of perfect surrender, possessed her whole being, and she felt the protecting arms of Christ about her.

The feverish chatter and rustle of the great audience grew still as she came slowly to the center, for something in her presence awed them—and besides, what ailed the beasts? Still crouching, still creeping, as if to spring, they came, but halted when a short distance from her, then turned and sped away like whipped curs, growling and protesting as they fled, and, stopping in a huddled group, gazed at her with red, angry orbs, sniffing the air discontentedly, and lashing their tails against their spotted sides.

Elizabeth, now in the center of the great oval, stopped and dropped slowly to her knees. She had had an instant of full consciousness, and realized that danger was near. She would meet it as she had met her arrest—in the attitude of supplication. Now was the time for the beasts to spring—why did they not?

The amphitheatre was as still as death, and every eye was fixed on that one slender Christian woman, who in heavenly contemplation seemed lost to all the world, and on those four wild beasts edging timidly away without offering to devour her, except with their greedy eyes. Suddenly Nadab sprang wildly up.

"A miracle!" he shouted. "God has saved her! The leopards dare not kill her!" and then fell back in a paroxysm of hysterical weeping.

The cry was caught up—the excitement spread.

"A miracle! A miracle!" yelled the changeable populace, wild with this strange new excitement of mercy, so uncommon and so delightful. "She is pure! She is innocent! The gods protect her!" And four times ten thousand upturned thumbs begged for the captive's life.

Nero, feeling the cold chills of awed amazement run down his spine, was glad to grant the favor, and his imperial nod revoked her death sentence. Amid a tumult that rent the air with shouts and set it all a-flutter with waving handkerchiefs and girdles, Elizabeth, still in a half daze, was led from the arena, free from all further persecution—and the Games went on.

CHAPTER XXIX.

TRIUMPH THROUGH FAITH.

THE noon recess was over, and the audience, rested by the movement and the meal, which many took in the building, was ready for fresh horrors. Nero was now accompanied by Poppœa and one or two ladies-in-waiting, and Cleotas had returned to his place, leaving Junius and Nadab with their restored Elizabeth, scarcely yet believing in their great relief. Salome also, seeing that the reunited could well spare her, had come with her husband to be a fearful witness, behind the women's gilded grating, of her brother's combat with the blustering Anisarchus. Gaius and Aulus were in their places, and Julia was with the party in the royal box. There was unusual interest in this event, not only for them, but many more. The singular compact between the Emperor and the centurion had been noised abroad, and all knew what royal interest and princely wagers depended upon it. Few remembered the humble Christian whose life hung in the balance, nor gave a thought to the anxieties which must overwhelm him in his cell.

But, in reality, Herklas was sustained as Elizabeth had been. He had long since given himself to Christ, not for prosperity and peace only—not for quiet days and restful nights—but for adversity; for old age and weakness, if they were to be his portion; for death in the prime of manhood, if such was the Lord's will. All he asked was to be able in some way to testify of Him. The flesh truly was weak, and shrank at

times from the brutality and shame of such a death in public; but the spirit was submissive and ready. If this soldier who had so oddly assumed his place succeeded, he must expect a degrading servitude; if he failed, he must take his place in the arena to be easily disposed of by the powerful Anisarchus. The details had been given him by the jailer, with many an oath and chuckle, and in either case his future did not promise much that was desirable. Yet Herklas "rested in the Lord and was glad."

It was about the eighth hour when the wrestlers appeared. There were several pairs, but Anisarchus and Hector absorbed the interest and led the little procession, as in the customary manner they advanced to the royal box and gave their strangely touching salutation:

"Ave Imperator, morituri te salutant." (Hail, Emperor! they who are about to die salute thee.)

Then each pair took the prescribed position—right foot projected, knees slightly bent outward, arms and chest extended, body supple and alert. The handkerchief fluttered down as a signal, and the clutching, writhing, swaying, twisting, and bending began, the audience sitting almost motionless in its interest over the intertwisted forms.

It was quickly seen that Hector, if slightly the smaller, was the more ready and quick, but few among those thousands understood whence came the wondrous strength and skill, the readiness to parry, the assurance in attack, that he soon developed; for he, like David of old, was "contending in the strength of the Lord,"—wrestling bodily for his brother's life, as he had long been wrestling, spiritually, with the powers of evil for his own soul.

The contest had proceeded but a short time when there was a yell of triumph, led by Nero—Anisarchus was down! But only for an instant. Regaining his footing after a bitter struggle of a few seconds, he seemed roused to fury by the disgrace, and for a while showed a strength which seemed invincible. Indeed, it was plainly observable that Hector had all he could possibly do to hold his own against him.

But the Olympic trick was swift and sure, and Anisarchus in his mad rage was not prepared for it. While he relied on his superior strength to down his opponent, he had not taken into account the watchful alertness that Hector had never lost for an instant, and just as he was ready to shout his triumphant "I have him!" feeling the sinewy figure of the Greek give way before him—neither he nor any one else knew just

Hector, kneeling above him, looked anxiously for the upturned-thumb signals of mercy.

what happened, but something quick and sinuous as a serpent's spring gave his left ankle a twist that caused a second's hot agony, and he fell so heavily that he lay still, utterly unconscious for the time being.

Amid the roars of applause Hector, kneel-

ing above him, looked anxiously for the upturned-thumb signals of mercy, having no desire for the death of his opponent; but instead down went the clenched fists that doomed, and instantly the cruel grappling-hooks dragged out the unconscious wrestler— no longer champion of Rome.

Then Hector, proud only in a strength not his own, glad only because of his brother, marched with stately tread around the arena with the four other victors, to receive the plaudits of the multitude, and as he bent low beneath the imperial party, Poppœa caught from her white wrist a blazing jewel and tossed it, with the cry:

"For Hector, victorious!"

But a bunch of roses flung at the same moment from the fair hand of Julia, his patroness, was to the man so newly born to better things a more welcome guerdon, for it meant the purest friendship.

The day was ended, and the sun had set in deepest crimson, giving promise of a fair to-morrow. Salome, thankful over Hector's victory, marveling over Elizabeth's escape, was crossing the court to seek Nadab and inquire how his mother was resting—for, with her hand clasped in that of her husband, the weary martyr had been sleeping some time—when she saw the youth crossing to her. A robe of white, stained and soiled, was thrown over his arm.

"It is mother's," he whispered, "and should be cleansed at once. It is tainted with the prison odor."

"Prison odor!" exclaimed Salome, noticing immediately the strangely pungent scent clinging to its folds. "No, that is something more. How singular it is! Not exactly disagreeable, but exceedingly penetrating. It makes me almost dizzy."

She took the garment from him and followed the court to the rear, where she sought the lavatory, presided over by a tall, dusky slave from Africa. The powerful woman had no sooner taken the soiled robe from her mistress than she started a little, then sniffed at it inquiringly.

A moment later she discovered the pale yellow stains of the powder spilled by Elizabeth the night before, when ministering to her dying companion, and looked up with a smile that displayed all her strong teeth in their perfection.

"Ah, ha! Leopard's-bane!" she cried. "This powder comes from a plant in my native land. It grows in our jungles, and all leopards shun and fear it as they do the great cobra that crushes them. They know its odor, and go far around rather than trample upon the plant. Whose robe is this?"

Salome's eyes widened. She had, with simple credulity, fully believed in the miraculous interposition of God to save her friend, and for a minute felt deeply disappointed.

As usual in perplexity, or trouble, she hastened to Cleotas, who was resting on a divan after his long and exciting day, and told him, with deep regret, of her discovery.

"It was no miracle, you see," she ended dejectedly.

Cleotas was wiser and only smiled. "But what is a miracle, my Salome? Simply some happening which transcends our powers of comprehension. Nothing is miraculous to the Almighty, and He works always through His own laws, only a few of which are intelligible to us. This event will always be a miracle to the Roman populace, who do not understand, though you and I have discovered its simple relation to a natural law. You like to think our Christ interposed to save Elizabeth, and so He did. Is it any the less His doing because He chose to work it out by natural means? Sometime, perhaps, my wife, we shall understand still more of these wondrous workings of the Divine mind, and there will be no more miracles. But all the same, God saved our friend to-day."

So Salome was comforted.

While she sat leaning against her husband in the soft twilight a servant entered to announce guests, and the two hastened to the atrium to meet Aulus Clotius and Gaius. Their manner was marked by suppressed excitement, and as Aulus requested the husband and wife to return with him to his palace, there to meet some old friends, the eyes of both rested upon Salome with much seeming interest.

"Is Hector there?" she asked. "I have thought it so strange that he did not come to talk over his great victory with us. Was it not grand! And how modestly he received the plaudits, and the gift of the empress! My whole being thrilled with pride as I watched him!"

"Hector is a wonderful man," returned Aulus with deep conviction. "He has a greater heart than even you have recognized. But come; he waits, with other friends, to greet you."

Salome sent a servant to excuse Cleotas and herself to their guests for a short time, and the four entered the man-car awaiting them outside, horse vehicles not being allowed upon the narrow streets after sundown.

As they neared the palace among the royal mansions on the magnificent Palatine Hill, Salome began to catch something of the excitement with which the air seemed vibrating around her. Who were these old friends? Whence had they come, and why had Hector so persistently absented himself since the close of the spectacles? Scarcely a thought did she give to the man whom Hector had saved that he might possess him as a slave—as all believed.

They dismounted at the guarded door in the street wall, and Aulus led them rapidly past the porter, with his dog, across the ostium, and through the atrium, to an inner room opening upon the peristyle, and consecrated to family use.

It was well lighted with many brazen lamps of quaint shapes suspended from the ceiling, and seemed quite full of people. The ladies, Pamphylia and Julia, came quickly forward, followed by Agistha, whose strange story Salome knew. But she hardly recognized the pale, sad lady of that day at the Three Taverns in this radiant creature with great, brilliant eyes, flushed cheeks, and smiling lips. What could it mean? Was not her husband one of those doomed to death as a Christian martyr? Could it be he had escaped?

Hector advanced to take his sister's hand, and drew her towards a wasted but happy-faced figure half reclining on a divan. The barber and the bath had made a great change in the appearance of Herklas. With tue removal of his beard youth seemed to have returned to his face.

Salome looked, and stopped—still gazed, and faltered forwards, with a faint cry:

"Hector, who—oh! is it—can it be—Herklas!"

The last cry was one of certainty, and she flew to his arms as he rose to greet her.

Then followed a scene almost indescribable. Everyone tried to explain, and tell the many-sided story, and in a whirl of wonder and delight Salome was clasped by Agistha, who called her "sister," and surrounded by the ladies of the house, who claimed her as one of the noble family through marriage.

"For you see," called out Aulus above the din, "Herklas being my brother-in-law, you and our brave Hector are also my sister and brother, while my dear mother would claim each and all of us as her very own."

It was an evening of unalloyed delight, following a day of fears and expectations terrible to bear. But we may not linger longer with the reunited. One word as to their future, though.

There is a certain portion of southern France most delightful as to scenery and climate, the name of which proves its Roman derivation. Laved by the soft waters of the Mediterranean and guarded by the Alps, its climate is ideal and the vine flourishes the year round. It is a Roman province, boasting excellent roads, fine buildings, and a certain degree of civilization. Here, in time, our families gathered, Aulus Clotius as the reigning Proconsul, with the honorary title of Legati Cæsar, and almost unlimited power over the lands and subjects about him.

Hector was at once appointed by him chief of the military forces, Cleotas first magistrate, and Herklas elder and governor of the first Christian church there established.

Junius was given an excellent civic office, and Nadab was delighted with the gift of a farm; and here, far from the restlessness of Roman life at the Capital, they lived in peace and comfort, loving and serving God in Christ, doing good to man as they found opportunity, and leaving their humanizing impress upon the ruder folk about them.

Thus they escaped the terrible burning of Rome, about three years later, and the fiery persecutions for which it served as cause, through which Paul, a stately figure and dauntless spirit, lived, wrote, and waited on the Lord until his triumphal martyrdom, fearing no man, because "One was his Master, even Christ."

THE END.

www.ingramcontent.com/pod-product-compliance
Lightning Source LLC
Chambersburg PA
CBHW082013170626
46817CB00009B/3086